Arcana

© *gipsika*

2013

Honeymead Books

www.honeymeadbooks.com

First published online 2013

Copyright © *gipsika, 2013*

Original Cover Design: Honeymead Books

ISBN 978-0-9922257-0-4

Arcana

1

Rain was sheeting down in a never-ending grey haze when Ivy Pennington opened the front door of her 4th level flat to brave another workday. Papers to file, files to study, she thought with irritation. When she'd set out on her career as a young accountant, she'd expected that companies would be a lot more up-to-date where e-filing was concerned. So she had to have the sodding luck to sign up with a store that had apparently never heard of computers yet – and in this day and age! She stepped out into the passage and turned in a fluid movement to close the door, her above-knee navy skirt swishing just a little too flippantly for the gravity of her professional image...

"Meow!"

That was when she glanced down. At the toes of her stiletto shoes sat a small, black kitten, staring at her with intent green eyes. The poor little fellow looked bedraggled from the rain. Ivy reached for it, meaning to scratch its ears; it backed away a little before allowing her to touch it.

"You poor little thing!" She put her briefcase down and returned inside to pour some milk into a flat tupperware, for lack of a saucer (she didn't own such old-fashioned things). When she put it down on the floor she realized that the kitten had followed her into the flat.

Ha, flat, she thought sarcastically. This was not a flat. It was a box. The walls were painted ever so tastefully light-grey in keeping with modern interior decorating, and while Ivy subscribed to everything that was fresh and young, somehow the colour grey didn't seem to make the grade. She wasn't even allowed to repaint.

Later, she thought impatiently, watching the little fellow – she didn't even know if it was a tom or a jenny – thirstily lap the milk. Her thoughts were working on hyperdrive now – she was running late. She'd need a place for him to sleep; and he needed to get out, to do his business - that would be a problem, on the fourth floor! And when she came home from work, she'd have to find out where he belonged...

The green eyes lifted to stare at her again, and a tiny pink tongue slipped out and licked a small black nose. There was a lot of milk left in the saucer, but the kitten seemed to have quenched its thirst.

"Have you lost your mommy then?" asked Ivy. "Did you lose your way? Where are you from?"

"Meow," came the quiet response.

Ivy decided that this couldn't wait. She took out her smartphone to text her boss – then remembered that the boss only had a landline. With an exasperated grunt she dialled his number.

"Oates and Son, how can we help you?" chirped the voice of the chicklet who manned the receptionist desk.

"Biljana, please tell Mr Oates I'm only coming in at noon," said Ivy. "Family crisis."

"Shall I put you through to him, Ivy?"

Those honeyed tones! As though being under twenty gave Biljana a preferred – hmm. Maybe it did, thought Ivy.

"No, just relay my message to him please," she said but realized she was speaking to a line in transit.

"Graham Oates; good morning."

Ivy gnashed her teeth.

"Morning, Mr Oates. I have to solve a family crisis this morning, it really can't wait – so I'll only be able to come in to work at noon – is that alright?"

There was a heavy sigh.

"Oh dear, Miss Pennington. There's a lot of work. I hope it's nothing too serious?"

"No – that is, not that serious for me, but it might be in future," she waffled frantically. *Just accept it and let me go, boss!*

"What's the matter?"

She had so hoped he wouldn't ask! It was none of his business; but to say that to your boss's face...

"My niece," she invented. "She's going to have a baby and she's still in school. I have to prevent greater disaster."

A momentary shocked silence, then, "Well, I'll see you at noon, Miss Pennington. Good luck!"

3

"Thanks!"

Ivy ended the call and stood for a moment, disoriented. How on Earth had that lie slipped off her lips? She was a dead-honest person, she *never* lied! Well, scrap that good record, she thought acridly. She gazed down at the kitten, unable to understand herself. She wouldn't have studied financial science if she'd had a dishonest hair – hmm. Maybe she would have, she thought with irony. Maybe, specifically.

"Come, baby," she murmured to the little black cat and scooped him up. He clung to her collar with little claws, his fuzzy baby hair tickling her neck. "Let's find out where you belong."

The funniest little sound came from the cat. It sounded like a mini motorbike trying to start its engine. She realized he was learning to purr, and it made her smile. Well, she'd better come up with a good explanation for her boss, backtrack and let him know that it had turned out to be only a scare and that her niece would be staying with her for a while until temperaments had cooled... gosh! She was spinning the lie further! She shook her head at herself, changed her shoes for more comfortable walking pumps, and left the flat – this time with a handbag rather than her briefcase, and the kitten nestling cosily inside on a towel.

It was mid-morning when Ivy sank into a corner seat at a little bistro. She had asked all the neighbours in the flat block, created a poster at the copyshop and put it up everywhere, called the SPCA to hear if there had been a call for a missing kitten, and made the round of all the local vets she was aware of.

Apparently the kitty was a tom. She decided to call him Peridot, after the colour of his intent eyes. If he didn't belong to anyone, she supposed she could keep him. He had been very well-behaved, sleeping quietly in her handbag. At one stage he had started scratching at the towel; at which point she had quickly put him into a flowerbed, where he dutifully did his business and even covered it up. She made a note to get a cat box on her way home, and a bed for him. And of course cat food.

And the call reached her.

"Ivy..."

Oh shucks. Here was her own lie, coming back to haunt her! Somehow that bastard of a boss must have investigated with her family...

"What's up, Bonnie?"

Bonnie Pennington, her niece with whom she didn't have too much contact. Unlike Ivy, Bonnie wasn't a fiery redhead but a gentle, sweet-natured brunette. The kind of kid one would wish to have. She was fifteen now, and never gave her mother a day of hassle.

That her boss had bothered her niece, irritated Ivy. To cause Bonnie such -

"Can I come and stay with you for a while, please?"

Ivy nearly fell off her chair.

No ways! She couldn't take Bonnie in right now – she'd just adopted a kitten! Argh! What kind of logic was that? But there wasn't space in her bachelorette box! It was tiny – just a place to crash, until she could afford better!

"Why, Bonnie, what's the matter?"

"Well, I'm not sure how it could have happened... there was this boy..."

No, something said inside Ivy, in disbelief. *It's not what I think!*

"... and ... we sort-of fell in love, and we... got together – and... and now..."

"...you're pregnant," completed Ivy.

"*No!* I mean – yes, but it wasn't like that! Mom wants to throw me out..."

I'm dreaming, thought Ivy. I'm seriously dreaming.

"Come and crawl in with me for a little while," she offered despite herself. "But Bonnie, there are house rules. Okay? And I have to find us a bigger pad, can't have you sleeping in the bathtub forever..."

"In the *bathtub?*" squeaked Bonnie, horrified.

"Kidding," said Ivy. "When will you be around?"

"After school," said Bonnie.

"Fine." Ivy hung up and proceeded to stare at the fifth dimension in confusion. Right.

"Can I help you, ma'am?"

Oh. She'd been staring at her waiter without realizing it.

"The bill please."

Outside, the rain was still falling persistently.

2

Ivy had cancelled the rest of her workday, too, much to her boss's annoyance. She promised to make a turn at the office just before five and collect her work so that she could do something she'd promised herself she'd never do – take it home. She had bought all the necessary bits for Peridot, including a little red collar. He clawed at this, trying to take it off.

"You'll get used to it," she informed him.

She had also gone to the camp shop and obtained an air mattress. Her niece's visit was *not* going to be a permanent arrangement. And she'd bought the papers – good old-fashioned newspapers, looking for a larger flat, or accommodation of any other sort.

Now she was home and sitting down for the first time, Peridot on her lap, and having a cup of coffee. Only her second, today. In her stressed job, she would be drinking her fifth, by now.

Her doorbell buzzed.

"It's open," she called.

The door opened shyly and in shuffled Bonnie, with her heavy school bag in one hand and a suitcase in the other. Ha! She'd known! She'd planned this before going to school!

And behind her -

Ivy shot to her feet after all, lifting Peridot back to her shoulder. "What -?"

"This is Jake ," said Bonnie, blushing as she gestured to the tall, sloppily dressed boy. "He's..."

"... the father," completed Ivy acridly. "Pleased to meet you, Jake – I think. Come in, I have to tell you my house rules too."

"Er... good day, ma'am," said Jake, off-handedly.

"This is Ivy, my auntie," Bonnie introduced her generously, then pointed to the only available beanbag in the place, "make yourself at home, Jake!"

Ivy gnashed her teeth.

"Put your luggage over there," she pointed to the far end, where her bed stood. "Then sit down and tell me everything."

"Surely not everything," giggled Bonnie.

"Well, no, unless you're about to start your own religion I'll assume this was a natural conception," Ivy cut to the point.

Jake sprawled over the beanbag that Ivy had vacated when the two had entered her flat. Ivy scowled at him. Peridot had retreated to the top of her shoulder and was digging his claws into her skin trying to keep his balance, his tail sticking straight up.

"Aw, that's so noo!" Bonnie giggled again. "Didn't know you had a kitten."

"Cute," commented Jake. "Can I hold him?"

"No!" snapped Ivy.

"And me?" begged Bonnie.

"No ways. Pregnant girls mustn't handle cats. You mustn't touch him at all. You know, toxoplasma and all that."

Bonnie's smile dropped. Ivy could see how the reply sat on the girl's tongue and was actively bitten back. Too bad, Bonnie, she thought a little smugly. Neither of the kids were going to be allowed to touch Peridot. That was going to be House Rule One.

"Right, kids," she said, settling down on the bed next to where Bonnie had dumped her baggage. *Next* to the bed, she'd told Bonnie, not *on* the bed. Aha. This was not promising to be easy.

"Rule number one. Nobody touches the cat."

"Why can't I?" asked Jake, slipping into familiarity a little too easily for Ivy's liking. She didn't know what Bonnie had told him about her – possibly that she was the 'cute little' auntie, instantly destroying any authority Ivy could have started with.

"Because he's my cat and you don't touch him," she replied. "He's tiny and he's shy. I don't want him picking up stress habits."

Jake released a derogatory snort.

"Second rule, Bonnie," said Ivy. "Jake is allowed to pick you up from here and visit with you at *his* mansion. Not here. This is a very small place, and three people breathing is too much, for me at least."

"I was just going to ask you, Ivy," said Bonnie, worried

wrinkles across her forehead. "Jake 's father has thrown him out too. Can he move in here with me too?"

"No," said Ivy before she had even recovered from being shocked. "Where in this box do you see enough space for both of you?"

"He's brought his camper mattress," Bonnie jumped ahead.

"So you were *planning* this?" asked Ivy, annoyed. "You simply presumed I'd agree?"

"Because you're such a cool person," said Bonnie.

"I'm not that cool," said Ivy. "He can't stay here."

"Where must he stay then, under a bridge?" asked Bonnie indignantly.

"You two ought to have thought of that before," replied Ivy.

Bonnie burst into tears.

Ivy watched her as she cried. There was something wrong with those tears. She couldn't quite pinpoint it, but the whole thing was starting to smell of a set-up.

"Look," she said. "You can tell Jake about the rest of my rules later. I have to go pick up some stuff at work. When I'm back I'll clue you in on them." She put Peridot back into her towel-lined handbag and got up, slipping her high heels on. And she looked pointedly at Jake .

"What?" asked the youngster.

"I'm waiting," she said.

"For what?"

"You to leave, so I can lock behind us."

"But -"

"But if you leave me alone in here, I'll be scared," protested Bonnie. "Someone might break in! This isn't the best area!"

"It's Putney!" exclaimed Ivy, annoyed. "It's a flipping brilliant area! Seven stops away from your home, girl! What the hell do you mean it's not a good area?"

"Well, there's the Heath; that's a bit too close for comfort..."

"Should have thought of *that* before, too," snorted Ivy.

"I did, that's why I brought Jake!"

Ivy's patience was up.

"No!" she snapped. "That's enough. Bonnie, see Jake to the door. Jake, it's time to go!"

"She told me you were nice," grumbled Jake as he picked himself up.

"Where should he go?" wailed Bonnie.

"The library," said Ivy. "The church. Lunar House. The job centre. London's a handy city, Jake. Plenty of places where you can get a job."

Jake slouched to the door. Ivy studied him as he passed. Deliberately run-down clothes; jeans frazzled at the lower seams, and hanging low on the butt. Tennis shoes that yawned. Holes in the T-shirt that was too old to be from Oxfam. His hair was plaited in dirty-blond dreadlocks – not very long dreadlocks and not very old ones, she recognized with relief, but the whole look said, marijuana. Or worse.

Bonnie shot past her to see Jake to the door, and flung her arms around him and engaged him in a downright indecent smooch. Ivy turned away and pulled a face.

"Cut it short, kids," she snapped. "Must I get a bucket of water?"

That did it. They released each other; Bonnie stared at her in horror and Jake muttered, "Bitch," as he left.

"How could you say that? It's disgusting!" shot Bonnie.

"Look, girl," replied Ivy, more than irritated by now. "Rule number three. You just *never* make out like that in front of me, no matter where we are. I'm really not interested in you demonstrating how you made that baby."

"You *are* being a bitch," Bonnie retorted angrily. "God!"

"Bonnie," said Ivy with a last strained attempt at patience, "you're here on sufferance. Did you think I'd jump for joy? I've worked very hard to get into the position where I can afford even this tiny box. For once I have my own space. I don't immediately need dependants. I'm offering you a spot to crawl into until Bex has calmed down, and that is all. After that you go home. Understood?"

Bonnie nodded silently, her whole body stance radiating rebellion.

"Now," said Ivy. "You have a choice. You call your mother and let her know where you are, or I call her, when I'm back. Which one?"

"I'll call her," said Bonnie.

"Fine. Now I've got to go. Make yourself at home – a little bit. There's coffee, tea, some bread... see what you can find in the fridge."

"Okay, Ivy."

Ivy nodded, picked up her briefcase, put Peridot who'd crawled out of the handbag, on his cat litter box, waited for him and stuck him back into the handbag when he was ready. Then she locked Bonnie into the flat and headed towards the bus stop.

It was only three pm, but she needed space. Gosh, what had she taken in? She had to be mad to agree to shelter that teenager! And Bonnie had become difficult since she'd last seen her – granted, four years back. Oh dear!

Ivy wasn't going to spend the last two hours of this day at work, not after this morning! She went into the local library and spent some time there, then browsed through some shops on the main street, remembering happy student days when she'd had a lot of time to do this.

The most important thing was to move into a larger place. Her bachelorette "box" barely suited her. Three 'P's had convinced her to rent it: Price, price and price. Her plan was to save up and buy the next place she moved to; not to spend more on a higher rent!

But maybe staying in an uncomfortably small spot would

jog her niece into action to get out of there again. With grey dread Ivy realized that the 'for a while' in Bonnie's plea had been meant to cover several years. And with a baby – Ivy shuddered. No. No, and no!

Bonnie had got herself into this predicament! She could get herself out of it again. Ivy strolled into a second-hand bookshop she hadn't visited in two years. Her studies had got too busy for her other passion: Reading. She drifted between the shelves, Peridot sleeping peacefully in 'his' handbag. She was glad the kitten was so adaptable, then considered that a lot of kittens spent a lot of time in carton boxes at his age, getting offered for sale or adoption.

Why had her sister-in-law thrown Bonnie out? She'd never do that to her own daughter! And Bex was a nice enough person, difficult at times but generally fair-minded... but to throw her daughter out because the girl was in a predicament? *May she grow hair where she doesn't expect it!* she found herself muttering under her breath.

"Can I help you, Miss?"

She looked up.

"You seem very intent," smiled the middle-aged owner of the shop. Ivy peered at him, taking note that in the two years his greying hair had turned a bit whiter – and sparser. But his beard was as full as it had always been.

"Is there something specific you are looking for?" he prompted.

"A book of hexes and curses," growled Ivy, then she

laughed. "Nothing really. I'm just here to distract myself. Got a situation to deal with, so it helps me to be around books."

"We have a self-help section," said the man and pointed her in that direction. She studied the books on the shelves. A weathered copy of '*How to Win Friends and Influence People*' sat there between gardening, cookery and other DIY books. The elderly man returned to his desk at the till.

"Here," someone stuck a book into her field of vision. She looked up in surprise, at a young man with middle-brown hair and stunningly azure eyes. They held her as though they wanted to hypnotize her. "You might like this one!"

Ah, she thought, feeling a little off-balance, a new shop assistant. She glanced at the book he was holding, then took it. 'Arcana', said the gold-leaf title; surrounded with coiling mandalas and animal sketches. It certainly looked interesting. She glanced back at the young man and found that he'd left. Oh.

Those eyes burned in her mind. A shade of blue she had never seen. And that intense stare... like a command! Ivy took the book to the till. It was in pretty good condition; nearly like new. The owner looked a bit surprised when he couldn't find where he had marked a price; but he was quick to make up one. It was nearly as much as for a new book. Ivy snorted and thought, maybe half of that or two-thirds, tops. She looked for the shop assistant to hand the book back. The man was nowhere.

"Let me have another look at that," said the owner – his

name was on the edge of her brain, just out of reach though. He took the book again, looked at it from all sides, then quoted her a price about a third lower. Ivy sighed, rolled her eyes and paid, pocketing the book. Nice. It was not usually in her repertoire to allow herself to be ripped off by the second-hand bookshop.

She continued to the office, picking up her workload early. Rats, if they'd had internet, her boss could have emailed it to her! She resolved to introduce this backward company to the modern world.

Mr Oates had already left, so there was only Chicky left to deal with.

"How's your niece?" she probed.

"Fine," said Ivy without enthusiasm, packing up what she needed to take home.

"And is she..."

Ivy nailed Biljana with a flat stare.

"It shall remain to be seen," she said coldly. "Now if you don't mind..."

"Was only asking," said Biljana sullenly. And she returned to her typing, muttering "*vešterka!*"

"Pardon?" asked Ivy reflexively.

"Witch!" said Biljana, more audibly, and proceeded to ignore Ivy.

The redhead snorted. May she break out in spots, she thought acridly. And she finished raking together what was hers for the night, snapped her briefcase closed, stuck her nose into the air and clicked out of the store.

Oates and Son (of which the current Mr Oates was in fact the son of a long-deceased Oates senior) was a retailer selling, amongst a selection of other things, mostly clothing. It wasn't a chain store; not a franchise; but a privately owned shop that had been of impressive dimensions a generation back. In this current climate of financial decline the shop had been cut back; even so it still had two stories, and – Ivy sighed – it needed to employ a junior accountant in training for CA to sort out years upon years of unprocessed finances. It was a forensic nightmare.

Smile, she instructed herself. It would certainly look good on her CV, all this experience. But it was difficult to smile about it when she didn't even have the remotest cooperation from Biljana, who was supposed to log sales into the sales book and enter them into the Excel file as she had repeatedly shown her. That was all the girl was supposed to do, except man the till – and people came in and shopped at far too large intervals. So mainly the teenage receptionist sat varnishing her nails and reading graphic novels when she thought Ivy wasn't looking.

Ivy shrugged impatiently as she made her way through the drizzle that had been with her the whole day, to the bus stop and waited there for the bus. She needed a small vehicle, she thought. Because this was maddening. It was no problem walking the distance to work on bright, dry days; but the drizzle was wearing her down, and taking the bus was tedious.

A scooter, or a small motorbike would do it.

"*Meow!*" said her handbag. She lifted Peridot out and smelled immediately that he'd had an accident on the towel lining. Just a small accident. The wet type, nothing more serious.

"Did you wet yourself then?" she asked him, holding him up to eye level. She sighed. "Sorry, my boy! You're not having a very peaceful day in your new home!"

Peridot gave her a lick on her nose with his tiny, raspy tongue.

"Oh, that's alright then," she smiled, and at that moment the bus arrived. Ivy boarded, paid and found a seat. There was one right in front; pure luck.

About seven stops on, she got off the bus and made her way back to her apartment. Damn, but she was going to turn that box into a home. For one. And a cat.

Curse that owner, that he wouldn't allow her to paint the walls! May his wife moan in his ears and his mother-in-law visit upon him, and may his daughter run away with a drug-using hippie so he'd soften up a bit!

But in fact she'd have to move anyway. No pets, her lease agreement said. Well, perhaps it was high time. She ascended the stairs – for four stories nobody had bothered with a lift – and unlocked her front door. And nearly dropped everything in shock.

Bonnie and Jake were both in there, on *her* bed, doing exactly what they had been doing that had got them in trouble in the first place.

3

Ivy stood speechless for a second. They ignored her and calmly carried on – or perhaps they hadn't heard her.

"What are you doing there?" she shrieked.

Jake turned his head.

"F* off, bitch, we're busy," he told her without pausing.

Ivy gasped for air. And she grabbed the nearest object she could find and lifted it, to fling at the pair in rage. It was a fork, left lying around on the kitchen top, amongst a fiendish mess the teenagers had made helping themselves to her food. She gaped at the pigsty her kitchen had turned into, in two short hours. And back at the two – calmly continuing as though she were air. Hell, she'd show them air! She raised that fork in mad fury, meaning to stab Jake in the bare butt, and -

There was a flash, and a smell of something singed, and Jake yelled, rolling down to the floor clutching his bum. Bonnie screamed too, in fright.

"What did you do to him?"

"Me?" Ivy gaped at the youngster who was writhing on the floor. A singe mark was now visible on his behind, shaped like lightning. He'd have a scar, thought Ivy disjointedly. Served him right.

"You burnt him!" yelled Bonnie, outraged. "You branded him!"

Jake had gathered himself enough that he could make a dive for the bathroom.

"I'll lay a charge," threatened Bonnie. "You injured him!"

This was enough.

"Out!" exploded Ivy. "Take your suitcase and go!"

Bonnie stared at her in shock, then was instantly remorseful.

"I'm sorry, Ivy! I didn't mean to shout at you. I'm just under such a lot of stress, you know, with the baby and all..."

Ivy knocked loudly on the bathroom door.

"I'll count to ten," she warned Jake. "If you're not out by then I'm calling the cops."

That worked. Two seconds later a fully dressed Jake emerged from the bathroom, grabbed his bag that was lying in a corner, and ran out of the door.

"So!" commanded Ivy. "Change of rules. He's not allowed near this apartment block within a radius of a hundred meters. Understood?"

"But Ivy..." begged Bonnie.

"And you," said Ivy, "are going to clear up here. Every bit of mess you made, and he made. And you're going to take my bedding off my bed and take it down to the laundrette, and bring it back washed and ironed. Is that clear?"

"But Ivy, I'm not supposed to work so hard in this condition!" objected Bonnie. She peered at the mess with an expression that told Ivy that not a finger would be lifted.

"Did you call your mother?" asked Ivy.

Bonnie shook her head.

"Then I'm calling her," said Ivy and started dialling. "Get clearing up!"

Bonnie ripped her own phone out and speed-dialled her mother, beating Ivy to it.

"Hi Mom? It's me, Bonnie." She swept a dirty plate off the box that served as a coffee table for Ivy's lounge, and sat down on the space she'd cleared. The plate shattered on the floor. Ivy watched speechlessly. "Yes, I'm okay, don't worry," trilled Bonnie with fake bonhomie. "Just spending some days with Auntie Ivy so you can cool down. Okay? - love you too, Mom!"

"You're totally not, you know," said Ivy, boiling over. Damn that girl! Too pregnant to clear up after her own backside! And that plate had been one of the set, the first set she owned, that her best friend had given her for a house-warming gift.

Ivy had consented to let her niece stay here for a while – not this rebellious, belligerent, sarcastic teen with the bad temper. She couldn't see herself doing this anymore. No ways. "You're getting on the bus back home, right now. Pack your things!"

"But Ivy, you said..."

Ivy pointedly started bundling up Bonnie's belongings which were already strewn far and wide, and stuffed them into her suitcase. She zipped it closed and stuck it in Bonnie's hand.

"There you go. Bye-bye!"

Bonnie burst into tears again.

"But it's already getting dark out! I'll be raped!"

"I'll walk with you," said Ivy resolutely.

"Then you'll get raped too!"

Ivy laughed brightly. "Oh no. That only happens to young girls who tangle with drug addicts."

"Who says Jake uses drugs?" challenged Bonnie.

"I can see it! Now come." Ivy waited for Bonnie to follow her reluctantly out of the door.

Ivy returned to her flat an hour later, having stuck Bonnie safely onto the correct bus home. She closed her door behind her... and gazed down into Peridot's accusing green eyes.

"Meow!"

"Yes, I know, my boy," she sighed and located a small bowl, and put some cat food in it for him, and some milk in another. And she raised her eyes and looked dazedly at the chaos that reminded her that today had indeed been real, not just some acid dream or something similarly crazy.

"I wish there were some good fairy that could just wave a wand and the mess would disappear," she sighed. Gosh, was she tired! But there was no way she'd be sleeping on that filthy bedding... how dared they? She ripped the bedding off her bed and carried it down to the laundrette, dumping it into one of the washers. She threw laundry soap on top and started the machine. And she realized that if she didn't go to sleep very soon, she'd be sleeping in the laundrette.

To hell with it. She left the machine to its washing and returned to her flat, realizing that she had left her door open. For a panicky moment she searched for Peridot, then located him at his food bowls, tidily washing his toes with his pink tongue.

"You're a lovely cat," she told him as she straightened the mattress protector which was all that remained of her bedding and fell onto it. The book she had bought, 'Arcana', lay there on the box that served as a coffee table; but she didn't even have enough energy left to reach for it. She fell asleep without switching off the light. Later on, Peridot jumped onto her bed and nestled up against her, purring like a mini-motorbike trying to start up.

Ivy opened her eyes the next morning to see what that incessant droning was about. Still halfway in alpha, she saw the apparition of Janet, the caretaker, going around her bachelorette box with a vacuum cleaner.

"Are you alright, dear?" asked the motherly woman. "You looked as though you might not be well, and then I saw all this mess, so I thought to myself, Janet, I thought, she's not well, that young lady. She's not feeling well after the ruckus yesterday, and she's too tired to clean up."

"What?" Ivy blinked, thoroughly confused.

"Your door was wide open, dear, and your light was still burning. Must've burnt the whole night through. And there you lay, on your bed in full office clothes..." She came closer and brought a steaming cup of something to Ivy. It was tea. Ivy propped herself up on one elbow and thankfully accepted the drink, though she didn't normally like tea much.

"I saw that little rubbish running out of here last night," added Janet, sitting down on the beanbag to supervise that Ivy drank her tea. "Don't tangle with him, Ivykins. he's bad news. Every druggie on the streets knows him. 'e's a dealer, he is!"

A dealer! Ivy shook her head. What it told her about Bonnie was worrying. She needed to contact Bex.

"You even left your bedding in the laundry," added Janet. "Good that I saw you going down there, dear. I wouldn't have known otherwise where to bring it back to."

Ivy nodded. "Thanks, Janet." She glanced at her watch. "Oh heck, is it that time? I must get to work!"

"Do you always work on Saturdays?" asked Janet.

"No! Of course not!" Ivy smiled. "Janet, thank you." She glanced around her 'box'. The place was spotless. "You are a sweetheart!"

"Worried about you, that's what," was Janet's half-gruff response. "Now you take today to rest, understand? Wish my own daughter would listen to me like you do!"

Ivy smiled. She remembered that Janet's adult daughters were far away, the elder married in Sweden and the younger in New York, having been head-hunted there by a computer company.

"May someone be looking after your daughters as nicely as you're looking after me," she said. This made Janet beam.

"Incidentally, did you see a small black kitten around the place?" asked Ivy.

Janet shook her head.

"I can see you have a cat," she answered, pointing to the litter box. "Wouldn't keep 'im if I were you; that's trouble with old mister Brown. But I haven't seen your kitty."

Ivy was up in a moment. "I have to find him."

"Will you be alright, dear?" asked Janet once more.

"Sure!"

"Then I'll be on my way," said the caretaker and left. Ivy went looking for Peridot.

A small *'meow!'* drew her attention to the curtain. High up, nearly at the pelmet, a small shadow appeared darker than the rest of the curtain, and she could see tiny claw-tips coming through the material. She lifted the curtain and there he was, behind it, hanging on for dear life.

"Oh you funny little silly!" exclaimed Ivy and freed him from his precarious perch. She cuddled him against her neck as she went the two steps to the kitchen to pour him some fresh milk and some more cat food. This time she offered a smaller portion, wondering if he'd eat it up and ask for more.

Janet had really cleaned everything, every last nook and cranny. Ivy marvelled at this, and accepted it gratefully. She went through her morning routine – today, mercifully, without time pressure. And then her eyes caught the newspaper ads that were lying open on her coffee table box.

That was right: She had been meaning to search for a place to stay. Because currently, Peridot had illegal fugitive status in this box. Her landlord would catch a harry.

She paged a bit, then an ad caught her eyes.

'Garden cottage, 1 bed 1 bath, smallish, beautiful setting' and a rental that was quite a bit lower than hers.

This was interesting!

"Coming out with me again today?" she asked Peridot.

"Meow!"

"Good!" So, no hard feelings about yesterday. Great! She realized that she hadn't changed the towel in her bag for him. Both the towel and the bag stank. She resolved to stick both into the laundry, found another sling-bag, lined it with a towel as well and put him into it.

"Don't get too used to this," she told him as she shouldered the bag. A muffled *"meow"* came from inside as answer. She could bet her bottom dollar that this cat understood every word she said!

The cottage turned out to be perfect. It stood sheltered under enormous trees in a fairytale garden full of flowers and herbs. It was detached from the main house which was a bit further down on the large property. The smell, the feel, the entire atmosphere of the place was peaceful. And it came – furnished.

It was irresistible. An antique *chaise-longue* with carved legs stood under the window; two equally old high-back chairs from two different eras complemented it. The coffee table was from nearly black wood, carved antique, too. The furniture was old and a bit shabby; nothing she couldn't fix though. This all stood on a wooden parquet floor from which some pieces were missing.

"I had a carpet in here," the young landlady, who had introduced herself as Alison, told her, "but it went bad, you know, so I took it out. You'll have to bring your own."

Ivy nodded and gazed at the windows. Alright: She would put her own curtains up, because that many flowers were just too much. But the burglar bars in the windows were pretty; they gave the impression of hand-wrought iron.

"Oh, those," smiled the landlady. "Yes... we found that there were break-ins in this cottage, so Marc – that's my husband – he found these on a fleamarket and welded them on. Somebody has hand-wrought them. You can really see the hobby-craft," she added apologetically. "Hope they don't offend! They work, at least."

"They're beautiful," replied Ivy with sincere appreciation.

"You'll have to bring your own bed though," said Alison, leading her further towards the back part of the cottage.

"Suits me," replied Ivy.

The kitchen was a little run-down, like the rest of the cottage. How Ivy with her usual standard of pristine, new and young could find this particularly attractive, she couldn't explain to herself. It was as though she were experiencing a world she had never yet been exposed to.

There were roaches in the kitchen. She set her teeth and resolved to get rid of them all. Every place she had ever looked at for renting, had had roaches. She'd had to clear out her current box from word go.

The bedroom had an old-fashioned wardrobe standing on feet. The bathroom was in need of repairs though.

"We're planning to redo the bathroom," said Alison apologetically. "It's the reason nobody wants to take the place."

"When do you want to redo it?" asked Ivy.

"The problem is a catch-22," said Alison. "We need the rental money first before we can look at that."

Ivy paused. This was a problem. The place needed a new toilet seat; the old one had been removed. The bathroom had been cleaned; this she could see. But there were broken tiles, a bad crack in the hand basin, and – she tested – the shower didn't work. She peered up. The shower head was calcified up. She reached up and tried to remove it to test whether the pipe worked. It didn't budge.

"We'll need a monkey wrench to take that off," said Alison.

Ivy made a note to price monkey wrenches. She glanced at the bathtub. It was old-fashioned; it stood on four clawed feet, similar to the wardrobe. The enamel coating on its inside was stained from age. It didn't look appetizing; but then again, it should not be replaced, thought Ivy, just re-enamelled. It belonged to the place.

She'd had enough of living in a grey box.

"Would I be allowed to paint?"

"Anything you like," said Alison, sounding relieved that this was one expense she wasn't expected to carry. "But please, first show me the colours you want to use."

Sure! That was no problem.

"I have a cat. Would he be allowed here?" Regardless how beautiful this cottage was, she thought, she wouldn't be able to move in here if he wasn't welcome.

"I never thought about that," said Alison. "A cat?"

"Yes," said Ivy and opened her bag for Alison to have a peep at Peridot. The kitten opened a sleepy eye and his tail-tip twitched. He yawned hugely and stretched.

"Awww!" Alison reached out and stroked him with her index finger. "Sure! Bring him! We have no pets ourselves, we didn't move in too long ago, still reeling from..." She shut her mouth, obviously realizing that she shouldn't give away too much.

"What do you think, Peridot? Shall we take it?"

"Meow!"

"That's sorted, then!"

She turned to Alison.

"I'd like to take it please."

The young woman got a worried crease on her forehead. "You dead sure?"

"Yes!"

"You don't mind that it's run-down?"

"It's charming," said Ivy. "I'll cope. The price is as listed?"

Alison nodded mutely.

"Anything else I should know about it?"

The landlady hesitated.

"There is something," smiled Ivy. "Isn't there?"

Alison gave a small embarrassed laugh. "The neighbours say it's haunted," she said dismissively. "I don't believe in that, do you?"

Ivy peered at her, smiling too. It looked as though Alison did indeed believe it.

"Done deal," she said. "I'm taking it, ghosts and all!" She paid the deposit in cash. "When can I move in?"

"It's available now," said Alison. "I cleaned it on Thursday."

It was Saturday. Ivy decided to take the leap right away.

Renting a service to help her with her minimal furniture was a quick thing. Few people moved in the middle of a month. Getting rid of the landlord wasn't as easy.

"I need at least ninety days notice!" he demanded.

"Whether you're in the flat or not, you owe me the rent for the next three months."

What? Three months? May he develop an itch where it was rude to scratch!

Wait - Ivy paused. She was sure she hadn't signed a contract with such ridiculous terms. She pulled out the file in which she kept it, and read it again, carefully. Nowhere did it specify even thirty days.

"It's for the whole flat block," the landlord told her. "Look at your house rules."

Ivy paged to where she'd filed the house rules. In there was a clause, "... and any other restrictions the landlord may consider."

"Those restrictions refer to *conduct*," she pointed out. "Not to the lease agreement!"

"'Any' covers all of that," the man insisted. "Ooh!" he added, sounding tortured.

"If it's not in the lease agreement, you can't legally claim it," Ivy replied angrily. She'd read quite a lot on the legalities of leasing, and house rules etc. House rules were not legally enforceable; the owner could merely levy penalties for broken house rules, or demand repayment for broken items, or terminate the lease. She was pretty sure that he had no leg to stand on.

"I'll call you back," came the abrupt answer. Click. End of call.

Not a chance in hell was she going to pay three months' rent, thought Ivy acidly as she handed her key to Janet.

"You're moving out?" The caretaker sounded shocked. Ivy felt guilty. Janet had just mothered her and pampered her, cleaning up the mess Bonnie and Jake had left her with.

"I've got to," she said with a sheepish grin, showing Janet the cat in the bag. Peridot awoke from his snoozing again and did his whole stretch-and-yawn routine.

"Ooh," cooed Janet. "So you found him. Isn't he cute! Y're right, I wouldn't give 'im up either."

"Come and visit me," invited Ivy. "But please don't tell anyone you know where I've moved to!" And she wrote down the address for Janet.

"That's a bit out of town," commented the caretaker, surprised.

"I'm in a cottage," said Ivy. "It's gorgeous. Come for coffee! Or tea, if you like." She smiled.

4

Five hours and a lot of caustic cleaning materials later, Ivy was relaxing in the huge, old-fashioned four-footed bathtub in her cottage. She'd bought a new plug for it, just to be sure. Peridot was exploring his new home, energized from a long day sleeping. He was zipping from one end to the other, playing tag with some dust bunnies that had come with the movers, and skidding on the smooth tiles of the bathroom which now featured his litter box.

Ivy hadn't let grass grow under her feet in dealing with the issues in the bathroom. She'd gone to a builder's shop and collected a monkey wrench, a new shower head, curtain rail and shower curtain, putty and a toilet seat. The crack in the basin was by now puttied up; she'd replace the basin and take all these materials off the rent, she had decided. She hoped Alison would go along with that, but in principle it was the right way to do it.

The toilet seat (one from dark wood) was brand new, but it did blend in with the look of the place. The shower head was something else. She had replaced the old head, but still no water came through. The problem must be in the piping. Ivy preferred to shower, but for now she'd have to make do with baths.

As she emerged from the bathroom, towel wrapped around her and another around her long, glorious red curls, she spotted the book she had bought yesterday. 'Arcana'. She pulled it closer and lay on the bed in only towels, browsing in it. It was an amazingly beautiful book; clearly angled at children who wanted to pretend about magicka, she thought. Magicka. That was how the book put it.

There was 'history' on arcane things such as ghosts and witches; boggarts, dragons and the whole lot of fairy fae; the oriental snake charmers and fire eaters; the tradition of Egyptian, Far East and European magic; modern-day witches, spells and curses -

Ivy laughed out loud. This explained the shop assistant pressing the book into her hands! She'd asked the owner for a "book on hexes and curses".

There was a sound outside the cottage. Ivy put the book down and went outside to investigate.

From under the trees, two eyes were staring at her, out of a large feline face. This cat was white, with black florets. But it was huge! And it had rounded ears with tufts. She realized she was looking at a white leopard.

She and the leopard stared at each other for a breathless moment.

"Whoa," she whispered. "Easy now, big guy." And she edged back to the door of the cottage, slipped inside and closed it firmly. The intense stare of the cat haunted her.

A white leopard! Alison had a white leopard on her property! Ivy dialled her landlady.

"Oh, you saw the cat?" asked Alison. "It's... around here. It lives in the vicinity."

"You mean, someone is illegally keeping an endangered predator on their grounds?"

"I have no idea. Could be it's wild, too."

"But you never asked the zoo to pick it up?"

"I did – but they can't find it. It's a secretive beast. They scoured the grounds, even used dogs... you know, that thing has never hurt anyone. Not that any of us know of. So I guess we should leave it in peace."

"What about my cat?" asked Ivy. This might be a problem.

"No idea, Ivy. Keep him close."

"Thanks." Ivy made sure that Peridot was on her lap when she settled back into reading the Arcana, trying to ignore the thought of that beautiful wild creature roaming around her cottage.

The Arcana was really engrossing. She read and read, finding herself immersed in marvellous ideas and phantasms. From a purely recreational point of view this was magnificent. She resolved to buy some candles, incense and crystals tomorrow at the fleamarket – they always had such paraphernalia – and decorate her cottage accordingly. Why not? It struck her as very suitable for this lovely old place.

She was immersed in discovering the Druidic traditions when her phone rang. She reached for it where it lay on the small table next to her bed, and answered.

It was Bex, asking how Bonnie was doing.

"Thought I'd leave you two girls to get on before bothering," she said apologetically. "Or I'd have called earlier."

Ivy's jaw dropped. Bonnie was not at home? Icy fear crawled all over her.

"Bex – I sent her home yesterday!"

A shocked silence. Then: "What?"

"They were laying waste to my flat," said Ivy. "Bex, this is – oh my god! So she never came home... Bex, call the police and put in a missing person report *right now!* It's been more than twenty-four hours when I last saw her – hell, it wasn't even properly dark yet! I put her on the bus, Bex – the one that stops right in front of your door..."

The shocked silence continued.

"Call the police," urged Ivy. "I'm going out to look for her!" She ended the call, got into a warm jeans, T and pullover from her not-so-distant student days, warm boots – it was nippy out there – and peered at Peridot.

"You're coming with me," she said resolutely. "I'm not leaving you here with a monster cat."

Peridot allowed her to put him into the bag again; she added a couple of kitty treats. He settled down to nibble on them.

Ivy grabbed a moonbag – from her student days too – and loaded her cards and identification into it. She locked the cottage and knocked on Alison's door.

The heavy, creaky back door of the old house opened and Alison peered at her.

"Is something wrong?" She looked stressed.

"Very," said Ivy. "My niece has disappeared. I'm the last one who saw her. I have to go look for her. Just wanted to let you know that I may be in late."

"You're going on foot?" asked Alison.

"Buses and the Underground," replied Ivy. "Mostly on foot though."

"Take my husband's motorbike," offered Alison. "It will be faster. You know how to ride?"

Ivy nodded. She'd done a license when she was sixteen, in case she'd ever get to the point of buying herself such a scoot.

"It's in the garage," said Alison. "I'd ask Marc to go with you but he's not home from work yet. He works on the building site," she added with a hopeless sigh.

Ivy agreed again. She didn't have the time for social chat now. "Where's the bike?"

Alison led her to it, chattering away as she did.

The motorbike was one of the smallest, lightest Hondas, just fractionally away from only being a scooter. It was black with flame detail on the sides.

"He bought it when he was only a teenager," said Alison. "He never uses it now, but it's a good machine. Works perfectly. A bit light, that's all." She took the keys off a nail on the wall, and handed them to Ivy. "Now go carefully please!"

"Thanks!" Ivy mounted the bike and started it up.

Peridot shot out of the bag and clung to her shoulder, bottle-brush tail straight up.

"You can't take the cat with you!" exclaimed Alison. "Here, I'll take him! I'll look after him nicely until you're back, alright?"

She tried to remove Peridot from Ivy's shoulder and got herself bitten.

"Peridot!" exclaimed Ivy in shock.

"He doesn't want to let go of you," said Alison.

"When he calms down, I'll put him back in the bag," said Ivy. "I'll drive slowly at first."

"As you wish," replied Alison doubtfully and saw her off.

The bike growled along the road back to Ivy's old home. Peridot relaxed and settled more comfortably on her shoulder, his claws hooked into the thick mesh of the pullover. At least it wasn't raining, thought Ivy. The whole day had been sunny and dry and surprisingly warm for October. Unnatural weather, she thought; but it was good. She had an emergency rain-skin stashed in her bag, in case the weather changed its mind.

Bonnie had gone missing! This was impossible! Ivy even knew the bus driver, as she knew nearly all bus drivers in the area – she'd grown up there, and buses had been her prime transport forever. She disliked the Underground, so wherever she went she always preferred the bus. Over many years she had got chatting with the bus drivers, getting to know the men and women who so patiently did their low-paid jobs, year in and year out. This particular guy, Fareed, she'd vouch for with her life. He was second-generation British born, and he had a wife – only one, contrary to the way prejudices ran – and four children, the oldest of which must now be in secondary school. Ivy had been chatting to him from the time he'd only had one baby he was insanely in love with. Fareed was a decent guy. He wouldn't have touched Bonnie.

In fact that was her first stop. With kitten crouching on her shoulder enjoying the wind – she even thought she heard him purring – she tracked down the bus, following it from stop to stop, then shooting ahead and pre-empting the next bus stop, getting off the bike and waiting there for the bus.

It arrived and stopped for her. The bus driver gave her a puzzled look. She wasn't aware how wild she looked, with her mane of red curls wind-swept and that intense look in her green eyes.

"Ah! It's you, Dayib! Tell me, which route is Fareed taking tonight?"

"Oh!" The driver recognized her. "Ivy!" He laughed. "I thought you were a... never mind."

Ivy scowled. "Dayib, this is urgent. I need to find someone. Fareed saw her last. Please, what route is he on tonight?"

"It's his night off," said Dayib.

"Then I need to find out where he lives," said Ivy urgently.

"We don't give out that information to the public," replied Dayib with a scowl.

"Dayib, I'm not the public, I'm Ivy! My niece has gone missing. This is urgent! Please tell me where he stays, I must speak to him!"

Dayib stared at her for a few moments, then he gave her directions to Fareed's South London flat. Ivy nodded her thanks.

"Dayib, you may have saved a life tonight." And she mounted the bike and zoomed off, the cat clinging to her shoulder, his tail straight up again.

South of London was a scary place at the best of times for a redhead like Ivy. It was as though the river called all sorts of low-lives to it who did their shady dealings based on predation – of what they could find north of the River Thames.

"Peridot," she sighed, "I wish we could get there somehow without touching the ground! I don't fancy those bands of drugged-up youths!"

The bike went over a large bump. The wheels cleared the ground entirely; a huge leap. The engine cut out, too. Ivy went rigid; she hoped the rock hadn't damaged her landlord's motorbike! Coming down, Ivy wondered how such a rock could produce such a leap – and when they were going to reconnect with the ground, actually.

They didn't. The motorbike went flying through the air. After a stressful few moments she realized that it still responded to all her controls, speeding up or slowing down as usual; she could steer it as though they were riding on standard road; but – it went right over the rooftops, street lights, it cleared the power lines and high-rise blocks. Beneath them the Thames snaked away in the moonlight.

Peridot was purring. They were actually flying! Alright, thought Ivy, I've had a serious crash and now I'm lying down there in a coma and having a dream of flying. I hope the local scum don't rob me or worse while I'm out cold – I hope that Peridot can hide!

Regardless, she had to find Bonnie. She located Fareed's flat block and directed the bike downwards, landing lightly on the pavement in front of the high security gate that fenced off the building from the road. The motorbike's engine sprang back to life as its wheels touched the pavement. She cut the power.

Rubbish was blowing in the nippy breeze. There were a few fires going in old gasoline cans, on the other side of the road; there were people camping around these. They were sitting up like sticks, staring across the road at her. She smiled. She'd probably not have to fear this lot – they feared her!

She pressed the doorbell of Fareed's number. There was no answer for a very long time, then a timid, "who is it?" by a scared female voice.

"It's Ivy," she supplied. "Fareed knows me. I'm a bus passenger. I need to talk to him, urgently."

"*Who* is it?" came the renewed demand, this time significantly less timid, sounding quite angry.

"Look, Neeva," said Ivy. "I'm a friend of Fareed's. Every time I take his bus he always tells me about you and the children – how much he loves you all, how you fill his life with light. But I need his help! He's the last one who saw my niece, yesterday. She's missing."

The intercom went dead. Ivy cursed, hoping that Neeva hadn't allowed her jealous response to another female to overrule common sense.

Three minutes went by in breathless silence; Ivy watched

how across the road the vagabonds cleared off, one after the other. Then there was a click. The safety lock had been opened for her. She pushed the bike into the flat block, took it into the lift with her – no ways was she abandoning Marc's magic Honda – and went up to the thirteenth floor where Fareed resided. She pushed the motorbike along the passage to the correct door and knocked quietly. Peridot had settled on her shoulder, the claw tips were coming out and going in as he exercised his balance. His tiny tail twitched.

Neeva opened the door. She was indeed as beautiful as Fareed had described. Pale olive skin like satin, flawless except for a few smiling lines around the eyes; long shiny black hair all the way down to below her butt. Hair to be jealous of, thought Ivy, thinking with momentary dread of the moment she'd have to brush her own wild red curls back into submission after all that wind tonight.

Fareed appeared behind his wife. She'd never seen him not smiling; but he was scowling now.

"Fareed," she cut to the chase, "Bonnie has gone missing. You know, the girl I put on your bus yesterday?"

"That one," said Fareed. "She got off only two stops after getting on."

Ivy rolled her eyes. "Oh merry hells!" So the kid had subverted her; not even told Bex – that phone call might even have been phony, thought Ivy with irritation. May Bonnie get a nasty cramp in her bum!

"Which stop was that?"

He gave her the particulars. She thanked him. At least, she thought, the silly girl had run off herself, not been abducted. But how long that could go well...

She called Bex. Her sister-in-law was understandably in a state.

"I'm tracking her," said Ivy. "At least I found where she got off the bus, yesterday. Bex, it looks as if she ran away."

The mother didn't answer; it seemed as though she didn't know what to make of that.

"I'll find her," promised Ivy. "Did you call the police?"

"They are here right now, filing the report," said Bex. "... what, officer? - Oh – they want you to come in and make a statement."

"Later," said Ivy. "First I'm trying to find her."

"What?... oh. The officer says that he can issue an arrest warrant for you if you don't come in and give your statement."

Ivy swore. "I *said* I'll give my statement later! I'm trying to find her first!"

"They say that they'll come and arrest you right now," relayed Bex. "They're sending a patrol to your flat."

"Bex," said Ivy, "you're being bloody dense." She cut the line.

Ha, her flat! They wouldn't even find her there! But she had to warn Janet. She called Janet's number, still parked with motorcycle in the passageway in front of Fareed's doorway, with Fareed and Neeva following the conversation, riveted.

Janet's phone rang; then a muffled, "hush, dear, I'm in

the cinema, I can't take your call right now!"

"Call me the second you're out," said Ivy. "Enjoy!" She cut the call with a smile. They wouldn't find Janet at home either; and nobody else knew where she'd moved.

Stupid Bex! Ivy thanked Fareed and Neeva for their time and pushed the Honda back to the lift, catching a whispered "she's a bit weird, right, Fareed?" and the reply, "She seemed quite normal on the bus!" She grinned as the lift doors closed.

Out of that security gate, back into the street, which Ivy noted was now deserted. The low glow of the fires was the only indicator of the vagabonds having been there. Ivy got on the bike, started up the engine – Peridot's tail again stood up straight and his claws hooked through the pullover into her skin.

"So how are we going to get this thing to fly again?" she asked the kitten as he shuffled for a comfort spot, clinging like a monkey – a spiky monkey. She started it down the pavement, picked up a bit of speed and then aimed for the curb to get into the road.

As the front wheel left the curb she lifted it a little, aiming for that moment of free fall. It worked. The bike jumped into the air; its engine cut out and it gained height, but not enough. A few seconds later it touched down on the road again and the motor sputtered back into action. It took Ivy a few tries until she realized that she had to go quite fast for it to gain enough height to clear gravity.

Now that they were soaring over the rooftops again, she

could see London beneath, with streets curving away like on a map. She passed over her old home – ha, 'old' only by half a day, and 'home' it had never really been – and spotted the blue lights converging on it. She cut the light of the bike. Should have thought of doing that earlier, she thought. If she were going to be a UFO, at least she might be an invisible one. She did a skidding turn with the bike in mid-air and followed the bus route two stops on from where she had made Bonnie board, and set down, cutting the engine even before the wheels touched the pavement.

So here was the bus stop. She looked around. Still Putney; still the good areas. She had chased Jake off and told him to take himself to the library, the park, wherever. Bonnie was crazily in love with a drug dealer. Wait. If he was a dealer, he shouldn't be that difficult to find. She pushed her scoot slowly along the road, looking for likely characters.

And she found them. More specifically, one of them found her, not too far away.

"Looking for Jake," she told the youngster in rags who was approaching her. The kid had a shifty look about him; any moment now he'd be ripping out a knife.

She was right. She saw the quite deliberate flash of metal.

"'and it over, lady," sneered the youngster.

"Hand what over?"

"Yo money! Or yo life!"

She smiled and reached into her pocket, looking for

inspiration. And she found *something*, though it didn't strike her as a good weapon. Her nail file. It was a nice nail file, metallic and pointy; at least if she aimed for his face with it -

"I'm tired of waiting, lady," stated the young hooligan. "Come on, it's not so tough..."

She drew the nail file and pointed it at him, saying, "khazam!"

It was only meant to buy a second, for her to get on the bike and take off; but lightning flashed off the end of the nail file and zapped across the kid's hand. He let go of his knife with a yell of pain and cradled his hand. He raised terrified eyes to her.

"You burnt me! What's that thing? Those are illegal! I'll take you to the cleaners, lady!"

She didn't lower the nail file. Khazam, she thought. Got to remember that command!

"No," she said slowly and expressly, as though addressing an idiot, "you'll take me to Jake. Sure you know Jake. Everyone knows Jake. The Man, you know!"

"You leave me no choice, lady," gnashed the hooligan and reached into his belt. But before the pistol was even pointing at her properly, she had sent another 'khazam' bolt to knock it out of his hand.

"You'll burn my 'and right off!" yowled the guy. "Alright, alright, I'm taking you to Jake – but after that, lady, you're mincemeat!"

"We'll see about that," said Ivy.

Not too much later they entered a fair-sized garden to knock on the door of a fair-sized, middle-class house. The door opened.

"She wants Jake," said the hooligan, turned and left her standing there, cat, motorbike and all.

The middle-aged man eyed her with suspicion.

"What do you want from my son?"

"Is he home?" asked Ivy.

"No."

"Where is he?"

"What are you, the social worker?" snapped the man angrily. "Kid ran off yesterday. Never said where he was going."

"Did you file a missing person report?"

"What are you, the cops?"

Peridot clambered from her shoulder onto her head, slipping down over her face. She caught him, looked at him and stuck him into his bag.

"Meow!"

"No," she replied to the man, deciding on the soft-touch approach rather than scare tactics – which, she realized, she had in her pocket in the shape of an unassuming nail file. "I'm the aunt of the girl he's with. She has disappeared, and I fear for her life."

"Oh!" The whole demeanour of the man changed. "Come in!"

After an interrogation of nearly an hour with the parents of Jake, Ivy had learnt a lot.

Jake hadn't come home yesterday. In fact they hadn't thrown him out; he'd left in a huff when they had refused to accommodate his girlfriend - "that little whore", as Jake's mother put it. That their son had impregnated a girl, didn't seem to worry them much. "Boys will be boys," was the father's stance, and he added that it was the responsibility of the girl to say no. "Luckily my daughter is in a convent school," he laughed. "They keep them out of trouble there."

You need an attitude transplant, thought Ivy acidly. May your toenails grow in until you change!

And as for the drug dealing?

"That's a lie," said Jake's mother with indignation.

"So how did this street lurker know where your son lives?" asked Ivy.

"How should I know? They're always hanging around in these areas. Jake is always chasing them off. He does it so gently, only talks to them quietly, doesn't disturb the neighbours..."

How could a mother be that ignorant, wondered Ivy. May she grow brains, soon! And Bex, too!

"Jake's a clever boy," said his father with pride. In his eyes Ivy saw clearly that he knew about the drugs. "He'll be rich one day."

Ivy glanced at the motorbike she had insisted on taking

into the house. She didn't want the lurkers to steal it. It was probably time to go, more or less; but first she had to get at least some lead where Jake would be hiding.

One thing was clear. The family wasn't harbouring Bonnie. They thought nothing of Bonnie; she was filth, in their eyes.

"So where would Jake have gone?" she asked. "Any preferential friends..."

"Oh yes," said the mother. "He's probably bunking down at his friend Zoro."

"*Zoro?*" asked Ivy with a frown.

"That's a nickname, obviously," said the woman. "We don't know his real name. Jake never mentioned it."

"So where does Zoro stay?" asked Ivy.

Jake's mom gave the address. It was in quite a well-off suburb.

"Do they have a number?" asked Ivy, tired of chasing after people. "Can we call them?"

"Never gave a number," said Jake's father.

Ivy sighed. She sat back, trying to think where to take it now. The trail of Bonnie may or may not run concurrently with Jake's trail. If she thought of that dangerous hooligan who had accosted her, she very much feared it ended not too far from that bus stop.

"I wish I could see where she is!" she uttered, very tired all of a sudden. She closed her eyes for a moment, trying to decide what next.

Before her inner eye she saw a wild place. Perhaps the Heath. Putney Heath. It looked a lot like that place. There was a fire going; a controlled small fire, inside something – a black pot, she realized. A tripod. A *cauldron*. And candles, tiny little lights like fairies, set in a circle around the few shapes that hunched around the fire.

Four shapes. One was standing, strewing with his fingers some or other powders into the fire, changing the colours of the flames. Chemicals then, obviously. Green flames, blue flames, red and bright orange. There was a murmur. She edged closer, trying to hear. The four shapes were muttering words in unison. She tried to edge past the candles and was repelled by a strong wind, catapulted back into Jake's parents' house.

"She's asleep," she heard Jake's mother say.

What? She'd only closed her eyes for a moment. Ivy opened her eyes, blinked a few times. The figure standing up had been Jake. And one of the other three had been Bonnie.

Peridot had climbed out of her bag and was nestling on her lap, purring his motorbike stuttering purr. And a loud banging on the door.

Jake's father got up from the table around which they'd held their conference and went into the hallway. Ivy heard him opening the door.

"Evening, sir!"

She suddenly knew she had to get away.

"I think I know where to look for them," she told Jake's mother, and following the woman, pushed the motorbike out through the back door. A number of steps led down into the back garden. This was great.

She started the engine in the kitchen and revved terribly, building pressure without moving. Then she released the brakes and flew out of the back door, down the steps; ripped the handlebars upwards, cleared the ground -

Up and away, with Jake's mother staring after her in stupefaction. And Peridot complaining because she'd stuffed him into the bag again.

I'm a witch's familiar, he seemed to be saying. *What do you think you're doing stuffing me in a bag?*

So, she thought, if that's the case, then I must be a witch?

The damned cops actually shot after her! Ivy sped up and ducked down low over the handlebar. Within seconds she was out of range.

May their guns rust and fall apart, she cursed inwardly. Her cellphone rang. She didn't know if there were laws against answering a cellphone in mid-flight, but if there were, she was breaking them now. Who was to stop her?

"Ivy?" came the flustered voice of her sister-in-law.

"Bex," she replied.

"The police says you moved out from your house!"

"Yea, I did, actually," said Ivy. "I adopted a cat. Stupid landlord wouldn't allow pets. So I had to move."

"The landlord says you left no address!"

"He wants three months' extra rent from me, which

wasn't in the contract," replied Ivy, watching the streets go by underneath. "Think I'll tell him where to send his thugs?"

"You think he has *thugs?*" asked Bex, shocked.

"Bex, have you had any news from Bonnie?" asked Ivy.

"No. There's no answer on her phone."

Duh, mother, thought Ivy scathingly. Think your runaway kid will answer your calls? She *faked* calling you last night, to try and manipulate me.

"I've been to Jake's parents," she told Bex. "She's not there, and neither is Jake. I think they are together. At least I hope so!" If her vision was wrong and Bonnie had fallen prey to the night life lurking in the streets behind that bus stop...

"The police tell me you escaped from Jake's place," said Bex. "Ivy, please, just stop and tell them everything! We'll work something out! I can raise bail money."

Ivy blinked.

"Bail money?" What? Was *she* now the prime suspect?

Of course she was! Bonnie had disappeared while under her care! Ivy cut the call, too angry to continue the conversation. May Bex turn old and fat, may her hair not accept any more artificial colour!

Now, if only Bonnie and Jake and their nasty little circle could stay put where they were...

A circle of candles? A *cauldron?* Someone conjuring with flames and chemicals? This was occult, thought Ivy with a jolt. Bonnie was involved in the occult!

Ha, that should be a hard one for her mother to swallow!

Bex was the naïve type, very superstitious – Ivy wondered what she'd say to a black cat. And a flying motorbike! That instant Ivy realized that she needed information – as much of it as she could get.

She turned the motorcycle which had been circling aimlessly over London, towards the west and aimed it at Putney Heath. There would be more heaths and greens than this one; but it was where she'd start looking.

5

Once again, Ivy cut the motorcycle's engine before it could make a noise touching down on the soft vegetation. Peridot complained softly in his bag; but she didn't let him out, because she was scared he might run away into the Heath. Then she'd never find him again.

She pushed the motorbike along the path, marvelling at how everything had become overgrown since she'd last been here, in spring last year. They had just mowed and tended the paths, at that point. Now?

She was glad it was dark; at least she didn't have to see all the rubbish up close that had to be floating around in this previously beautiful park.

There were a few crickets that simply wouldn't give up. But for the rest, it was quiet. Not the lively park it was in summer! A small shadow whooshed away ahead in the path. Probably a fox. No, Peridot was definitely staying in the bag for now!

What was she going to do against four big teenage thugs dabbling in occult – with a nail file? Suddenly her courage deserted her. Going on the hunch that Bonnie was definitely here, she'd been planning to pick the girl straight out of that circle, force her onto the motorbike and return her home, into the mob of waiting cops. Damn, that was all Bonnie deserved! How could she do this to Bex?

But she'd need more than a nail file. She could throw 'khazam' lightning at one or two, but she'd be outnumbered and beaten down in a second. She glanced around and found a good, thick piece of a branch lying on the path. It was longer than she was tall. She picked it up and put it across the handlebars of the motorbike and continued pushing the bike to where she thought she had seen them.

And there they were, indeed! Firelight shone through the trees. She rounded the bend and saw the circle of fairy lights and the burning cauldron, and the four occult revellers around it. They weren't yet aware of her. She reached for her 'staff' and her nail file, leaving her flying scoot standing on the path, and walked up to the circle, slowly, but without crouching.

Tiny claws dug into her shoulder. Ag, Peridot! He'd got out of the bag! Well, she had no time for a scuffle with a kitten right now, so he could just perch on her shoulder and hang on.

Should she try to be nice first?

"Bonnie," she called.

The four faces swivelled to her.

"Intruder!" screeched one of the girls, pointing an awful finger at her. All four of them picked up something from what was lying scattered amongst them on the ground – a crystal, a dagger, a stick – *wand,* corrected Ivy, after all they were practising occult. And they got up and converged on her, slowly, menacingly.

They're on the Dark Path, she thought distinctly, though she had no idea where the knowledge came from, that within the occult there were degrees.

The four looked drugged up to their ears, in fact.

"Bonnie!" called Ivy, this time with significantly more authority. "Come here!"

"It's your auntie," Jake sniggered. "Coming to check that you're not being naughty! Have you been a wicked girl then, Bonnie?"

Ivy studied them. This was a dangerous game. Each one of the incidental implements these children had picked up, could do serious damage. Jake, in fact, brandished a ceremonial dagger the length of his forearm.

They're not supposed to use such a large one, came the thought. *Looks like they're sacrificing things with it.*

Whether fear made her do it or whether she was suddenly fed up with these young hooligans abusing a sacred legacy, she couldn't clearly discern; but she rammed her 'staff' down on the ground in anger.

Lightning shot out of the upper end of it and crackled above her head. The four youngsters recoiled in surprise; but their response worried Ivy as they recovered in a moment and continued to approach.

"Your auntie's a witch, Bonnie," taunted one of the four. "Lookit her playing with lightning magick!"

"Careful," warned Jake. "She's crazy. She knows how

to burn."

Her time was running out. She stomped the ground a second time with her staff, shouting, "Bonnie, this instant! Come here!"

Bonnie didn't obey; the other three, less surprised by the second show of lightning, only made remarks such as, "impressive show!" and "ooh! She's getting angry!"

That was enough. Ivy hit the ground with the staff a third time, this time shouting, "khazam!" Blinding lightning flashed; while everyone was reeling, blinded, she lunged forward, grabbed Bonnie's arm and dragged the resisting girl to the motorbike, dropping the stick in the process. Bonnie fought and battled; but Ivy was stronger and forced her onto the seat.

"Khazam," she shouted, pointing her finger, envisioning a glue gun. Bonnie tried to wriggle off the motorbike's seat and found herself stuck down. Ivy climbed on behind the girl, grabbed the handles past the struggling teenager and revved up the engine. And off they went, over stick and stone, in wild circles around the witches' fire, looking for a suitable place to release gravity.

"What are you trying?" screeched Bonnie. "Are you mad?"

The others had by now picked up the lightning staff and were hammering the ground with it shouting "khazam"; all without the slightest spark coming from the branch. When this failed, they threw the stick in the way of the approaching motorcycle.

Bonnie screamed, shouting at Ivy to avoid that stick or they'd be done for. Ivy aimed straight at it; then at the last moment lifted the front wheels off the grass and let the stick provide that essential airborne moment for the rear wheels.

It worked. They flew away into the night, Ivy battling to steer with Bonnie in the way.

"Duck down!" she instructed her difficult niece. "Can't see where I'm going!"

Bonnie obeyed out of pure fear. Now that they were in mid-air she had stopped trying to escape; she was rigid with terror.

Ivy headed towards Bex's home, landed her scoot on the doorstep and rapped like Santa Claus on the door. The place was swarming with police; it was one of those who opened the door for her.

"The errant daughter returns," she said cynically. "Where's Bex?" And she freed Bonnie with another "khazam" and shoved her inside, an iron grip on her shoulder.

"Ow! Ow! You're hurting me!" moaned Bonnie.

"Well, you're not running away again," replied Ivy. "Where's Bex?"

Bex entered the room, spotted Bonnie and ran to her, clasping her in an embrace. "You're safe, my darling! Thank God!" And she looked up at Ivy. "There you are! Finally!"

Finally? wondered Ivy. She didn't wonder long.

"This is Ivy," said Bex. "The suspect."

"The *suspect?*" exclaimed Ivy. "Why, damn you! May your milk go sour in your fridge!" She only had time to rip out her nail file as two policemen and one -woman converged on her, the woman carrying handcuffs. "Khazam!" she shouted heartily.

Lightning fizzled around the police officers' hands, and double around the handcuffs. The policewoman dropped them in shock. Ivy added in her mind, *but don't hurt them, only scare them!* She waited for them to recoil, to give her half a gap, and slipped through it, running outside to her motorcycle. She mounted the flying bike, revved its engine, and took off right off the steps from Bex' front door, leaving them all staring after her.

Damn Bex! She'd have her arrested for bringing Bonnie back! After all that Ivy had been through, she wouldn't have expected this. She directed the scoot to the cottage, taking care to keep the lights off; and after a good few minutes of flight, she landed on the driveway and drove the rest of the way to the garage.

Alison had heard the noise and came out to greet her.

"Any news?"

"Found her," said Ivy, out of breath and suddenly dead tired.

"Is she..."

"Alive, Alison. I'll tell you in the morning." She parked the Honda and turned towards her cottage, but stopped. "One thing, Alison. This is a super machine. If Marc wants to sell it to me, please tell him to make me a price."

Alison's face lit up.

Oh honey, thought Ivy, suddenly feeling terribly sorry for the young woman – barely her own age, but already so steeped in financial trouble. It will come right! May there be enough this month to pay all your bills! And may that terrible worry release its grip on you – you're making yourself sick! You're too young to be that worried!

"Is he home yet?"

"Marc? Sure! He came home around eight. He's fast asleep – say, Ivy, you know what time it is?"

"Witching hour," said Ivy with a grin. "Finding her wasn't simple. I'm beat."

"Go to sleep," said the landlady. "We can chat in the morning."

"You sure the leopard doesn't hurt anyone?" asked Ivy.

"Nobody," insisted Alison. "It's shy. It never even comes up close."

"Leopards are stealthy," said Ivy. "They attack from a hiding place."

"Well, I don't know," said Alison. "It's been here forever, about, and it's never done anything. I think it may be tame. May actually belong to a neighbour."

"They shouldn't let it roam," said Ivy pointedly.

"How do you restrain a cat?" Alison asked back.

Ivy marched across the lawn, looking out for the white

leopard. At least its light colour would give it away; she needed to keep her eyes open. But she was also quite sure suddenly that a lightning spark would frighten it off – though she'd hate to singe that beautiful white coat.

She unlocked her cottage's door, dead tired, and locked it behind herself again; put down the bag – Peridot crawled out of it; he'd gone to hide in it himself during that insane ride with Bonnie on the bike – and crawled into the fresh sheets on her bed. Peridot snuggled in with her, cuddling up at her throat. She stroked his soft tummy until he fell asleep.

What a day, she thought. And now the blasted police were hunting her. And Bex – had she looked greyer than before? Her hair was ageing quite fast, thought Ivy. And then she recalled the curse she'd launched at Bex.

That was interesting! Did her curses actually work? She had been using them as a tacit way to vent her feelings, just about forever. It was probably only a fancy notion – Bex could easily have aged from the worry about Bonnie.

Well, they deserved each other, thought Ivy. The police would do a drug test on Bonnie and find whatever it was the girl was using. Ivy had a good mind of tipping the police off as to where that group held their little circles. In fact, that was what she'd be doing first thing in the morning.

Kids like those give the Craft a bad name!

She had no idea where that thought had come from; she suspected it of leeching out of the book next to her bed, 'Arcana'. With a sigh she closed her eyes. Come what may now – after tonight, no ghost was going to scare her. She was simply too tired.

Perhaps the white leopard was the 'ghost', she thought. Enough to scare tenants away indeed.

"We'll have to be careful of that crazy witch," said Chatz. "Lightning magic! Definitely insane."

"We've got to watch out anyway now," said Charlotte. "They got Bonnie. The cops will look for us now."

"The cops are the least of our concerns," growled Jake. "I had no clue she's that powerful! There's only one chance."

They stared at each other in silence. Then Chatz started nodding slowly; shortly after, Charlotte did too.

"But how does she do that levitation spell?" complained Charlotte. "It never works for us! All that we ever do is invoke -"

Jake put a finger across his lips. "Shoosh. No bad vibes now, Charlotte. We're all-powerful if we focus. I think we must call in Spirit, and another Water. We've lost Bonnie. Whom do we ask?"

The next morning dawned bright and clear, if quite windy. This was a reprieve; the rain had given Ivy a break yesterday and was giving her another today. One complete weekend. What a pleasure.

She stretched in her bed, taking in her surroundings. She was utterly pleased with renting the cottage. In fact she ought to make Alison a bid for it. She'd like to keep it. It suited her beautifully. And if she'd ever need to move away – well then she could rent it out, to a retired old lady or someone. Who was not scared of a single leopard. That should be no problem.

She got up and realized that she was still wearing those dirty, stressed-up clothes from last night. She treated herself to another soak in the bathtub-with-feet, and dressed once again in comfortable, old clothes. There was something she hadn't taken into account. There was no washing machine; she doubted that Alison had one either. So she'd need one, at some point. But that should be no problem.

Today she was going to the fleamarket to flesh out her home a bit. She had almost forgotten that the police had nearly arrested her, last night. In any case that whole episode felt more like a fever dream the more she thought about it. Had she really found Bonnie in a circle of kids practising black magic? And had she really – she shook her head. Impossible that she could have been flying on an ordinary motorcycle.

Peridot was meowing at her. She filled his food bowls and sorted out his litter box, and made sure that all the windows were closed so he couldn't get away.

"Today you stay in here, my boy," she told him firmly.

"Meow!"

"No. You can be my familiar at night. In the day I have

to be human. And you have to be a cat. I'll bring you a surprise," she promised, smiling. "Be good now, I'll see you later." She made sure every last window was closed tightly, shut the cottage door on his accusing eyes and locked it, and headed down to Alison's place.

"Where's the cat?" was Alison's first question.

"In the cottage," said Ivy. "He has to learn to be by himself at times. I can't take him to the office on Monday, either. Say, Alison, did you speak to Marc?"

"He's very happy to sell you his motorbike," replied the young landlady. Marc appeared in the doorway behind her and nodded, smiling.

Ivy jarred, and had to check herself. It was seldom that one met such a handsome man. He was tall, broad-shouldered and muscular; his hair quite dark like that of a Spaniard; but his eyes, underneath dark, focused eyebrows – deep-blue, nearly indigo eyes – shrouded in... *something*. They were intense eyes, to say the least. Lined all over with laugh-lines; together with the deep suntan, it led her to conclude that he spent a lot of time in the sun.

He'd noted her moment of surprise, and was smiling, pocketing the unspoken compliment. His appraising glance told her that he didn't think her too shabby, either. He stuck out a large, well-muscled hand for her to shake – on touching, she felt that same unease again.

Oh my god, Ivy, the man is married, she scolded herself. She wasn't the type to chase after men that were taken. She

67

glanced at Alison, wondering if the girl had picked up on this exchange. The landlady looked so young, innocent and vulnerable! No, she'd noticed nothing – or was brilliant at hiding her reaction.

"Pleased to meet you!" said Marc, with a strong baritone voice.

"You work in construction?" she asked, reclaiming her cool.

He nodded. "Trained for an architect, but you know – those jobs are so scarce! I'm a professional bricklayer," not without cynicism.

Ah! And there was that flash in his eyes that told her that, even if he'd been single, she would not have wanted to tangle with him. A streak of coldness, professional anger. He was probably a passive-aggressive type.

"That's right," Alison chipped in. "We thought if he studied architecture, there'd be a good job for him. Forget that! - But come in, Ivy! We're having breakfast. Won't you join us?"

So Ivy sat down to enjoy a breakfast of home-baked scones and strawberry jam with Alison and Marc. The strawberry jam was the cheap jelly sort; Ivy felt a bit guilty that she was helping this couple eat up their provisions.

"How long have you two known each other?" she asked between bites, in part to focus the attention on their marriage. She had not enjoyed being taken off-guard like that in response to a male, and was going to discourage anything he thought she might have implied by – what? Doing nothing?

A knowing, intimate smile passed between Alison and Marc.

"Since grade school," said Alison. "We started going out in A-levels."

"Had my eye on her long before that," added Marc with a grin. Alison, cascading black hair and white skin, smiled. Snow White, thought Ivy. And the Hunter. Well, not quite. Alison was a – witchy name...

They did make a gorgeous couple, though it seemed to her as though something was amiss. She hoped she wasn't the cause of that. Three seconds after meeting the male. Right!

"Tell me about this house?" she prompted.

"The property belonged to an elderly gentleman," said Alison. "We bought it from him when he wanted to retire to Hawaii. He sold it furnished and all. We suspect the cottage belonged to his mother. Got the whole deal at a total bargain. Total throwaway price. All he wanted was out."

"The neighbours say she died in there," said Marc with a laugh, not catching the furious warning glances from his wife.

"How did she die?" asked Ivy. "Not attacked by something?"

"Natural causes," said Marc.

"Did you sleep alright?" asked Alison, concerned. "No funny noises, geyser clonking..."

"Things going bump in the night?" asked Ivy, laughing. "No, Alison! I slept like a rock! Saw nothing unusual except that big cat... Actually wanted to ask you – three things."

"Shoot," said Alison.

"First. How much does Marc want for his Honda?"

"Two grand," said Marc.

Two grand? Ivy scowled. The seven-year-old machine wasn't worth that. But... it flies, said a little voice in her head.

The man was smiling – but by now it wasn't the dripping-sex-appeal style smile but a rather calculating one. He was shrewd. And possibly desperate for money.

Hold on. Let's make financial sense here.

"Okay, I'll give that some thought," said Ivy. "The other thing was, you're not maybe thinking of selling the cottage? White leopard, ghost and all?"

A look of complete new possibilities entered Alison's eyes.

"Marc – if we did – we could afford -"

"Shoosh, Allie, not here! - We'll have to think about that, Ivy."

"If you do, with all furniture please," she added. "And a patch of garden surrounding it, and the garden behind it."

"Two million and you've got yourself a deal," said Marc.

"Two million?" She doubted the whole property was worth that. "I think I'll get it assessed and see if -"

"Five hundred G," Alison cut in quickly. Her husband gasped. "But we want in the contract that if you want to sell it, you have to sell it back to us first."

"First option," said Ivy. "Hmm. It can be arranged. I

really want to get an assessor to -"

"It's worth more than five hundred grand," said Alison. "Much more! It would be a special price because we like you."

Marc scowled at her.

"Let me think about it," said Ivy. And the third thing: Alison, do you want to come to the flea markets with me today?"

"I'd love to," squeaked Alison delightedly. "I need a day out! This place with all its issues is driving me round the bend!"

"On one condition," said Marc darkly. "That you girls don't cut deals behind my back! I won't stand for it."

Ivy smiled sweetly at him. "No problem! That's not the reason I'm taking Alison along. I don't feel like going alone."

It turned into a glorious day. Ivy and Alison trawled through the flea markets, sat down at a bistro for lunch, and picked up a lot of items.

"I can't really afford all this," said Alison guiltily. "We're saving for a baby."

"Oh!" exclaimed Ivy, surprised. "Are you..."

"Not yet," said Alison. "We first have to get our money right. And Marc is such a grouch these days..." She clapped her hand over her mouth and grinned. "Too much information, right? But with his attitude, getting him even halfway in the mood..."

Ivy laughed. "You're right, that's too much information."

"It's the money," Alison said. "The payments on that old home are breaking our backs. We got the whole place for two million – not bad for a full hectare, and a five-bedroom family home, a huge garden and a granny flat."

"How on Earth did Marc get a loan for that?" asked Ivy.

"I was working, then," said Alison. "For an estate agent. But Marc doesn't want me coming home late, that is too risky now with all the crime and that, and so we sold the car and we're trying to make do on one income..."

"Surely a bricklayer's income can't..." Ivy trailed off. Why on Earth had Alison given up her job? "Whose idea was it that you stop working?"

"Marc's," said Alison. "He said, when I have children I won't be able to do it anyway, so we should train to make do now."

Financial nonsense! Ivy didn't even realize how she was shaking her head. "Now that things are tough – why don't you take your job back?"

"The jobs are all taken," said Alison. "Anyway Marc wouldn't like it."

"And would Marc like it if the bank repossessed your house?" asked Ivy scathingly. So that was why Marc had wanted two million for the cottage. Pay off their whole loan in one go! Ha! He should be so lucky!

"If he could only get a job as an architect!" sighed Alison.

"Are you even allowed out of the house in the day?"

asked Ivy suspiciously.

"Oh yes, sure! But where would I go?"

Ivy shook her head again and purchased a colourful woven rug for Alison. She knew where *she* would go, if she were in Alison's position – even without money. The library – the second-hand book store...

In fact, she needed to get back to that store in Putney. There was something she wanted to ask that shop assistant. His unusually blue eyes came to mind. One rarely saw that shade.

Marc had dark-blue eyes. Striking, yes. But something lurked. There was hidden violence there; she didn't envy Alison. That shop assistant's eyes had been different. Blue like the sea around a tropical island. Or the sky on a – no, the sky was never that shade of blue. Ivy realized that she had really only seen the eyes of that assistant. And only for a split second. She wouldn't recognize him.

How on Earth had he known that she'd be dealing with the occult?

"Tell your hubbs that I'll take the Honda for *one* grand," she said. "As for the cottage, that really has to be assessed before the bank can give *me* a loan. Banks don't allow people to sell property above its real value."

"But if you had the cash..."

Ivy laughed out loud.

"Oh, sure – do I look like someone who has five hundred grand stashed away in cash somewhere?"

By the time Ivy opened her front door, it was five o'clock. She and Alison had spent an equally enjoyable afternoon at more flea markets. And by now she knew a few things.

Firstly, Marc was probably a force to avoid. Alison had only sweet words for him; but all around the edges, evidence of his temper and his scathing moods came crawling out. No thanks, thought Ivy. In fact, she was going to find Alison some support and some counselling.

Secondly, the couple was in deep dire straits, financially. Ivy resolved to find Marc a job as architect, and Alison some lightweight work, too.

And thirdly, Alison's need for company and friendship bordered on the pathological. The girl had laughed and giggled like a teenager, so thankful to go around the markets with a friend. Poor Alison! To sit cooped up in that house all day just because of an overly jealous husband!

Peridot came to greet her at the door, meowing accusingly. She picked him up and cuddled him, and checked his food bowls and gave him some fresh milk, which he lapped greedily.

She sank down on the chaise-longue and put her feet up, kicking off her shoes. Those pumps had had their fair share of work, today. But they fitted nicely, so her feet weren't sore, just tired. She leaned back and felt the wonderful wave of weariness wash over her.

"Peridot, can't you just bring me my book..." She smiled. The kitten jumped on her lap and walked up her chest, and put a paw on her nose. He then curled up on her chest, nestling against her throat, and started to purr. And the young man who'd been sitting in the chair watching her, got up and handed her the 'Arcana', for the second time.

Ivy sat bolt upright, barely catching Peridot in time. The bookshop assistant. How had he got in here?

"I'm Alison's neighbour," he introduced himself. "Bryan Woodwright."

"Two questions," said Ivy, her eyes darting about to find something she could use for 'khazamming' him. "How did you get in?"

"That's one question," said Bryan with a winning smile, strikingly blue eyes and all. It really was a winning smile. It won so thoroughly that it very almost won her trust. Only almost. That made her very suspicious of him.

"Well?" she prompted, picking up a small *athame* she had obtained at the fleamarket, and toying with it. She was quite sure it would *khazam* nicely – it had the right shape.

"Marc let me in," said Bryan. "He said you'd probably wanted to meet me."

And so he locked the door behind Bryan and let her walk into this, like into a trap?

What if Peridot had slipped out, got lost and had been eaten by that leopard?

"And secondly, how did you manage that I didn't see you right away?"

"I'm sitting in the chair with the back to the door," said Bryan.

She allowed herself to breathe, a little. Gosh, she was as jumpy as a kitten!

"Your cat's good company," Bryan pointed out.

"So Marc let you in here..." said Ivy, trying to put this together.

"I was over for a couple of beers," said Bryan. "He told me he has this luscious girl who moved into his garden cottage, so of course I had to come and have a look."

Luscious, huh?

"Alright," said Ivy. "I'm presuming here that you're not a burglar, and that you're sincere you just wanted a look. What have you stolen?"

Bryan laughed and turned his pockets inside-out. "Nothing, see?"

"And besides... how did you know it was the Arcana I wanted to read?" she asked pointedly.

Bryan laughed again. "Because it's the book I sold you two days back. Ivy, don't be scared. I want nothing, just to make your acquaintance."

"I'm not scared," she snapped, pointing the *khazammer* at him. Lightning crackled over it, subdued.

"Shoot me with that," invited Bryan.

"Ha, you really want that?" Ivy pointed the athame and

commanded, "khazam!"

Lightning short out of tip of the small ceremonial knife. It streaked towards Bryan quite satisfactorily – and dispersed over a slightly glowing, golden shield he had cast around himself. The shield disappeared with the lightning.

Ivy stared.

"You see," said Bryan with a smug smile, "you need me. You want to learn about the Craft. But books can only tell you so much, until you need an experienced mage taking you in hand."

"How the hell did *Marc* know..."

"He doesn't! Marc is the sceptic in this equation. He doesn't believe a word of it. Alison on the other hand... quite an adept little witch, but her husband keeps her under his shoe."

"So I gathered," said Ivy. "If you're so clued up, Bryan, can you give me an insight into what's happening with Bex and Bonnie?"

Bryan stared at her without comprehension.

"Coffee," she said. Outside, the light was fading.

"I'll make us coffee," volunteered Bryan. He got up and found his way around her kitchen, pottered around making coffee and arrived back with two large mugs, handing her hers. And he smiled smugly. That irritated her.

"Thanks," she said with a sweet smile back at him and took the coffee. He had some gall coming into her house like that! May that manipulative little smile cause him -

"Stop that," said Bryan, holding up a hand as if warding her off. "You have to learn to think twice before you curse someone."

"How the hell did you know I was cursing you?"

"You were muttering," he smiled. "You must understand the first few rules, Ivy."

"Rules, aha," she echoed, waiting for him to elaborate. And resolving not to mutter. Some cheek! Walking into her home like that and then talking about rules.

"I wanted to give you my number in the bookshop," said Bryan. "Nobody should start on such a path without solid guidance! But you disappeared. So I tracked you to work, and to where you stayed – and I was too late. You'd gone missing. That caretaker knows where you are but you think I could get a word out of her?"

Ivy peered at him. "You *stalked* me?" Oof! Last thing she needed, on top of all the rest: A stalker! This was getting creepy.

"No," said Bryan patiently, "I tried to *track* you. Normally I'm good with that. But you vanished off the face of the Earth."

"So why did you stalk me, then?"

Bryan sighed impatiently and gave up on that. "The Arcana is good background, but it's not enough," he explained. "You've no clue how long it took me to procure this copy!"

"What?"

"And now I'll have to get myself another copy," he said

with a grin. "That book is rare – there was only one very limited edition."

"Why did you give your copy to the second-hand store?" asked Ivy, baffled.

"I didn't! I gave it to *you*. Because you need it."

Ivy shook her head. "You're nuts! I wouldn't sell my best book second-hand to some stranger in a bookshop! Were you hard-up for cash or something?"

Bryan laughed.

"Not exactly. I could see some huge damage happening and I had to prevent it."

"Why? What's it got to do with you? Surely I can't be that fascinating?" She'd had that kind of response from men and boys all her life. It was the hair, she supposed.

"It's not about who *you* are but who *I* am," he popped her bubble. "In our circles, once you set someone on a path, you are responsible for them until they can stand on their own feet."

What an ego!

"*You* didn't set me on this path," laughed Ivy. "And I *can* stand on my own feet." She indicated the athame.

"Khazam," replied Bryan, grinning. "Nice one! Why not 'abracadabra' or 'boom'?" He shook his head. "You can't, you know. You're like an infant thrown into deep water. Half the time you don't even understand what is happening around you, never mind what you're doing."

"I'm a fast study," said Ivy condescendingly. "And how do you claim to know all this anyway?"

"Your cat is quite talkative," smiled Bryan. He held out a hand. Peridot jumped down from her lap and onto Bryan's. Ivy bristled.

"Ivy," said Bryan seriously, "better tell me everything."

She was instantly suspicious.

"You're not a cop, are you? Did Bex send you? How did she find me?" That would explain how Marc would have had to let him in.

"No, and I don't know who Bex is," he replied.

"But you're not *really* Marc's neighbour?" she asked sceptically.

"Actually I am," said Bryan. "If I believed in chance I'd say, pure coincidence. But it's not. It's synchronicity."

"Sync *what*?"

"When things happen the way they should to produce a highly unlikely result," he summarized. "What's this about cops?"

"They're after me," said Ivy lightly, stretching out her hand for Peridot again. The kitten jumped off Bryan's lap and came back to her. "You're one confused kitty," she scolded him as she scratched behind his ears. "You're *my* familiar! You don't know this person from soap! Can't trust him, you know!"

Bryan grinned.

"Biscuits," said Ivy, jumped up and went to rummage in the cupboards of the kitchen. There was only a low wall between the lounge and the kitchenette; she didn't lose sight of

Bryan and could watch that he didn't get up to nonsense.

She found the packets of biscuits she'd bought yesterday and ripped two open into a bowl, and offered some to Bryan. He took one. She placed the rest on the antique coffee table, took one herself and settled back on the chaise longue, comfortably pulling her legs in under her.

"Ivy," said Bryan seriously, "if the police are after you, it's worse than I thought. You must tell me everything."

She smiled smugly. "It's all under control," she told him. "They have no way of finding me. I moved, quite by accident, without leaving any address."

"I wouldn't count on that," he said. "The caretaker at your old place may be resistant to strangers fishing, but she can't resist the law – she'll legally have to give them your address. Is there any *mundane* reason they're looking for you?" he probed.

"'Tis none of his business," she said lightly to Peridot who had settled down and was curled up next to her again. And she wriggled her varnish-tipped toes. "I'm apparently a witch, Bryan. That makes me off-beat to begin with; different, strange, whatever you like to call it. Apparently weird things happen to us. But it's no problem."

"No problem?" he repeated. "Let me give you some background, Ivy. Usually it's teenagers that start tangling with the Craft. They start off playing glassy-glassy; next thing people like me have to climb in and clean out the mess of demons they've invoked. Real deceased spirits have better

81

things to do than hang around teenage séances. So it's inevitably the rubbish they call up."

"If you believe in that nonsense," she strewed in.

He arched an eyebrow. "And you don't?"

"Ghosts," laughed Ivy. "You've got to be kidding."

"That's the trouble. By the time a witch is a few years older, she – or he – knows all the rules. And they have decided by then to follow either the right-hand or left-hand path. The left-hand path is steeped in bad karma. Those who follow it, conjure demons, sacrifice animals – sometimes children – they use drugs – you hear what I'm telling you?"

"Sacrifice *children?"* asked Ivy, horrified. She had been wondering about that enormous knife Jake had brandished.

"Sometimes they get pregnant for that specific purpose," said Bryan.

Ivy stared at the bags she'd brought home from the fleamarket without seeing them. She felt icy. If this was what was going on...

Bryan was watching her.

"Better tell me about it," he prompted quietly.

"Why should I?" she asked back. "It's my troubles, not yours."

"Because I'm one of the clean-up squad," he replied. "I don't have a badge but think of me as... the psychic police. If you're in any way entangled in black magic or Satanism, you need heavy guns to back you up."

Ivy nodded. Heavy guns. Yes. That would have been

handy last night. She'd had a few close shaves; it felt to her as though her next tango with the Dark Craft may not be that lucky. And it was far from over.

Yes, she could use a powerful ally. She studied Bryan critically. He did have that look of power about him.

"How should I know that you're not one of *them?*" she asked him. You didn't get to study CA by being gullible.

"You know," smiled Bryan. "You have intuition. And so does your cat."

Good point. Peridot had not let anyone near except for her, so far – and Bryan. Animals knew about such things.

So she came clean. Bryan sat listening to her story, his face intent.

"It was Esbat yesterday, of course," he commented when she was done.

"What?"

"Full moon," he explained. "Special forces at work."

"So you say the moto won't fly for me tonight?"

"Of course it will," said Bryan. "It's *you* doing that."

"Me?"

"The same with that 'khazam'," he said. "You used it with a fork, a nail file, a fallen tree branch and an athame. You could be saying any other word, too. But keep 'khazam'." He smiled. "It's a bit unique." And his smile dropped again. "But it's not enough, Ivy. Can't go through life with only a 'khazam' and a flying Honda. You need to know what you're doing!"

"So you're proposing to tutor me?" she asked.

"Exactly. You could do with that, right?"

Ivy considered for a while and then nodded. "When do we start?"

"Right now," he said. "Emergency Wicca, speed course." He pulled an old-fashioned leather school-bag closer and dug in it.

"That was your grandfather's?" joked Ivy, pointing at the bag.

"It was, actually." He produced a pad of A4 exam paper and a pencil. "See here. First the rules. Wicca – that's the right-hand path, the good guys – it comes with what we call a 'Rede'." He scribbled on the paper. She craned her neck.

First rule: Harm none.

"That's easy," she said.

Second rule: Be careful what you witch for. It may be granted.

Ivy grinned. That one was predictable.

Third rule: What you send out, comes back to you. Good or bad – times three, up to times thirty-three.

That rule bothered her. "So if I curse someone..."

"That's the point at which I decided you need me," said Bryan, glancing up. "You were muttering curses. I don't want them catching up with you."

"I've been muttering curses since I was thirteen," Ivy pointed out.

Bryan grinned. "Oh god, what a lot of bad karma!"

"I never have bad luck," she replied. "So there!"

"You were a clueless child," was his response. "Ever wondered why you get picked for such a lousy job while others in your class..."

"My job!" exclaimed Ivy. "My lousy job! Oh my god! I'm in such trouble! I took a whole day's work home because I bunked Friday – and I totally forgot about it! Bryan, I hate to do this, but I have to ask you to leave right now, I have an ungodly amount of work to catch up."

Bryan stared at her.

"This is more important," he said intently.

"Than keeping my job?" asked Ivy. "No ways! I can't afford Oates throwing me out! I haven't even started my career – what would that look like on my CV? I'd have my bad karma then," she mocked.

"Ivy," said Bryan gravely, "listen to me. This is more important. Oates won't throw you out. But the bad eggs might find you and your life will definitely be in danger."

She sighed. Damn Bex for setting the cops on her; damn Bonnie for getting involved with a drug dealer. And for tangling with – what did Bryan call it – the *left-hand path.*

"Bryan," she said, "the cops are one thing. But that lot of blundering kids – come now. How big is the chance that they'll find me here?"

"They won't find you here," said Bryan. "But the moment you're outside the property, anything goes."

"Why won't they find me here?" she asked.

"What do you think?" asked Bryan. "It's a sanctuary. You've got a policeman of the Craft as neighbour. This place is shielded."

Ivy nodded. It wasn't particularly more cooky than the rest of the stuff going on. And sadly, the rest of it was depressingly real.

"Wish I could see what they're up to," she said.

"Scry it," said Bryan.

"What's that about?"

He got up and rummaged until he found her black ceramic oven dish. He filled that with water from the tap, threw some salt into it and made some symbols over it with his fingers. Then he gave it to her.

"Clear your mind and look into the water," he instructed.

She tried it.

There was nothing in the water. But before her mind's eye she saw Bonnie, back at home, sticking her arm with a needle; and Jake, out in the streets with about seven other hooligans (some of which dressed like rich kids) on their mission to somewhere.

"They're gathering," said Bryan when she told him. "A coven is strongest at thirteen. Depends very much what they're planning. I can tell you it's nothing good. They're after you. If I have to predict, I'd say they're planning to do something for Halloween."

"What?" She laughed. "Will they come trick-or-treating?"

"Halloween is no children's game," warned Bryan. "It's the night the gates between this world and the underworld are open."

"Right!" she said flippantly.

"You had better start believing all these things, Ivy," warned Bryan. "You're in the middle of them. A lot of modern magic lore is based on the old superstitions."

"I don't even know if I want to believe in modern magic," she replied.

Bryan laughed. "She flies on a motorbike and waves lightning out of her wand and says she doesn't believe in magic!"

"Those are just – effects," said Ivy.

"You're right," agreed Bryan. "They are effects. Because you have no cooking clue what you're doing."

"But I really have to do my accounting now!"

Bryan sighed.

"You're stubborn. You know where I am now. Call me if you need me." He pressed a small card with his number hand-written on it, into her hand. "Any time, day or night. Don't be scared to wake me up. Understood?"

She nodded at him. "Thanks!"

Bryan led the way to the door and let himself out, with her following. It was dusk outside.

"Good night, Ivy. Hope they give you a break tonight. Remember, you can call me, even if it's three a.m."

And he turned and walked away, not in the direction of

the driveway or even the house, but towards the opposite wall where Ivy spotted a gate for the first time.

"Thanks," she called, and waved at him as he went through the gate. He waved back, and was gone.

Neighbour with a gate! That might just explain some of the hauntings in the cottage, she thought with a grin. Ha, Marc, your secret is out of the bag! It threw a rather sinister light on her landlord though. Why would Marc want to scare people away from a cottage he could be profitably renting out? What game was he playing with Alison?

She scowled. She'd have to look into that! Suddenly she felt quite protective of her new-found friend. Alison was so innocent; young and gullible. Well, she'd get behind what was going on.

She closed her cottage door and went to her desk – one of the four items she'd actually brought from her box, the others were her bed, fridge and a tall bookshelf – and she opened her laptop. Peridot purred around her feet, then pounced on her toes as she settled down to work. She played with him for a while, then picked him up into her lap so he'd quieten down. He slipped back off and started chasing phantoms around the floor.

Ivy smiled and fetched a small cottonwool puff out of the bathroom for him. Within seconds he was immersed in playing with it. She watched this for a while, then knuckled down into filing. It was past midnight before she finally shut down the computer, locked everything, switched off her lights and crawled into bed. Peridot jumped up and found his spot in the hollow under her chin, purring.

6

A small raspy tongue was licking Ivy's nose. And in the background her alarm was going, straight from the smart phone. A stupid alarm that she promised herself to change, every time, and she always forgot. Sounding like a cuckoo clock.

She got out of bed – surprisingly she felt rested. She attributed it to the cat effect. Weird dreams still buzzed in her head, worry about Bonnie and her unborn baby, the cops hunting for her, that book 'Arcana' only having come out in a ridiculously small edition, her filing, which she had almost completed. And a shield over this property that made it impossible for the little black coven to see her. She got up, and dressed.

Work: A short beige skirt, above the knee, that kicked out just a little bit – to show that inside that accounting professional there was actually a real, live person. A stylish black blouse with lace detail covering her neckline. And she put on her sheer black lace stockings and slipped into her black stilettos with the closed toes. She lifted the curtain a bit: Yes, she'd pre-empted the weather correctly, it was melancholy outside. She slipped her warm business jacket on, the lined one that sat so nicely tailored; brushed and confined her terrible hair with a heartfelt wish that it were better behaved and wouldn't tangle as much – and then remembered what Bryan had said. Be careful what you wish for. Wishes – and curses too – could come true. She stared at her mirror image over the cracked and puttied sink in the bathroom, then applied just the right amount of make-up, covering up freckles with base, touching up her key features.

Peridot was around her feet; she nearly fell over him when she turned to move to the kitchen.

"Alright, my boy!" She put out food, milk and, after thinking for a moment, also a bowl of water for her little cat.

"Listen now, Peridot. I've got to go to work. I'll try not to be home too late. Please try not to be too sad. Maybe Uncle Marc will sell me his bike today, then we can go flying again tonight."

"Meow," came the answer, and accusing eyes.

"Oi, Peridot," sighed Ivy. "I'd love to take you to work. But you'd be dead bored. *I'm* dead bored, what do you think. There's nothing to do there for a kitty."

Peridot focused on his food. Ivy understood that she was being cold-shouldered. She picked up her briefcase, found a bag to stash the pile of notes in to take back to work, and left, locking the door behind her.

Marc had a key to the cottage and could come rummaging at any time. This didn't suit her at all. Especially not as Peridot might slip out and become leopard-kibbles. She needed to complete the deal, get that bank loan, make the little spot her own. So she could change the locks.

91

Travelling to work by bus was tedious this morning; the bus route was a lot longer than from her Putney flat. And there was a lot of walking in the rain and mud to get to the bus stop, that wasn't good for her shoes at all. But eventually she got to the store.

One glance at Biljana told her something was amiss. The girl's face was absolutely covered in red spots.

"Biljana, your face!" exclaimed Ivy. "Do you have measles?"

Biljana's eyes were red from crying.

"I don't know what this is," she wailed. "The doctor says it's acne! I've never had acne! I don't know where this comes from!"

But I know, thought Ivy guiltily. "May it get better really quickly!" she muttered. "Sorry, Biljana. But you don't look bad, really not."

"I look gross," sobbed Biljana. "How can I do my job if I look like this?"

"I think it's stress," soothed Ivy. "Go home, catch some rest. I'll pick up here for you."

"You mean that?"

"Just clear it with Mr Oates."

Biljana did. She emerged from his office, smiling a bit.

"You know, Ivy, I think you're right, it's stress," she said. "The moment I relaxed, it stopped hurting so much."

"They *hurt?*"

"Course they do!"

That was too much for Ivy.

"Let me try something," she said. "Sit down, and close your eyes."

Biljana obeyed.

Ivy grabbed the nearest object – a pencil, and concentrated. "Khazam," she whispered. And she directed the lightning like a laser treatment, erasing the spots. It was no fun; it eked her, but, she reminded herself, it was her fault, so she'd better fix it!

Her treatment worked. When she was done, the horrible spots were erased, though the general skin was a bit red and irritated.

Ivy hid the pencil in her hand. "You can look now."

Biljana got up and looked into the mirror, and gasped.

"You made them all go away! How did you do it?"

"Lightning pencil therapy," said Ivy glibly. "It's experimental. But you must go home and rest anyway, so that your skin can recover." Biljana's skin did look as though it needed a day's rest. Biljana thanked her profusely and left, quickly before the boss could come in and see that there was really no visible reason for her to go home.

Ivy noticed an elderly lady staring at her. A customer! She'd been in the shop for a while; Ivy hadn't been aware of her.

"That was phenomenal," she exclaimed. "Will you give me treatment too? For wrinkles?"

Ivy thought very fast.

"It's experimental," she said. "There's no guarantee it will work. We're testing out this new tool."

"Let me be your test subject," volunteered the woman. "I've never seen anything like it!"

"If you like the results, I'll ring it up for hundred pound," said Ivy quickly. "If you don't like the results or don't see any, you don't owe us anything. I need you to sign here that you're agreeing that this is at your own risk, and you will not hold us liable for any unwanted results," and she handed the lady an order form that was folded so that only the bottom part was visible.

"Sure!" The lady signed the paper and took the chair. Ivy bent over her face.

"You need to close your eyes and not open them at all during the treatment," she said. "Remember, at own risk! No remedy for something going wrong."

"I'm feeling brave," smiled the elderly lady. She was quite well-padded; but she was right, her skin could do with tightening and rejuvenation. No wonder, at an age when one wore one's hair white.

"Then just relax," smiled Ivy and took out the pencil again. She whispered, "Khazam!" and carefully traced every wrinkle, every line with the lightning pen as though she were operating a magic eraser. The lady's skin tightened and straightened out.

Wait, thought Ivy as she also treated the woman's neck that was more wrinkly than her face, let me push this a bit.

After she finished, she dived into the cosmetics section of the shop and fetched the cooling cucumber gel. That stuff was very expensive, but worked wonders on a hot and irritated skin. She should have thought of it for Biljana!

"How is the skin feeling?" she asked.

"It burns," said the lady without opening her eyes.

"I've got a cooling gel here," said Ivy. "Top quality, from Lancôme. But it comes separately. Fifty pound. You want it?"

"I'll take it," agreed the lady. Ivy opened the little pod and applied some cooling gel all over the woman's face and neck.

"That's wonderful," sighed the customer.

"You can go look now," smiled Ivy, standing back, chuffed with her work of art.

The lady took a look in the mirror – and gasped.

"I look twenty-six!"

She took out her purse and paid Ivy; the redhead placed the money in the cash till and carefully wrote the sale down in the sales book, both of a "lightning therapy" and the 20ml pot of gel. Hundred and fifty quid, for Mr Oates to boost his business.

You're on the right path, she heard that invisible commentator in her head.

When Mr Oates came out of his office for a break and a cup of tea, he couldn't believe his eyes. There was a queue longer than at the tax office, to the door of his shop. And Ivy was emerging from one of the change rooms with a customer, making the young girl look in the mirror, then taking money from her mother and booking it down properly as a sale and stashing the cash in the till.

"What are you doing, Ivy?"

She looked up at him. "Morning, Mr Oates. I'm very sorry – I didn't finish the workload over the weekend, there was more family crisis going on."

He scowled at her. Ivy looked at him with sympathy. Poor old man! He had a bad case of manager sickness; his stomach regularly acted up; he'd packed on weight around the middle; and he was stressing himself to death. No wonder, with his finances in such a mess, and debts eating him up. She discreetly angled the pencil at him from under her palm, and whispered, "khazam!"

"Family crisis?" he probed, and his eyes widened. He took a deep breath and smiled. Colour returned to his grey face.

"Yea, nothing world-shaking," said Ivy vaguely, smiling back. She knew that his stomach ache had just subsided.

"And what are you doing now?"

"I stumbled on this experimental beauty treatment," she said. "Lightning pencil. All these customers want me to treat their skin. I'm putting the money into the business," she added dutifully. "This is my work time, after all. But Mr Oates, I can't do this for long. I need to get back to my filing."

"Do it as long as it works," he said, amazed. "I'll see what I can do about the filing." And he went off to the kitchenette to make himself some coffee.

"Next," called Ivy.

By four that afternoon she knew that, regardless how she had swelled the coffers of Oates today, she couldn't do this permanently. It was boooooring! And her energy was flagging; the treatments didn't come out quite as khazammy as the earlier lot.

"Enough for today," she told the disappointed crowd that was still waiting outside the door.

"Where can we buy such a pencil?" asked a woman from the crowd.

"The Paper Chain," she said before she could stop herself. It was an ordinary pencil. Luckily the woman appreciated what she thought was a joke to protect a trade secret, and laughed heartily.

"We'll be back tomorrow," she promised.

"In the meantime," suggested Ivy shrewdly, "why don't you get the gel, the cleanser, toner and night cream from this range?"

The customers stampeded the cosmetics section. For the next forty-five minutes Ivy was hopping like a flea writing down all the beauty products people were buying.

She glanced up at quarter to five – nearly quitting time and she hadn't done a single keystroke of her actual job.

"Go home early, Ivy," said Mr Oates generously. "I'll lock up here. I feel better than in years! I wish the Missus were well, I'd take her out for dinner tonight to celebrate."

"What's wrong with her?" asked Ivy.

"She has a back that will just never recover. We've already had three fusion operations for her but it simply progresses."

"I'm sorry," said Ivy and sent a wish to Oates' wife that she should recover, and that tonight she'd have no back pain at all. She sent a silent "khazam" with it for emphasis; there was no telling if it would work or not.

"Take this," said Mr Oates and opened the cash till. He gathered up a good third of what Ivy had earned for him today, and stuck the wad of notes into her hand. "Bonus. You were brilliant today."

She smiled and stuck the money into her briefcase. Lucky, lucky, she told herself. That bit of cash-flow would pay for things. Depending on how much it was.

She left the shop and headed to the bus stop, and out, rattling along an endless rocky road, towards the little place she called home, where a kitten was waiting for her.

In fact, more than Peridot was waiting for her. Once again, Bryan sat in that high-backed armchair. He got up as she came in.

"Bryan!" she exclaimed, startled. He'd let himself in again!

"Evening, Ivy," said Bryan with a smile and those amazingly blue eyes. "How was your day?"

"You know," she said, a little indignant, also at herself for the breathless moment those intense laser eyes cost her yet again, "when one has been giving thirty-six beauty treatments and worked with old-age wrinkles and teenage zits all day instead of doing one's proper job – one expects to come home to a quiet house and relax, not entertain visitors!"

"I'm sorry," said Bryan. "I thought you'd enjoy the surprise."

"In general I only like surprises when I get fair warning," she said.

"We need to carry on with your studies," pushed Bryan, turning serious. "There's not much time – only two days to Samhain, and they're most definitely planning something vile. I can feel it."

"... in yer bones," completed Ivy. "'Tis the old wooden leg that gives the game away, och aye! - Look, Bryan. I appreciate your concern. But I really need to be alone a bit before I can focus on anything."

"Shall I come over later, then?" he suggested.

"Make it around eight," she said, then amended that. "Seven. I can't let it get late tonight. This weekend was a killer."

"You don't even know what you're saying there," he growled.

Ivy stopped, and stared coldly at him until she knew she

had his full attention.

"Oh, I do know," she said darkly. "Believe me!"

She was soaking in a bath – a nasty habit, she could get used to too easily – when there was a knock on her door.

Was it seven already? Had she fallen asleep in the tub? "Wait!" she called, getting out as quickly as she could, drying off and slipping into her jeans and jersey, and answering the door.

It was Alison. In fact it was only half past six.

"Come in!" invited Ivy.

"I brought you the Honda," said Alison. "Marc is prepared to sell it for one thousand."

Ivy cheered, and opened her briefcase. Not much later, she parked the beautiful machine in her kitchen for lack of a better place. She didn't want to leave it out in the threatening drizzle.

It was raining properly when Bryan joined them half an hour later. As Ivy opened the door he came in, looking wet, rained-on and unkempt. There was something boyish about him as he grinned his greeting at her. That was quite endearing. Ivy forgave him his earlier intrusion.

He looked surprised to see Alison. A look passed between the two that Ivy couldn't quite interpret. Was he annoyed to see her landlady there? Or – worried?

"I've got to get home," said Alison hastily. "Ivy, thanks for the chat, and the coffee." She patted her pocket. "And the cash! Marc will be thrilled."

"Hope so," smiled Ivy. Even one grand was a little overpriced for a second-hand machine, but the Honda was in good condition, and – well – it could fly.

"What was that about?" she challenged Bryan when she'd seen Alison off.

"What?"

"You and Alison," said Ivy. "What secrets?"

Bryan laughed. "It's not what you think," he said.

"With you, I never know what to think," she retorted.

"I'll take that as a compliment." He opened his leather school bag and removed the notepad and a few books.

"Can you give me a few solid things I can work with?" asked Ivy. "Hypnotizing people, invisibility spells and so on?"

"That's advanced stuff," replied Bryan. "Let's start at square one."

"I'm dealing with an advanced enemy," countered Ivy. "Baby steps won't help now."

"If you could start listening and stop wasting time?" challenged Bryan. "We don't have forever and it's quite a lot of work to cover."

The time flew by, and before Ivy realized it, it was ten.

"I think we'll have to call it a night," she said, looking up from the book she had been given to study.

"We're nearly at the exciting parts," said Bryan, watching her from his armchair over the tenth cup of coffee.

"You keep saying that," she laughed. "These *are* exciting parts. Just not very useful."

"You need to understand the principles at work before you can start operating with them," he said patiently. "For instance, it explains why I said they're planning something for Halloween. Understanding ritual structure makes it rather predictable."

"Who needs rituals?" she asked, surprised.

"Most people," Bryan smiled. "Most can't simply snap their fingers and *voilà,* magic!"

"And the rituals make the magic work for them?"

"For some," he said. "See, the teenage poltergeist can be awakened by dealing with a lot of arcana."

She peered at him. "Tell me one thing," she asked. "I might not be much of a witch, but I'm quite a - erm... I'm no idiot with finances. So how the hell can you afford a house out here on a shop assistant's salary? Did you inherit it? Even so, how can you afford the rates?"

"Shop assistant?" asked Bryan, baffled. "Who said I'm that?"

"You *were* in the bookshop selling me a book," she pointed out.

"Ivy, you don't understand," said Bryan. "I happened to be in that shop at the same moment as you. I was reading up on things, and had my Arcana with me to compare. I saw what was happening and decided you need the book more than I do. There wasn't a single book in the shop that would have measured up."

She stared at him. "Whoa," she said then. This was seriously weird. Had he meant to *give* her the Arcana? And that opportunistic old man who ran the shop – for the life of her she couldn't remember his name right now...

"Right," said Bryan before she could mention any of that. "But I have to get home. I can see you're not focusing anymore. Tomorrow, try not to work so hard in the day, we only have tomorrow left before they strike."

7

It was amazing to fly along the roads on her own little motorbike, even though the Honda absolutely refused to lift off the road today. Maybe she had dreamt the whole episode, she thought, drawing her raincoat closer. She'd need a more heavy-duty raincoat. Heck, she'd need a diving suit for this rain! Her hair that had poured out under the helmet, had been confined under her warm jacket, and covered over with the raincoat.

Still, to drive – to swim, more accurately through this amazing rain, on this cool machine – she was mulling where to park it, at work. Would Oates allow her to take it indoors? To prevent it being stolen?

Good that Peridot wasn't perched on her shoulder – he'd have been whipped right off by the drops. Perhaps she should calm down, put on gumboots and take the ordinary bus to work on days like these, and keep the moto for sunny days.

As she arrived at work, there was already a huge crowd outside the shop. They were waiting for their lightning pencil treatment, she thought dismally, longing for her nice clean numbers. She'd invest in some latex gloves for this. The gruesome reality of people's skins – all colours, shades, conditions and reflections – was getting under her *own* skin.

She steeled herself on the inside, wondering if she could in any way train Biljana to take this over from her. No doubt the young girl would enjoy it, she was so into her beauty.

The crowd was probably the reason she didn't spot them in time. And before she could say "khazam", the police had surrounded her and roughly grasped her by the shoulders and wrists. Someone clicked her wrists into handcuffs behind her back.

What you send out, comes back to you, she thought uneasily as they bullied her into the police van. Her moto! She saw how Mr Oates came out of the shop, gaped at her in shock, and then took the bike inside. Aw, boss, she begged inwardly, lock it into your office, you've no idea... She dismally watched the shop recede in the distance.

Thousands of curses sent out... yesterday's right path was not enough to compensate for all this, she thought. Aw – rubbish! This was Bex's doing!

And she was right: Bex and Bonnie were waiting for her at the police station. She glanced at Bex's hard face, and at Bonnie – and recoiled from the sheer hatred she saw.

The girl was on some or other hard drug right now; she'd bet her bottom. Dollar. Her bottom dollar. Not her bottom. She'd hate to lose her bottom; she'd better amend that little idiom that she'd misquoted more often than she could count.

She didn't understand this. Bex was her sister-in-law; they had mourned her brother together when he'd passed away in a lethal motor accident coming home from his law office -

he had been a barrister. And Ivy had tried to keep close contact with Bex and Bonnie; but her own life had got busy, she hadn't visited them in four whole years...

Drugs, she reminded herself. It wasn't her fault. The girl was on drugs.

She was pushed into a holding area, in view of the waiting room but barred from it. Where she sat was really just a corridor next to where the officers at the main desk were working. There was no real barrier dividing her from that area, only a half-height door with a small bolt, quite accessible from both sides.

She eyed the proceedings mutely, trying to understand what they'd do next. This was a bit of overkill for a simple statement, right? Bex had her down for something or other she'd supposedly done to wrong Bonnie. Because she couldn't claim abduction anymore – the girl had been returned home. That was, she could actually.

Ivy ground her teeth. She'd fight this in court. Bex had no chance! In the interim, poor Mr Oates was losing out, both on business and on his bright and shiny young accountant.

Bex's eyebrows had got a lot bushier, she noticed idly. And the woman was growing a moustache. Was she aware of it? She also sported some interesting tufts coming out of various facial moles. All the hair was grey, going on white. Her head hair was patchily stained; as though it wouldn't take any more artificial colour and she was still unable to accept that she should wear it natural. Patchy auburn interrupted with light grey made her look a bit like an Appaloosa.

And Bonnie? She was sitting most uncomfortably, shifting from one buttock to the other. Ivy remembered, and had to grin. A cramp in her buttocks. Indeed. Well, if these curses cost her karma, it was karma well spent.

Her old landlord, Mr Brown, came in. Her spirits plummeted. This was the last thing she needed. His face was red and he was sweating despite the cold, incessant rain outside. And his hand reached down and – Ivy couldn't believe her eyes as he scratched himself heartily in public, where it was rude. This was gross. Ivy looked away.

"Has anyone read you your rights, girl?" asked one of the policewomen, passing by. She shook her head. Girl! Lady, or ma'am to you, she thought.

"You have the right to remain silent," the woman in uniform rattled off. "Anything you say can be held against you." And down the whole list of rights.

"The right to one call?" asked Ivy.

"To call your lawyer."

"Don't have a lawyer." He's in heaven, thought Ivy. Her brother had been an honest man.

"You can call someone else too, a family member maybe."

Ivy shrugged, and motioned with her head at Bex, who glared at her. "There's my 'family'."

"Then what's the problem?" asked the policewoman. "They're here!"

"They're the ones prosecuting," said Ivy.

The officer looked taken aback. "A friend then, maybe?" she prompted.

Ivy considered. Her old friends had one by one disappeared over the three years in which she'd been so focused on her studies that she'd visited nobody. They wouldn't appreciate this.

And her new friends? No, she couldn't heap this on Alison. The girl had enough worries; and no transport; and no personal power at all; in fact, she'd probably have a nervous breakdown hearing about this.

And Bryan? Was he a friend? Sure, he bullied her into learning Wicca at night, probably for his own sinister purposes – the weird things people thought redheads were good for – but... He'd said she could call him whenever she needed help, and help she needed, but this was the wrong kind of emergency. He'd meant, *magic* help. Against wicked teenagers doing a demonic ritual.

She thought back whether she could direct the policewoman to find Bryan's number on her phone. No, she hadn't saved his number. It lay on a little handwritten card on her coffee table – or under it by now, probably. She hadn't even had time to decorate her home with the witchy paraphernalia she'd bought at the fleamarket; it was all still in its bags.

She looked up at the policewoman and shook her head.

"Well, bad luck, cricket," replied the woman and turned

her back, to focus on the waiting queue.

Bad luck. That was it, exactly.

No! Ivy refused to accept this. Blast Bryan that he hadn't wanted to teach her invisibility or hypnosis yesterday! The only thing she could do was try whether 'khazam' would work for her even if she didn't point any object. She watched the proceedings and waited.

"Yes, she tried to cheat me out of three months' rent."

She glared at her previous landlord. Damn that man! That rent was never due; but now it was used as aggravating evidence against her in whatever crime she was supposedly to have committed against Bonnie.

Yes, the wonderful police, she thought acidly. When London was burning in 2011, and shops were looted in hordes, where were the wonderful police then? Hiding in their offices. But they were brave enough to arrest a defenceless young woman on high heels, on her way to her honest work.

Khazam, she thought pointedly, precisely knocking the pen out of the officer's hand who was taking Mr Brown's report ... and all without lightning! The pen flew across the waiting room. The police officer went through the other half-door to retrieve it; fat and out of shape from not hunting enough real criminals and letting too many real crimes pass. She reached out with invisible lightning tentacles and gave him a tiny shove in the hindquarters as he labouredly bent down to pick the pencil up – and he went sprawling across the room and landed on his knees with his face in the lap of a fat lady who swatted at him hysterically with her handbag.

"Do I get to make *my* statement at some point?" Ivy asked. "I have a job to get back to."

The other police officer behind the counter looked at her as though he'd only just become aware of her.

"No," he said. "You're a suspect. You have the right to remain silent."

That ticked Ivy off.

"I'm not a damn suspect," she said heatedly. "I would have been a witness – if there had been a case. The point is, that girl over there -" and she motioned with her head at Bonnie - "that's my niece. She tried to run away from home; first tried to camp in my place, and when I sent her home, she escaped and ran away again, and *I'm* actually the one who rounded her up and brought her home. There – that's my statement, that you arrested me for! Write it down and let me go!"

"I'd stay quiet if I were you, lady," warned the police officer. "You're under arrest for trafficking drugs, harbouring fugitives, resisting arrest and inflicting injury on a minor."

"What?" exclaimed Ivy. "You're accusing me of *what?*"

"Lady, stay quiet, or you'll be charged with contempt of an officer on top of the rest," warned the policeman.

Ivy snapped her mouth shut. May your feet start itching uncontrollably, *right now,* she thought. *Khazam!*

Seconds later the officer started shuffling around; this got worse and worse until he abruptly left the room.

The other officer, the fat one who had by now retrieved the pencil and apologized to the lady, returned to finish taking Mr Brown's statement.

Ivy boiled inwardly. She had no idea how this would end; but it was irritating, and it was wasting her time, she ought to be at work lightening Mr Oates's filing cabinet and training Biljana to take over the lightning pencil treatment. But here she sat instead with all these unenlightened time-wasters.

One day to go to Halloween. Today was the last chance she had to learn more from Bryan before she was going to go up against a crowd of teenage hooligans tampering with black magic. But that felt so far removed from reality right now...

She had to clue the police in about where that vile coven was meeting! But not now, she thought. They'd find a way to turn it against her. She'd do it later, anonymously, from a public phone booth.

"Ninety days," said Mr Brown. "Three months' worth of rent, sir. That's what she cheated me out of."

Oh, that Mr Brown! May he brown his pants! *Right now, khazam,* she added and watched with satisfaction how her curse took effect. Under great discomfort and embarrassment, the dishonest landlord excused himself and ran from the police station, holding onto his trousers while still scratching madly at that rude itch.

The police officer wrinkled his nose at the mess and beckoned a cleaner, who had been taking a first-thing-at-work break, to clean the floor. She went ahead with an extremely sullen expression.

Ha! By now Ivy was mad with everyone. That stupid cleaner! She had a job! Alison wasn't even allowed to work and earn money! And cleaning was a job description. Not a brilliant one – for heavens' sakes, better yourself, you lazy cow! Go and jog that sluggish brain, read something, study something – you're getting it for free! The state will pay for it!

That mop *daaaaaawdled* its way to the bucket, and the cleaner – almost as fat as the first police officer – bent cumbersomely over the bucket to wring the water out of that mop – and suddenly the mop twisted itself in her hands, gave her a wet smack over the head with its fibres, turned itself the right way round again and danced a Devil's waltz with her across the floor. She was hanging on for dear life – after all people couldn't know that she couldn't let go. Somehow her hands were stuck on the mop, and that mop was hexed. Within two minutes the whole floor was sparkling clean; the mop jumped back into its bucket and the cleaner sank to a chair, drenched in sweat and out of breath.

Ivy. You're being naughty!

She chuckled softly. This was worth a whole lot of karma to her. What about those other people's karma? Surely their dishonesty and negativity earned them karma too? What if the reason she'd been lucky with her curses so far, was because she was using their own karma against them?

Then it had nothing to do with her! She resolved to discuss this loophole with Bryan. Did it exist or had she just made it up?

The point was, this arrest wasn't her bad karma. It was Bex and her dumb intrigues – or even Bonnie and her shrewd intrigues.

"Next!" called the officer behind the counter. Bex started getting up, but he gestured at her. A set-up!

Jake's parents walked in through the door. Ivy's jaw dropped. Jake's father spotted her and shook a fist at her as he came to the counter.

"Want to press charges against *that* there," he said, pointing a finger at her. "She abducted my son and got him addicted to drugs." And his right hand moved jerkily to his face, and he slapped himself. He gaped at his hand, and slapped himself again, and then started indiscriminately picking his nose. This seemed to upset him; the more agitated he got, the faster he picked his nose.

"Go do that in the bathroom!" scolded his wife. Jake's father hobbled off. Ivy tried to remember if his difficulty walking had to do with her too, and remembered that she'd wished him ingrown toenails.

Jake's mother took over where his father had started. *Force you to speak the truth,* thought Ivy. *Khazam!*

"Please erase all that, it's not true," said Jake's mother, much to her own surprise. She shot Ivy a puzzled look. "We're here to file a missing person report. My son hasn't been home in the last five days. We thought we knew where he is, but he's not there."

"Five days?" asked the policeman. "Didn't you leave it a bit long, lady?"

"He often stays over at friends for a few days," said the mother. "Only this time he wasn't at the friends."

Ivy spoke up from her position behind the bars. "I can help with where you can find him."

The police officer shot her a venomous look. He opened and closed his mouth, but nothing came out. Eventually he blurted, "I have the right to remain silent", clapped his hand reflexively over his mouth and stared at Jake's mother.

"Where is Jake?" she asked Ivy.

"I don't know where he's right now," said Ivy, "but I'm pretty sure he'll be at the Putney Heath tomorrow night. But you've got to be careful. He's into black magic and they are planning something nasty. You must take people with you to protect you."

"That's not true!" protested Bonnie from her seat. "He's not into anything of the sort! He's a decent kid, Jake!"

Jake's mother turned and studied Bonnie for a scathing moment.

Positive, khazam! thought Ivy.

"Bonnie, thank you for defending my son!" Jake's mother gasped and clapped her hand over her mouth, too. The officer was still blowing mute bubbles behind the counter.

"He..." Ivy could see how Jake's mother was battling to formulate what she wanted to say. "...needs help, Bonnie. He *is* taking drugs. This is the truth. So we must... work together to help him."

"Send him to rehab," shot the police officer, both surprised and relieved to have his words back.

"That's what I'm considering," said Jake's mother.

Ivy left it at that. Jake deserved more than rehab – though with the way the rehab centres were, perhaps that was the worst punishment anyway.

"Then you can stick me in rehab as well, if that's what you're planning," said Bonnie belligerently. *Khazam,* thought Ivy. *Granted!*

Bex looked shocked.

"What now, lady?" the officer prompted Jake's mother. "Do you want to file a missing person report or not?" He smacked himself on his cheek, looked up and said, "mosquito", and went behind.

A few minutes later a female police uniform supplanted him. "Can I help you, lady?" And she looked disoriented. "Lady? Where are you?" She went behind, shaking her head.

"She couldn't see me," said Jake's mother in bewilderment.

Ivy scowled. This kind of havoc was fun, and came quite easy; powered by Loki, no doubt, the God of Mischief. But what she was trying now, would be more complex...

There was a burning sensation as the handcuffs on her left wrist heated up, and cracked open with an audible 'pop'. Ivy stuck her burning wrist into her mouth, biting back a cry of pain. The amount of agony this had brought with it wasn't worth a repeat. Her hands were free now, even though the handcuffs were still on her right wrist like some weird circus decoration. She got up.

There were by now no police officers in the office at all; and a pretty fed-up queue waiting. *Happy thoughts, khazam,* thought Ivy. Temperaments calmed down a bit.

She viciously pointed a finger at the lock of the gate that kept her captive and broke it with a directional lightning bolt. Moving to the counter, she grabbed a pencil and labelled a blank piece of paper 'Statement', and then wrote down her side of events ending with a tip-off on where to find the dark coven on the next night. Then, for good measure, she pointed the pencil at the gate to the public area and broke that lock, too. She could simply have opened it from inside, but by now she was angry enough to leave another sort of statement. Let them figure it out when they surfaced from their various predicaments.

Bex was on her feet, in outrage.

"Your prisoner is escaping!" she yelled at the empty front desk.

"Sue me," invited Ivy, stalking past her and her daughter towards the door. And Bryan entered the room.

She nearly collided with him. He shook his head at her. "In trouble again?" And he raised his hands and said some or other word...

A kind of golden mist settled over the room. Bryan grabbed her by the arm and hauled her out of the door, steering her to a huge Land Rover.

"In!"

Ivy obeyed without questioning.

"My motorbike is at work," she said.

"Let's pick it up." He glanced out into the grey streets. "What miserable weather to bike to work!"

She shrugged, offering a small, apologetic grin.

The first stop was Ivy's workplace. Bryan found a convenient parking space and locked his car while Ivy went in.

The crowds had dispersed. Mr Oates was in his office; he looked beaten. When Ivy came in, he looked up with sad eyes.

"What happened, Ivy?"

"False arrest," she said. "Those family issues over the weekend? They got their numbers scrambled. I was only supposed to be a witness, and they got it wrong and arrested me for a suspect."

"I hope it was sorted," he said gravely. "It's cost the shop a lot of reputation."

"Reputation?" asked Ivy, getting angry again.

"You understand that after this, I can't keep you on," said Mr Oates. "The crowd was here for your treatment, and next thing they witnessed your arrest. There is a nasty rumour that you deal in drugs. Of course nobody wanted to touch our merchandise after that."

No. This was not okay. Ivy's blood boiled. Now Bex

and her machinations had cost her the record of an arrest, her job, and her employer his business!

"Firstly," said Ivy through her teeth, "let me quickly take care of something."

"Go ahead," said Mr Oates.

Bryan appeared behind Ivy and put a hand on her shoulder as she turned. She shrugged his hand off and moved to one of the computers, opened a document and typed a notice for the door.

"Statement. Oates and Son has never been, and will never be, involved in anything illegal. Neither has any of the staff committed a crime. The wrongful arrest of one of our staff is currently under investigation, the results of which shall be disclosed to the public on completion. We are temporarily closed but will reopen on the first of November."

She held the notice up for her boss to read. He nodded in approval.

"For all I'm concerned we're finished," he said morosely. "We might as well not reopen in November. You really think you can solve this in two days?"

"On one condition," said Ivy. "I keep my job. - oh, two conditions. You allow me to train Biljana?"

Mr Oates nodded. Biljana arrived in the doorway, pushing Ivy's Honda.

"Ah, my motorbike," said Ivy. "Thanks, Biljana."

"But -" started Biljana, looking at Oates.

"I told her she could keep the bike," said Oates. "It's

only fair; your arrest has ruined our business and I can't pay out her salary."

Ivy gnashed her teeth and motioned to the notice she held in her hand.

"Do you want to give this a chance, Mr Oates?"

He nodded. "Biljana, we're not closing shop yet. We're taking a two-day break. In November we reopen and try again. Ivy is pretty sure of her case."

Biljana looked disappointed, gazing longingly at the Honda.

"That's my motorbike!" said Ivy. "Give here!"

Biljana pushed it across the tiled floor towards Ivy with a sulky glare.

"Look, Biljana," said Ivy, deliberately staying calm and sweet though her patience with sulky teenagers was worn to shreds. "How would you like me to train you to do what I did yesterday?"

"Can you?" asked Biljana, instantly excited.

"That's a good question, but I'll try!"

"Yes please!"

"You'll find it worth more than a second-hand bike," said Ivy, taking her moto back. In her mind she added, then *you* can deal with people's zits and impurities! *Khazam! Granted!*

It might take a bit of teamwork, and investment from Mr Oates. Into real beauticians' tools. Biljana had it in her. She was not suited to an admin job.

They would need another admin. Ivy smiled. And she

knew someone who was sweet and gentle, and even overprotective Marc would not have a problem allowing Alison to go work under the supervision of Ivy. Haha – and while this was the case, she could develop Alison further, show her options and study courses, introduce her to the second-hand bookshop...

"Let me put this notice up," she said, and rummaged for the Stickydots. She shut the glass entrance doors, stuck the notice she had just typed in place, and hung the 'Closed' sign under it.

"When we restart," she told Oates, "what we need to do is advertise some special feature. I think the beauty therapy is just the thing."

"Advertise, how?" he asked.

"Leave it to me," she said. "I'll work on it. Do I get an advertising budget?"

He groaned. "This is taking a risk! Alright, fifty."

"Fifty?" That would not go far. "Let me work on this." She pushed her motorcycle out through the glass doors, followed by Bryan, and rode home through the rain with him following in his Land Rover.

This was beginning to feel like a massive puzzle. Not only did she have to sort out and set the police on that young coven dealing in the 'left-hand path'; she had to straighten out Bex's and Bonnie's heads - though the only thing that prevented her from simply breaking with them was the memory of her brother. While Bex's hair was indeed growing in strange places, the second curse – or blessing – didn't seem to have taken effect yet, that of her growing some brain. Or maybe the brain was growing in the wrong ways.

Well, may she take up the tuba as a hobby and practise it to distraction! That should nicely keep her out of mischief! Ivy parted ways with Bryan's car and headed towards Alison's entrance; up the long driveway, and through the wet grass, to the back cottage. She navigated the machine into her kitchen, scowling at the dirt it brought in. She really had to take care of things soon; even putting up a simple roof-and-cage would help.

She heard Bryan's engine across the wall, and not too much later he came through the gate.

"Come over," he invited. "I think we've got to talk."

She grinned brightly, thinking of all the Loki-derived mischief she had wrought in that police office. No harm to anyone; what was a bout of diarrhoea? And a dance with a mop-stick? Dealing out smacks to oneself, picking noses – nothing that damaged anyone. She had not breached the Wiccan Rede; she could still call herself on the Right-Hand Path.

"So what took you so long?" she asked with a smirk when she sat in one of Bryan's highly modern, leather armchairs with a steaming mug of coffee – laced, she noticed, with some brandy.

Bryan's living quarters were far too spacious for a

bachelor. But the energy here was purely male. She couldn't detect even a trace of female presence. Yes, this was his pad. She was more curious than before what he did for a profession.

"You had fun today, didn't you," was his caustic comment back.

She reared up. "Damn you, Bryan! If you think it's fun to be framed for drug-dealing, harbouring fugitives, injuring a minor -" She paused. "Actually, I *am* guilty of that last one," she admitted and hummed a few bars from a well-known film. "I gave him a lightning scar. But he'll have to produce the evidence that I did, and..."

"... the burn is on his backside," laughed Bryan. "He deserved that!"

"More specifically the evidence has gone missing with the minor," she pointed out.

"Harm none," warned Bryan. "You broke the Rede."

"That was my very first khazam," Ivy protested. "I had no idea it would actually do that!"

"I suppose, after that you modified it that it didn't burn holes in people?"

"I did, actually," agreed Ivy. "It only needs to scare them, not injure them. I got quite a fright with that burn."

"I guess you may be forgiven for that one, it wasn't really in your control," said Bryan.

"What are you, the psychic police force?" asked Ivy. "Oh, right, you said that's what you were. Great – from one police office into the next!"

Bryan got up and fetched something that looked like a letter opener, and knelt down next to her armchair. He took her right arm and inserted the pointy end of the implement into the lock of the handcuff that was still rattling around on there. He muttered something and the lock came apart, without any pain or heat. Ivy dared to breathe again; she'd braced herself for considerable agony.

"Thanks!"

"Show me your other wrist," commanded Bryan and picked up her left arm. The burn mark on that was significant.

"Harm none includes yourself," he scolded. "Sit!"

She was already sitting; so she just watched him disappear into the depths of his house.

The house was another old farmhouse; but the inside had been renovated and modernized completely. On the one wall of the lounge was a huge plasma screen; the coffee table had a glass top and metal legs without any frills; there were low cabinets from dark wood with closed doors, and here his strange sense of interior decorating manifested. On one of the cabinet tops was a strangely shaped piece of driftwood. Only that. Another housed an empty vase, Japanese-style, of beige stone; it was angular but sleek with no frills. Almost as though he'd given decorating a shot – but to him it was a foreign language.

She couldn't contain her curiosity; she nipped over to the low wooden cabinets and opened one, and peered inside.

Books. Titles on flying, landscape photography; more

titles on flying; wildlife; more on aeroplanes. Wow! But the books were covered in dust of ages. They had clearly not been referenced in years.

There was a bar in the corner, with a drinks cabinet that contained – she looked closer – only two bottles of wine, one white and one red. And a half-empty bottle of brandy sitting on the bar, obviously just having been used. The dust layer on all three bottles told her its own story.

She returned quickly to her seat and took a deep sip of coffee. The brandy in her coffee relaxed her. And Bryan was back with a toolbox; he knelt down on the other side of her armchair, unlocked his toolbox and opened it. It was in fact a first-aid kit. Ivy laughed when she realized it. She'd had no idea what to expect, but from this man, anything from hammers and wrenches to crystals and ceremonial daggers. But a plain old first-aid kit?

He smeared some antiseptic salve on the burn on her wrist and bandaged it, with surprising tenderness for someone who was that chronically critical of her. Then he closed the toolbox but didn't bother packing it away.

"That was the easy part," he said.

"My soul being the difficult part?" she laughed.

"Your *karma* is the difficult part," he corrected. "Let's retrace our steps, Ivy. Every bit of magic you used needs to be accounted for. Did you hurt anyone else?"

"Well, in self-defence, you know, I zapped quite a number of people with lightning," she said. "But not to cause injuries. It burns for a while, then it's finished. No trace. Not like this," she added, indicating her wrist, "but I had to melt through metal, you know!"

"You didn't damned-well have to. You had to call me! Why didn't you?"

"Haven't saved your number yet," she admitted.

He grunted. "You're obstinate. Can you remember injuring anyone with your curses?"

She thought very hard, but couldn't remember a single instance that had caused more than momentary pain or embarrassment. Well, except that itch. And the ingrown toenails. And, she supposed, Bonnie's ongoing cramp.

"You need to lift those," he warned.

"Why? They deserve them! It's *their* karma, not mine!"

Bryan leaned back in his chair, studying the ceiling.

"Return of karma," he said, shaking his head. "She finds the principle by herself. You're a sly fox, Ivy. Return of karma is the *only* way a Wiccan can cast a curse and get away with it."

"I land knee-deep in the faecalia and defend myself admirably," complained Ivy, "and *I'm* the one on trial? Why the hell don't you go and grill Bonnie?"

"Because I don't care about Bonnie," replied Bryan. "Bonnie's not my problem. I have to keep your record fairly clean."

"What for? For introduction to your brotherhood of some sort?"

"Oh, for heavens' sakes! You don't understand what

you're up against tomorrow night!"

"I've tipped off the police," said Ivy. "They'll be there to arrest the little filth before he can get up to anything serious."

"Don't count on it," said Bryan. "You know how efficient the police are."

Ivy said nothing for a while. Then:

"Great! Are we going to learn any more Wicca today?"

"I think I had better show you some psychic defence moves instead," said Bryan.

8

When Ivy returned to her cottage around dusk, she found Alison waiting.

"So nice to see you getting on with Bryan," said her friend with a suspiciously sweet smile.

Ivy snorted. 'Getting on' was about what one could call it. The man was relentless; he made her practise something until it came out of her ears; made her focus until she thought her skull would split, and did not stop until she had reached what he deemed perfection. And she still hadn't discovered his motive. She suspected by now that he did lead a coven of his own, somewhere, and was grooming her to be adopted into it.

As though she wanted to join a witches' coven! Gracious! All her life she'd resisted organized religion of all sorts; the occult struck her as worse. Even what little common sense lived in religions was missing from that. She just wanted to finish with this insane stretch of life, lock the little drug addicts safely behind the bars of a rehab, get Bex off her back, and then return to business as usual.

"Come in, Alison," she invited. She unlocked the door. Peridot came stroking around her shoes.

"Are you in love with him?" asked Alison.

Ivy gave her a quizzical look. "Bryan? No. Are you?"

Alison vehemently shook her head, but she blushed. "How can I be? I'm married!"

"To a man who treats you like an acquisition and keeps you on an extremely short leash." Ivy switched on the kettle and retrieved the bowl of biscuits as she peered at Alison. "Have one. He *is* rather charismatic and powerful, isn't he?"

"Who, Marc?" Alison misunderstood her deliberately.

"No, Allie. Bryan."

"He's a womaniser," said Alison. "I'd be careful of him if I were you."

Ivy laughed out loud. She poured a sink and while it was running, she fed Peridot.

"As long as nobody steals my Peridot and my moto, I'm fine," she said. "Don't need more males than that in my life."

A womaniser! Of this, she had seen no evidence around his lounge; how were dusty old books on flying going to seduce a woman? Bare stone floors? Colour scheme of black and stark? His wine was not looking overly used either. But it didn't touch her in any case – she wasn't in the market for a love-affair. She smiled and shook her head, aware of Alison peering intently at her.

"You haven't had any spooks?" probed Alison, crunching another cookie.

"Not in this cottage anyway," said Ivy. "You'll have to lower the rent! You promised me ghosts, and not a single one!"

Alison looked stressed. Ivy laughed.

"Seriously though, Allie, I want to buy this place. When would it suit you for an assessor?"

"I don't know," said Alison. "I'll have to ask -"

"Marc," completed Ivy drily. "Say, did you say you were an estate agent?"

"I worked for an estate agency," said Alison.

"Look, nothing is fixed yet," said Ivy, "but I'm going to try and organize you a receptionist job where I work. Would you like that?"

Alison smiled. "Sounds like a good idea. But I'll have to talk it over with -"

"Marc," completed Ivy with a sigh. "I get it. Say, would it be better if I discussed such things with Marc directly?"

"Oh no, he'd think I'm saying bad stuff about him."

"You have a problem, girl," said Ivy.

Some time later, after eating a bite and having her nightly bath, Ivy for once found herself and Peridot alone in her little witch's hut. She opened the Arcana, but couldn't rally any enthusiasm to study more. Where she was concerned, she'd be going in with a police squad, encircling the little Satanic sect and arresting them. And finished. Bryan's whole 'defence against the Dark Arts' act was probably not even going to come into play. A wand didn't stand up against a tazer gun, and magic flames did nothing against tear gas. End of story. She scratched Peridot behind the ears until he turned around and grabbed at her hand with all claws, and gnawed at it.

"Hey, you little savage!" she exclaimed, laughing. Her hands and forearms, even her toes, bore witness to her owning a kitten.

This intrigue between the neighbours didn't suit her at all; but it was in essence none of her business. She loaded up her laptop and browsed idly among the current news, as she liked doing on a quiet evening.

Her phone rang. She answered reflexively, and then cursed herself for not checking who it was first.

"Ivy Pennington speaking."

"Ivy, this is Bex."

Ivy went completely quiet. Bex! May her teeth fall out! *Kha- wait.* Not yet.

"Ivy," said Bex, her voice tearful, "she ran away again!"

"Sorry, lady, you've got the wrong number," said Ivy coldly and switched the call off. She sat there shaking with rage, unable to even think of words to answer Bex's audacity.

It's a trap! That little warning voice in her head. Sure it was a trap! Bex wanted to lure her out. That was what. Her phone rang again; Bex again. This time, Ivy killed the call without answering. And she put the phone on silent and let it ring, and ring, and ring... Peridot crawled onto her shoulder and refused to budge from there. She stroked him, thankful for his sensitivity.

Someone banged on her door. She jumped sky-high, then went to open it, but first she grabbed one of the heavy metal candlesticks she'd procured at the fleamarket on Sunday. That should do for socking an intruder on the head that he didn't know who he was. Completely free of magic and its complicated karma.

"Ivy, it's Bryan," came his urgent voice from outside. "Open up!"

She hurried up and unlocked and unbolted the door. Instead of coming in, Bryan grabbed her by her forearms and pulled her outside.

"You've got to hide! They're coming *now!*"

"They, the Magic Maniacs?" she asked.

"No, the police. It was a just matter of time, Ivy."

"How the hell do you know they're here?"

"Listen!"

She heard the sirens howling. She switched off the light, locked her cottage door and headed for her moto, which she had parked around the back of the cottage under a plastic sheet Bryan had given her for it, after her intense study session at his place. Rats, now she'd left her computer on, and all her money... and her smart-phone!

Peridot, at least, was clinging to her shoulder. Tonight there was no bag. She hoped she wouldn't lose him because of that. She put on her helmet.

The blue lights pulled up the driveway. Bryan hurried her and her bike through the garden gate and locked it behind him. They heard the car doors going.

"Your bike takes two," said Bryan. "Take me along, Ivy.

You'll need me."

"You don't have a helmet," she objected.

"I do," he said and led her to his garage. They could hear the voices coming nearer to the wall; police interrogating Alison as she was forced to show them to the garden cottage.

"Poor Alison," said Ivy.

"You can say that again," agreed Bryan. He picked up his motorcycle helmet from a shelf and put it on. "Come!"

She got onto her Honda, wondering if the larger, more powerful bike parked in Bryan's garage wouldn't do the trick better for two. But it might not fly. She beckoned to Bryan, and he climbed on behind her, and she rolled her Honda onto his driveway without making a sound.

"Is there something we can use as a ramp?"

"It's quite a steep driveway, and the gate is open," said Bryan.

"Let's hope that's enough," said Ivy, revved the engine and careened down that driveway. Towards the bottom, at the steepest part, she lifted the front wheel of her bike off the ground and *wished.*

It worked. The back wheel cleared the ground too, the engine cut out and the Honda ascended into the skies. She switched the headlight off.

Peridot clung to her shoulder, and Bryan to her middle. She felt a bit crowded on her broomstick tonight.

She analysed the situation. If Bex had called her to get the police to trace the line, then there was one place the police were not: At Bex's place. In fact, Bex was probably not even home but at the police station.

"It's your fault," she accused Bryan over the wind. "Should have shown me how to do hypnosis and invisibility."

His reply was muffled by the helmet, and blown away by the wind. Where to? She decided to give Bex a nasty surprise.

Bryan beckoned to her to set the motorbike down somewhere. She circled aimlessly; they were over Putney again, not too far from where Bex lived. She landed on the roof of a tall building. Bryan took his helmet off.

It had only stopped raining a bit earlier; everything was soaked.

"What's wrong?" she asked him. "Airsick?"

"No. We need to discuss things."

She removed her helmet too. In any case that helmet disoriented Peridot. She fastened it onto the holder of the handlebar. You didn't need a helmet if you were a witch on a broomstick. At Bryan's request she fastened his, too.

Peridot slid down her shoulder and tried to nestle in the hollow of her neck. She steadied the kitten.

"What now?"

"I bet you they're already at the Heath, rehearsing for tomorrow," said Bryan.

"So what are we going to do about it?" asked Ivy. "Tipping off the police tonight is no good. They're after *me*."

"There's something you don't know," said Bryan. "There's been a disappearance."

"You mean, Bonnie has actually run off again? That wasn't just a lure?"

"Not Bonnie," said Bryan. "It was in the news. A toddler has disappeared from Hayward Gardens, right off the Heath."

Ivy iced as the implications sank in.

"But... you don't think *they* would..."

"They would," said Bryan with conviction. "Think Halloween. They'll try to invoke something."

She considered for a moment.

"They wouldn't do their human sacrifice tonight, would they?" she asked.

"Unlikely," said Bryan. "But not impossible. We'd better check."

Another detail bothered Ivy.

"Bryan – Bex. Think she's in on this?"

"Why?"

"She's trying to get me out of the way. We're just about the only ones who can stop this, and she's not aware of you."

He stared at her.

"You're now starting to be paranoid," he said. "That's good. Exactly the kind of thinking we need."

Eventually they decided to check on the circle on the Heath first. Ivy cruised the bike over the Heath in the dark until she spotted the circle of fires. Bryan had been right.

"Now, leave the magic to me," he said softly. "Only use

yours if you have to defend yourself."

They cruised a bit lower, and then set down behind a copse of trees, out of sight of the fires, and crept closer, Peridot clinging to Ivy's shoulder for dear life.

There were thirteen youngsters. Quite a bit more of an intimidating group than on Saturday. And in the centre of the circle, where Jake was standing doing his conjuring thing, there was something small they all had their attention fixed on, chanting and muttering in unison. Ivy edged closer to see what it was.

A small child, maybe three years of age. She couldn't see if it was a boy or girl. The little one seemed drowsy; but awake. It was crooning constantly, as though it had been crying for hours and given up on crying.

"They'll have told the kid they're sacrificing her," whispered Bryan next to her. "The terror of that is part of their ritual. The idea is to harvest fear." He listened closely, then took out a directional mike and pointed it at the group, sticking an earphone into his left ear.

"They're planning to invoke Baba Yaga," he whispered with a scowl.

"Who?"

"Wicked old witch that eats children. She's a Russian spirit essence of evil." He nodded, satisfied that he'd judged the situation correctly. "They're 'preparing' the child for the slaughter. Anointing her, pouring goat's blood over her..."

"Which they got where?" she challenged.

"Butchery. There's a black market going for such items. We have to be quiet, Ivy!" If they all hadn't been chanting, they'd have heard her.

Bryan pulled out binoculars, even though they were quite close, and used them to peer into the circle.

Ivy watched in trepidation. Four of the youngsters were now taking the child at hands and feet and stretching her out on the ground. She cried and resisted, terrified.

"Bryan, we have to intervene! They're going to kill her!"

"Not yet," said Bryan. "That's for tomorrow. What *are* they doing?"

One of the youngsters brought a small black shape to over where the little girl was being kept stretched out on the ground. Two others started removing her clothes.

"That's a cat!" Bryan's whisper was nearly a gasp. Peridot clawed into Ivy's shoulder. She shot upright, raising her hand in which she held the athame she'd found in her pocket. And she screeched.

"Leave that kid alone!"

Lightning shot forward from her athame and crackled around the heads of the thirteen. The boy who had been holding the cat, let go of it in fright, and it shot away and right up a tree. The four who had held down the girl were also so surprised that they released the toddler, who curled up into a bundle and whimpered hysterically.

"It's her," yelled Jake. "The Lightning Witch! Get her!"

Thirteen wild young demon invokers stormed at Ivy as she lunged forward to grab the child. Lightning kept on dancing all around her, and between the members of the mob. Someone tripped her as she surged past the mob, and she went flying. Peridot disappeared into the back of her pullover; she'd have scratches all over her back in the morning, but that was the least of her worries. She reached for the crying child, and a teenager blocked her way and sat down on her arms.

Bonnie.

Ivy sent lightning coursing out of her own arms, and Bonnie jumped up with a scream.

"I'll deal with you later," warned Ivy, and then she had the toddler in her arms and turned – and faced a huge black monster, snaking over her like a cobra.

"You with your fluffy kitten," sneered Jake the Snake. "My familiar is a bit bigger than yours!"

Ivy cringed in reflex as the black spirit cobra hissed and struck. She shielded the little girl with her own body, already feeling the icy touch of that evil entity.

"Ward!" Bryan shouted at her. She threw her golden protective shield over herself as he'd taught her; at the same time she sensed how the cobra was restrained – probably by something he was doing. She looked up.

Green glowing threads had sprung up out of the ground and were growing up the cobra like vines. It twisted and turned, trying to get rid of them, but they turned into a mesh and brought it down, immobilizing it. It lay thrashing on the ground. Ivy noted how twelve of the thirteen Dark Mages were lying on the floor in a daze; Jake was wrestling valiantly with this condition, but was losing.

And then the sweet noise of her motorbike growled in her ears. She gathered the little girl in her arms, mounted her bike in front of Bryan and revved. Peridot crawled back out of her jersey to perch on her shoulder; the toddler clung to her neck, terrified but aware that she was being rescued. Ivy revved the moto to high heaven, then released the brakes. They shot forward, and at the first rock they hit, they cleared gravity and flew out of the Heath.

"Where to?" asked Ivy.

"Get the baby home," said Bryan. So she steered the scoot towards Hayward Gardens.

They landed in the road, cut the engine, and Bryan pushed the machine alongside as Ivy was carrying the little girl who had discovered Peridot and was holding onto the kitten like a fluffy toy.

"We'll have to rescue that poor kitty too," Ivy pointed out. "What were they going to do?"

"I'll tell you later," said Bryan. He rang the first doorbell, and a brown woman answered.

She took one look at the baby and screeched. And she yelled something into the house. A boy appeared, probably around twelve years.

"Mpho, go and tell Justine," yelled the woman. "Quick!

Amy's back! They found her!"

The boy ran while his mother burst into tears of joy, clapping her hands and touching the little girl's wispy blond hair, just to ascertain that Amy was indeed alive. All over the flat block, doors opened and neighbours came streaming out. Some quick-witted souls took snaps with their cellphone cameras and instantly posted them to the social media; a practice that made Bryan bare his teeth.

"Stop that! You're endangering her! They're going to come back for her if you post where she is!"

The youngsters who were doing this, stopped in shock. Amy's mother Justine came flying down the stairs from the fifth level, and took Amy from Ivy, and hugged her tightly, crying loudly.

"This is the point at which we disappear," said Ivy.

"No. Wait." Bryan parked the motorcycle and raised his hands. "Listen, guys. You have to stick together now. Amy was abducted by Satanists. They will try again. Watch all your children. Don't let them play outside in the next few days. These monsters are out hunting children, and they mean to kill them. You have to protect each other. Look after each other and keep an eye on each other's children. Is that understood?"

"Yes!" - "We will!" - "Sure!" and so on echoed as reassurance.

"Good," said Bryan, turning to Ivy. "And *now* is the moment we disappear."

"Peridot," she pointed out.

The kitten was struggling in Amy's little hands. The girl didn't want to release him. It cost persuasion and gentle force, both from Ivy and Amy's mother, to get the kitten released. The second he was free, he clambered up Ivy's pullover again and hid inside it, against her shoulder.

Ivy mounted the bike and waited for Bryan to get into the pillion seat before speeding off, away from the mother's overwhelming thankyous.

On the side road there were a few traffic bumps. Ivy picked up speed and used them to climb back into the sky.

Peridot nuzzled against Ivy's neck. She reached over and patted him.

"You alright, kitten?"

"Meow." It sounded a bit worried.

"And you?" asked Bryan behind her.

She laughed. "Sure! Where now?"

"Bex," said Bryan, wiping his brow. "Thank the angels that we were in time to stop that rubbish! But now Bonnie is in danger."

"Bonnie? Why?"

"Didn't you say she was pregnant?"

There was a point beyond which Ivy couldn't take on more stress. All she could come up with was a sigh. "In that case, may the angels protect her, khazam," she said half-heartedly. "Because her auntie can't be everywhere."

"That will only become relevant tomorrow," said Bryan. "We'll be ready for it then."

The car engine hovered outside for a while; then there were doors clapping closed, some unintelligible calls, and the sound of the car moving off. A key in the door; the door opening; high heels click-clicking along the tiled floor, coming closer, rounding the corner to the spacious lounge...

Bex saw who was parked comfortably on her lounge suite. It took her a second of disbelief; then she screamed hysterically. She scrambled for her cellphone in her bag.

"Khazam!" said Ivy casually, sending a lightning bolt that disabled the cellphone. "You're on your own, madame."

"You're here – you've come to finish me off -" stammered Bex, and retook the screaming.

Oh for heavens' sakes!

"Khazam!" Her voice lost its strength and went down to *mezzo-piano*, though she still tried to scream with it.

"Sit down, Bex," ordered Ivy, pointing her lightning-stick – her athame – at a sofa in the plush lounge her brother had left this woman with. This was not the time to get emotional. She had to keep in mind that Bonnie was all she had left from her brother. So Bonnie had to be rescued, period.

"I – the police," uttered Bex.

"The police have nothing to do with this," said Ivy scathingly. "You know exactly where Bonnie is, don't you? Truth!" she commanded.

Bex nodded.

"So why the hell are you supporting Bonnie's Satanism?"

"What?"

"She's dabbling with the Dark Craft," said Ivy. "Come now, Bex. Don't tell me you didn't know this!" Gee, Bex was really growing hair in odd places! Her nose hair had started lengthening and was nearly down to her upper lip; her ears had got bushy, too. Her eyebrows were beginning to meet in the middle. And the patchy effect of her head hair was even more pronounced than before. Places where the hair was rejecting its dye, taking its clothes off.

"Yes, stare at me," snapped Bex. "Bonnie says this hair trouble is *your* doing!"

For a moment it was on Ivy's tongue to say that Bonnie would indeed accuse her of anything; but Bryan touched her arm, lightly, steering her, keeping her on the Light Path. Which, if you read the fine print, didn't necessarily include complete honesty to a non-Wiccan. But for tonight, she had to stay spotless.

"Yes, that was me," she admitted. "I can take it back; but give me one good reason why I should."

"I tried to stop her," said Bex. "You know. When she started dating that Jake. He's bad news. A drug dealer. Belongs in rehab, the little scum."

"In prison," corrected Ivy angrily. "You won't like what he was doing tonight!"

"They're just toying with weird rituals and stuff," said Bex dismissively. "Kid stuff. They think it gives them magical powers."

"Weird rituals?" asked Ivy. "Have you been to one of those yet?"

Bex denied this.

"Involving goat's blood, cock's feet, disembowelling a cat, sacrificing a human child," said Ivy. "Still think it's kids' stuff?"

"That's just evil myth," said Bex angrily. "See, this is what nasty rumours people spread about magic."

"There's magic," said Ivy, "and then there is murder. I don't think on a magical level they're up to much. But they're evil, Bex. Extremely evil. And that's what Bonnie has been tangling with."

"Bonnie decided to get herself pregnant by that good-for-nothing," said Bex angrily. "I thought, if she wants to escape to you for a few days, you'll be able to talk sense into her – but you betrayed me and just sent her home!" She raised her hands in exasperation. "Ivy, how in the world am I supposed to raise another baby now? I'm old! I'm thirty-six! Look at me!"

"Thirty-six," repeated Ivy pensively. Yes, she remembered the wedding, even though she'd only been four. Her brother getting married at a terribly early age, to a woman he'd landed with child... Bex must have been twenty-one when she gave birth to Bonnie. And Ivy's brother had gone on to become a hugely successful barrister, for the next nine years, until his sudden death. But he'd been so well insured that whatever he hadn't already provided for the family, like this house and furniture, could still be bought or paid from the endless fund of the insurance money. He'd appointed his best friend and colleague to do the administration of his estate, and that man had done an excellent investment job, so that Bex didn't even have to worry how the monthly money got into her account.

But at thirty-six, to look like an old, warted and hairy hag...

"Some women have their first baby at thirty-six," she pointed out. "But Bex, there won't be any baby. Any idea what she got pregnant for?"

"What a nonsensical question," snapped Bex. "You don't get pregnant for a purpose."

"In her case, you do," said Ivy. "Let me tell you again. They are planning a human sacrifice for tomorrow. A child. They had a toddler there that they'd stolen, but we rescued her, so they'll be going for second best – performing a live abortion in the ritual."

Bex frowned. Ivy waited for the emotional impact. It was slow in coming.

"She's twelve weeks now," said Bex. "I was wondering why she was waiting so long to abort! I thought she wanted to keep the baby."

"Twelve weeks," repeated Ivy, shooting a glance at Bryan. She couldn't keep the tears from glistening around the edges of her eyes. "At twelve weeks, the baby is ten centimetres long. Like this," and she indicated with two fingers. "It is perfectly formed and has everything it needs, eyelashes, earlobes, even fingernails. All it must do is grow. This is why twelve weeks is the legal cut-off for elective abortions."

"She's had abortions before," said Bex. "She only told me afterwards. 'Mom, I was pregnant, but don't worry, I already took care of it.' She's responsible that way."

"Responsible?" gasped Ivy, with another loaded glance at Bryan. Was he taking all this in? "How is that responsible? How many has she had?"

"Two or three, I'm not sure," said Bex uncertainly.

"And you let her?"

"What should I do?" asked Bex with a shrug. "It's her body, she's got the right to decide if she wants to bugger up her life with a pregnancy."

"She has that right to decide before she allows a boy to jump her," shot Ivy, angry. "Afterwards, once there's a baby, it's not only her body! It's the baby's body too!"

"Ah," said Bex, "you're a pro-lifer."

"And you're a life-denialist," shouted Ivy. "You'll let this happen? You'll let them do an amateur, hand-botch abortion on your daughter to feed some dark ritual? You realize she can die?"

"They won't," insisted Bex. "It's hogwash, all that."

Ivy got up. She'd had enough.

"I'm locking you in," she said. "You're going nowhere tonight! And then I'm going to take care of my brother's little girl. And his grandchild if I can help it."

She raised her athame, and a "khazam" danced around the house. Burglar bars grew denser; doors bolted themselves; locks fused so they could not be cracked.

"You have everything you need in here," said Ivy. "Bed, toilet, water, food, bathroom, heating, entertainment... a nice prison, this is. Your cellphone is out of commission. Your alarm and panic buttons are out – because I'm not expecting burglars here tonight."

"You're a wicked witch yourself," screeched Bex. "Look at you, dabbling in black magic. Curse you! May you -"

"Ward!" said Ivy quickly, raising her athame. The 'rot in hell' fell on a wall of sizzling lightning, and dispersed, to add to the general bad vibes in the house.

She let herself and Bryan out of the front door and re-fused the lock, with Bex yelling curses after her.

9

"That was weird," said Ivy when she, Peridot and Bryan were back in his lounge, relaxing. Bryan had decided that it wasn't safe for her to go home to her cottage yet.

"Are you alright?" he asked as he poured a bit of brandy into two tumblers and handed her one. "You teared up there when Bex told you the age of the pregnancy."

Ivy nodded and sipped her brandy.

"When I was young and dumb I volunteered for some social work," she said. "It's an eye-opener. I went to help in a mercy clinic, assist the doctors who perform elective abortions... Bryan... some of those kids come at sixteen, even twenty weeks and they've tried to do an abortion themselves and... we sit with the rest," and she wiped impatiently across her eyes. "The convent school sent me there to get in touch with life. I didn't turn Catholic; but man!"

Bryan nodded gravely.

"Bet you didn't expect this little accountant to have experience in blood and gore," she laughed and sniffed the tears away. "It put me off studying medicine."

"You? Nothing surprises me about you by now," he replied. "There's something really bad in that house," he added. "The evil vibes are everywhere."

"Wasn't like that when I last visited them," said Ivy. "Four years back. When Bonnie comes home, she'll find all the doors fused locked," she added thoughtfully.

"Bonnie won't come home tonight," said Bryan. "They'll keep her close, so that their second-best option doesn't disappear too."

"We have to rescue her!"

"She's safest where she is right now, believe me," said Bryan. "They'll be guarding her like gold. Unnerving, but safe. Tomorrow at dusk we dive in there and snatch her up, and away."

"An attack from the air," said Ivy. "Good idea, but how do we do this? The moto is not a broomstick, after all."

"You put it on its side. You wheelie in the air. We can practice it in the dirt, tomorrow morning," said Bryan.

Ivy yawned.

"Bryan, I'm beat! Won't you let me go home?"

"The police will have set a trap for you," he predicted. "Something that triggers when you go in there."

"So what must I do?" She hated the plaintive tone that crept into her voice; but she was really very, very tired.

"Come," invited Bryan and gave her a hand up out of the armchair. Peridot nearly fell off her lap where he'd been sleeping; she caught him and cradled him against her shoulder. Bryan led her out of the lounge, and into the dark of the house. He switched on a number of lights.

The interior of his home continued to be sleek, male and minimalist. Some black-and-white photos of small planes graced the walls of the corridor, and a few photos of people she didn't know.

"Who are they?" she enquired, pointing.

"My father," said Bryan. "He was a flyer. A pilot, with his own small plane. His big dream was to join the Hurricane Hunters. He did eventually, a few years back. Almost too old to fly. They took him because of his experience. He had flight hours like few."

"And?" prompted Ivy.

"And then there came the day he went flying and never came back. His plane disappeared with him, another pilot and two scientists, inside a hurricane. I guess it's the sort of way he would have chosen to go."

"He owned this house?" asked Ivy.

"Yes. Bought it after my mother passed away. I grew up not too far from here, but when Dad and I moved in here, we decided to make a clean break from all the clutter. He detested clutter. I've been honouring his memory and keeping it clear."

Ivy nodded. She could associate with that.

"And you've got brothers, sisters..."

"A brother somewhere," said Bryan. "He's a drifter, gambler, lucky fish. Wanders all over the world clearing out the casinos and amassing it all. He lives in a tent most of the time. Asked me to look after his bank account, that's how I usually know where he is."

"Sounds like a man on a mission," grinned Ivy. "And you are unemployed and share in your brother's winnings?"

Bryan laughed shortly, with an edge of anger. "Fine things you think of me!" He opened a door to a guest suite. "Hope this is alright."

Twin beds with comfortable puffy duvets on them shared a single bedside table between them with a stark, black desk spotlight on it. The linen was white; the table was of dark wood.

"It looks comfy," said Ivy. "But it will get hellishly dirty, because I am. You don't have more down-to-earth blankets?"

"Only on my own bed," said Bryan. "You want to crawl in? You're welcome to!"

She smiled. "Er... no, thanks." Nice try, Bryan, she thought. Womaniser. Aha! Just as she was beginning to think that he really cared...

"Consider that one declined invitation," he said lightly, and smiled. "Don't worry about the linen, for heaven's sakes, Ivy. We've got bigger fish to fry. There's a bathroom across if you really must have a bath right now, but you look too tired for that. Am I right?"

She nodded apologetically. "Tomorrow morning," she said.

"Then sleep tight," said Bryan and closed the door, leaving her and her cat alone in that stark, pristine guest bedroom. Alone with her thoughts; having to wonder at herself, where that pang of disappointment had come from.

She wasn't aware that he wove powerful shields around the room, and then his whole house, before returning to the lounge to clear up and then take himself off to his bed without a lady in it.

In the middle of the night Ivy woke up, breathless from a nightmare. She lay in the dark, trying to block out the images of the poor kitty they had been meaning to sacrifice. Had they managed to catch it again?

Peridot was nestling in his favourite spot, under her chin, as always, sleeping peacefully. And Ivy realized that the rumbling and bumps she was hearing came from across the wall, from her cottage.

The bastards! Were they turning everything upside down searching for her? Had they damaged her computer? She dreaded what she would find in the morning; she was sorely tempted to go out there and *khazam* them while they were at it.

May their fingers turn pitch black wherever they touch my stuff, she thought. And she released a resigned little sigh and closed her eyes, trying to block out all these things: The nightmare, thoughts about Bonnie or Bex, what was happening in her cottage, and what she had lived through, tonight. Sleep was going to fix it. She only hoped she was actually safe in Bryan's house.

Now that she was awake, she needed the bathroom. She opened the guest room's door and slipped across the passage without putting any lights on. The bathroom was right across, as she'd noted when Bryan had shown her to the room. She crept into the bathroom, not wanting to wake up her host. There was enough moonlight coming through the window that she didn't need to switch on any lights.

When she re-emerged, she moved across the passage back to the guest room's door – and froze.

Eyes peered at her from the dark of the passage.

She stared back at the huge cat that was stalking closer, noiselessly.

Don't let it smell your fear!

It was the white leopard! How had it come in? Had it jumped through a window? Fearfully she remembered something she'd read on the internet recently – that the original *homo erectus* at the Cradle of Mankind had been hunted out by leopards. The Assassin of the Grasslands, the article had called the animal.

The leopard moved right up to her and pushed its head into the palm of her hand, and rubbed up against her. Her fear transformed to electric excitement; this wild creature was acting exactly like a house cat seeking affection! She unfroze slowly and scratched it behind its ears, and heard it make a noise like a soft, rumbling purr. The leopard purred! She went down on her haunches and took its big head between her hands and cuddled it. The white leopard put one paw on her shoulder as it cuddled her back.

This was unreal! Ivy remembered all she'd learnt about

leopards; at some point she'd had a fascination with the stealthiest animal of the bush, and had devoured information. One thing was clear: Leopards were solitaires, they *never* bonded with humans. They didn't even bond with each other! How they procreated, was a little mystery – Ivy suspected, by wind pollination. A leopard could be hand-reared from a cub, but the second the cub was fully grown, the keeper would be reluctant to interact, because the animal would generally get aggressive and stand-offish. Dangerous! And this white leopard, this magical creature, was doing exactly the opposite of what leopards were supposed to do.

If it got snappy she could 'khazam' it, she thought, but that was a fleeting thought. It was far from reality. This leopard, somehow, was tame; it must belong to Bryan.

Aha! And there was the answer to some of the mystery surrounding the man. He was probably part of a syndicate that smuggled rare animals. That sounded feasible – but it didn't explain the pure affection of this particular white leopard. Well, it was quite likely that some smugglers – who no doubt liked animals, or they'd be smuggling drugs instead – fell in love with one or two particular specimens and decided to keep those, while keeping the trade going. She wondered about his clientèle; found herself mulling whether there were any really rich, good-looking young Shahs amongst them.

"You are such a beautiful cat," she told the white leopard as she *shmoozed* with it. The purring never slowed. And then she thought of her own kitty and decided that she'd better make sure he was safe. Because no matter how unusual the leopard was towards humans, it was still likely to regard a tiny black kitten as a snack.

"I have to get back to Peridot," she said apologetically. "You wonderful creature! Thank you for your visit! I love you!" And she closed the guest room's door on the white leopard, cuddled into her pillow where she found Peridot fast asleep, and closed her eyes, dreaming of a wild white leopard.

Halloween morning dawned dark and drizzly. Ivy woke up thinking of her computer. She'd promised to design an ad campaign for her boss before the first of November. She had to be insane! And this ongoing thing with the police – that had to be cleared. There were only two legal ways; if she allowed the whole procedure to roll over her and waited for court, for them to try and fail to prove her guilty; or for Bex to drop the charges. For that, Mr Brown also had to drop his – wait! His charges had never been filed. Well, maybe by now he had completed that form. So she'd have to find something to blackmail him by... something that was more important to him than trying to crook three months' unearned rental out of her.

And Bex? How could she be pressurized to drop her charges? This was a riddle. Bex hated her with a passion; Ivy knew this now. She had no idea why.

Maybe, she thought, it was time to get legal help.

Bryan had a nice breakfast waiting for her as she came

down to the front. The smells directed her to the kitchen, where porkies and eggs were frying.

"Good morning," he greeted her. "Feeling alright today?"

"More rested," she admitted. "But I'm missing my four-poster bathtub."

Bryan laughed. "My Jacuzzi-style tub doesn't cut it?"

Ivy pulled a face. "It's not my home zone," she explained and took a seat on a high barstool at the sleek, bar-style breakfast surface. "Say, Bryan..." She petered off and smiled.

He glanced up. "Shoot," he invited.

"What do you know about the white leopard that roams around here?"

Bryan smiled broadly. "Ah! You've met him!"

"He's a beautiful animal," said Ivy dreamily. "So affectionate!"

"I'm glad he likes you," said Bryan. "He doesn't take to everybody."

"What's his name?"

"Name?" echoed Bryan. "He's a wild creature. I call him Leopard." He grinned and returned his attention to the frying pan.

"But I do worry about Peridot with him around," mentioned Ivy.

Bryan looked up, seemingly puzzled. Far away in distant countries, she thought. Was everything alright with his syndicate, or was there trouble? She wondered how he managed to keep it all hidden from view.

"Just keep your kitty close," he advised.

She tickled Peridot who was perched on her shoulder. He jumped off and landed squarely on the table.

"You don't own the leopard, do you?" she asked suspiciously.

"Nobody owns a leopard," replied Bryan. "Zoos and circuses sometimes think they do. And sometimes the leopards correct them on this."

"And... you don't maybe run a racket with wild animals?" With a smile. She wasn't going to betray him!

Bryan laughed out loud and served her a plate with all the necessary bits of an English breakfast. He indicated towards the coffee machine, for her to help herself to the freshly brewed beverage.

"D'you know a lawyer?" asked Ivy as she poured herself coffee.

Bryan looked up in surprise. The flash that passed his expression was gone in a split second, covered up behind a scowl.

"A lawyer," he repeated. "Why?"

"The little demon conjurers out there," she specified, then laughed. "Oh, Bryan! Not to press charges against you for owning a rare wild cat! He looks happy and well looked after. He's in good hands."

"You never hear a word I say," commented Bryan. "But

regarding those little criminals - they're breaking the law, Ivy. This is a criminal matter, no lawyer needed. You only need one for civil matters."

"For defending myself against Bex's charge," said Ivy. "And Mr Brown's."

Bryan half-smiled. "You moved in here pretty suddenly," he mentioned. "*Are* you in trouble with your rent?"

"No!" She snorted. "Fully paid up! But the old bastard wants to invent a clause that was never in the contract and press three extra months of rent out of me. For a place where I no longer live."

"It's nowhere in writing?" asked Bryan.

"No."

"Then he has no leg to stand on and I wouldn't bother with a lawyer," he replied. "If he wants to sue, he must carry the legal cost. Remember he needs to produce proof that you owe that rent. I hope you kept all your proofs of payment?"

"I'm an accountant, Bryan," she reminded him.

"Ah. Of course you kept them. Let him proceed. Let him bump his nose. I can tell you now that he won't. He knows he can't win this."

"But in conjunction with Bex..."

"Bex is the problem," said Bryan. "Damn! I'd love to go back there and find out what smelled so bad in that place."

Before he allowed her home, Bryan investigated Ivy's cottage.

"All clear," he said then, beckoning to her where she stood in the garden gate. "There's no trap."

Ivy steeled herself for what she'd find. But there was no getting around it; Peridot needed his food. He'd been good and not had any accidents inside Bryan's house; instead he'd let himself out the second she had opened her bedroom door, and made a beeline for the outside.

Poor kitty, she thought. No cat should have such a hectic schedule. And her thoughts returned once more to the cat at the dark ritual.

"Bryan," she said as she cautiously approached her door, "those kids – ah!" She walked through the rooms of her cottage in disbelief.

Everything was just as she'd left it the night before; even her computer was in the same spot, and still on; hibernating by now.

"Didn't they search this place?" she asked, baffled.

"Doesn't look like it," said Bryan.

"What on Earth did I hear banging around in here last night?"

He peered at her. "You heard banging?"

"Yes! Anyway I was sure the police would turn the place upside down looking for..."

"... a fully grown woman," completed Bryan as she went silent, seeing the breach in her own logic. "Sure."

She shrugged. Whatever she had heard – imagination? Wind? She remembered her little curse that she sent after the perpetrators. Well, time would tell. She was going to the police office anyway today.

"Make yourself comfy," she invited. "I'm going to pick up here quickly, then I must design an advertising campaign for Mr Oates and a program to train Biljana – Bryan, those kids. Some of them were from good homes. I can't imagine all of them playing truant today? All thirteen?"

"Unlikely," he said. "They'll be in school."

"Then..."

"Remember, if you want to arrest them you first have to prove that they are in possession of drugs," he said.

"They arrested *me* without any proof of anything," she pointed out.

"Ivy," said Bryan, "you're jumping the gun. If we get them arrested for possession of drugs, they'll be out before dusk, on bail. We want to catch them red-handed."

"So we wait until they start cutting up Bonnie?" she challenged, and shrugged, exasperated. "I'm going to find her and prevent this. Even if I have to keep her tied up tonight!"

"Good luck," said Bryan drily. "Remember she got herself pregnant for this in the first place."

"I'm finding her," said Ivy resolutely. "If last night was not enough evidence to get them convicted – abducting and terrorizing a toddler, attempted murder – then tonight won't be either. She'll have to confess."

"How will you get her to confess?" probed Bryan.

"Put her under pressure!"

"Like the Spanish Inquisition?"

She went silent.

"Ivy," said Bryan reasonably, "how would you even find her?"

"That's no problem," she replied and took out the black oven-proof bowl, pouring tap water into it.

"It doesn't work with tap water," mentioned Bryan.

"Really?" She gazed into the water, knowing that she had probably forgotten the whole recipe for preparing a scrying bowl.

Darkness. The black bottom of the bowl. And then, in her mind's eye, some other darkness. A warehouse, or the back entrance of a shopping mall. In... she nearly had the name of the street. She became silent, listened...

Now she had it. Just off Upper Richmond avenue. She peered into the bowl, clearing her mind, imprinting the image... she knew this place. She'd seen it before. She knew exactly where it was.

Bonnie was crouching in a dark corner, her knees drawn up to her chin. Three of the gang were hanging around, guarding her. Bonnie looked scared. She might just be amenable to being rescued, for once.

"I'm going out," Ivy informed Bryan. "Please feel free to stay here as long as you like. When you go, just bolt the door from outside and put the jay-lock on."

"Going where?" demanded Bryan.

"Picking up Bonnie."

He got up, angry. "You're incorrigible! You can't go alone! Give me a second, I'll bring my car round."

"Done," said Ivy. But you won't be controlling me, the way Marc controls Alison, she thought. And then she scowled at her own thinking.

Think of the devil, Ivy said to herself when Alison appeared in the open doorway mere seconds after Bryan had left.

"Hi Ivy. I want to invite you to a little Halloween party for tonight."

Ivy smiled. A party would... tonight? She shook her head.

"Allie, I can't. I've got to..." Rubbish, she thought. If things went well, Bonnie would be in protective custody by five o'clock, and the rest of the gang under police surveillance. No need for her to attend their little Satanic rite personally.

"Sure, I'd love to," she amended. "What time?"

"We're starting around six. But the idea is to go through until after midnight. Is that alright? I mean, I know you have to work tomorrow," she added, "but your house is right here, so if you get tired, feel free to leave early. Is that okay?"

Ivy smiled. "Super. What do I bring?"

"I think, if you can come dressed up..."

Whoa. "Does it have to be something witchy?"

Allie hesitated.

"Well, you could come as a ghost," she suggested.

"Can I come as the Anonymous Accountant?" asked Ivy. She really didn't have any Halloween costumes and didn't feel like inventing one. She'd probably just pick up a mask at some party shop.

"Sure," said Allie, relieved. "As long as it's clandestine. And sinister. All in black, maybe?" She giggled. "Some of us are coming skyclad! Hope it stops raining. If it doesn't, we'll have to do the whole thing inside. But actually we're planning a bonfire, so maybe wear something not too fragile."

Hmm. So not her black outfit. "I'll think about it," said Ivy. "And do I bring something...?"

"Maybe a bottle of wine," said Alison.

Ivy nodded. "Allie, I hate to do this, but I have an overload of work and a niece to pick up. I'm trying to organize you a job. I can't really visit right now."

"That's okay," trilled Alison, clearly happy that Ivy was coming to the Halloween bash. She left, skipping a little.

Ivy got into fresh clothes, cleaned herself up as quickly as she could and was just putting on sneakers when she heard the hum of Bryan's engine. She met him as he parked on her lawn, wondering if this vehicle could be made to fly as well.

"Where to?" he asked as she climbed up to the passenger seat.

"Putney again. Upper Richmond Road." And she considered something. "Bryan – just in case, can we take the moto along please?"

"The Flymo?" he joked.

"Yes!" She grinned.

"Help me lug it into the loading area then," he said, cut the engine and jumped out.

A few minutes later they were on their way to Putney.

The place was actually the cargo area behind one of the large modern warehouses. Bryan parked his van in the loading zone, and Ivy jumped out. She patted her right pocket, where her athame was stashed, and her left one where she carried her small handy tear gas spray that she'd purchased an age ago when she had moved into a flat alone. She hoped it hadn't decayed from age.

She moved between large boxes full of goods; aisles upon aisles of them. The place was huge. She nearly tripped over some beer bottles in the dark; they clattered as she accidentally kicked at them. She cursed. The hum of the aircon was fairly loud; but it wasn't impossible that they had heard her.

She rounded the next corner, and – wham! Something slammed into the box behind her. She ducked, late; and she took out her athame and sent a flash of light. Just light. Doing this, she realized that she was giving her position away, and ducked to the side.

In the instant the light flashed on them, she saw the group; as in her scrying bowl. Bonnie sat huddled in a corner, looking very frightened; two others, a boy in designer clothes and a girl in full Gothic gear, sat to her left and right. The third, Jake, was standing, peering into the darkness looking for her.

Alright. There was only so much one could do with lightning. She concentrated. What she wanted, was a silent, hypnotic sleep spell. She pointed at them, and in her mind she hummed a lullaby. *Hush-a-bye baby, on your tree top...* She sensed Bryan's presence behind her even before she felt his hand on her shoulder. *Not now, Bryan... When the wind blows, the cradle will rock...*

A barely visible blue mist rose from the point of her athame. Her eyes were getting used to the shadows; she could see some points of light, reflections of something or other.

And then the weather played a nasty trick on her, and the sun broke through outside, and the warehouse lightened enough that she could see them all – and they could see her.

Something came flying at her head. She ducked instinctively and it slammed into the box behind her. She lifted her athame and redoubled her efforts. *Hush-a-bye baby...* she sent another, gentler flash of light to see what was happening.

Damn, this wasn't working. The two youngsters on either side of Bonnie had drowsed off, and Bonnie was looking very groggy; but Jake was still standing, wielding his massive ceremonial knife, weaving some sort of spell. Probably to ward off her magic. She tried it out by sending a lightning bolt. It fizzled around the invisible shield that Jake had woven.

Fine and well, she thought as she suddenly knew her own

strategy. She sent some seriously blinding flashes his way; he was kept busy blinking and blindly waving his dagger, reinforcing his shield. Light went straight through that shield. She kept the bright flashes coming, and advanced on him, and when she was at arm's length, dodging that waving knife, she sprayed the tear gas into his face.

That he had not expected! He roared, and collapsed, coughing and retching and trying to scream at her at the same time. She beckoned to Bryan, and together they picked up Bonnie and carried her as fast as they could back out of the warehouse and to Bryan's Land Rover. They put her on the back seat, Ivy jumped up next to her, Bryan took the wheel. As they pulled away, Jake came staggering out of the warehouse entrance, still coughing dismally, and pointed his knife at them. Something black detached itself from its tip and hurtled towards the windscreen.

"Ward!" yelled Ivy, blocking physically with her hands. A shield of lightning crackled across the glass, and the black thing exploded into droplets and dispersed. The Land Rover's tyres screeched as it took off. Jake ran after them. Bryan navigated the Jeep down the fairly narrow lane running next to the warehouse. A large truck came towards them. The driver stopped and gestured at Bryan, quite explicitly. Jake closed in from behind.

"Reverse," exclaimed Ivy. Bonnie, half conscious, mumbled something. Bryan scowled at Ivy and reversed back towards Jake, who caught up and jumped up on the Jeep, holding on and looking for an opening to get in. Ivy countered the stream of curses he was spewing by maintaining the lightning shield.

Bonnie mumbled something as the Jeep went around the corner. Ivy ignored it. Bonnie raised her voice.

"Let him in," she demanded.

"Oh no, my girl," countered Ivy. "Not a damn."

Bonnie started screaming. Ivy lifted her athame and pointed it at her niece.

"Quiet!" she commanded. Bonnie's voice fell away though she still tried to scream.

But that gap was all Jake had needed. Something black hit Ivy in the back, right at the height of her solar plexus. She gasped and collapsed in pain. Bonnie sat up and opened the window for Jake. Bryan reversed the van into the wall. And night folded around Ivy.

When she awoke, she was in her bed. Alison was sitting next to her, holding out a cup of some hot brew for her.

"What happened?" she asked. "Where's Bonnie? Where's Bryan?"

"Bryan's over at Marc's, organizing some things," said Alison. "Bonnie has been taken to hospital."

"Which hospital?" asked Ivy, electrified. She tried sitting up, but found that she had absolutely no energy. "Where's my motorbike?"

"Was totalled. It was in Bryan's van."

Ivy was ready to scream. "Which hospital?" she repeated, frantic. "Where did they take Bonnie?"

"Queen's," said Alison. "She's apparently having a miscarriage."

Ivy closed her eyes and exhaled, not knowing how to respond to that bit of news. On the one hand, it put a nice stop to the horrors that were planned for tonight. On the other, she'd hoped to save that poor baby. And on the third hand, probably it was for the best – for Bonnie as well as for the poor little foetus who had only been conceived to be sacrificed. Better to miscarry naturally, in a clean, medically equipped hospital under supervision of a doctor. Ivy's ears were ringing and she couldn't help tears slipping through her closed lashes, for that poor little soul whom she'd never meet now.

Alison's slender hand stroked her forehead. She appreciated that.

"Come now, Ivy," said the girl. "Have some tea. Things will feel better after that."

"You could have adopted him," muttered Ivy. "There was no reason for her to throw that baby away!"

Alison sighed.

"Sorry, Allie," said Ivy. "Didn't mean to bring it up."

"You've been through a lot," said Alison, stroking her arm. "Don't worry." But Ivy could hear the tears in the other girl's voice. She sat up.

"So Bryan's van is totalled?"

"No, just the bike is. I'm sorry, Ivy. Bryan's van is

pretty badly damaged too, some heavy boxes fell on it. It'll cost him quite a bit to get it fixed."

"Shit! And Jake?" asked Ivy. "Where's the boy who was in the van?"

"He went to the hospital with Bonnie. He's her boyfriend."

Ivy took a deep breath and sat up. She felt dizzy; but this had to happen. She pushed herself off the bed.

"I need transport," she said vaguely. Peridot, who had been lying on the blanket at her feet, scampered up her clothes and went to sit on her shoulder.

Right. She'd forgotten to take him along. And now her athame was gone, her bike was gone, and most critically, her niece was still in the hands of the guy who'd probably murder her too, for a sacrifice.

"Sorry, Peridot. I won't forget you again."

The kitten purred, digging his little claws into her shoulder. Somehow she felt better; her energy was returning.

"Ivy, where are you going?"

"See my niece in hospital. I can't leave her alone in this crisis."

"Her mother will be there," said Alison.

"Her mother? Ha!" Bex was still locked up in her house. Not only that, but Ivy doubted that she'd care enough even to check on her daughter.

She resolutely staggered down the path. If she didn't have a bike, she had two legs and the bus. And she'd get there, before the hour was out. Damn that Jake; he wouldn't break Bonnie. That much Ivy had resolved.

At this point she couldn't give a rip that she had all sorts of work deadlines for tomorrow. Hang that. She stumbled forward down the path, hearing Alison running towards the main house.

A few moments later both Marc and Bryan were emerging from the front door. Ivy lifted her chin and marched on down the path, not glancing backward.

"Ivy, where are you going?" Bryan had just about caught up with her.

"Rescue my niece from that damn drug dealer!" she snapped. "And just you try to stop me!" She lifted her hand in warning, pointing her index finger at him.

"Stop that," said Bryan.

"Ivy, be sensible," Marc chimed in. "You can't go anywhere in your condition."

She ignored them both and continued walking. She was at the garden gate now; her pace had picked up significantly.

"Let me take you, then," said Bryan.

"You must be mad!" Marc berated him.

"I know what I'm doing," replied Bryan.

Ivy laughed bitterly, never slowing her pace. "You can't take me, Bryan. I'm very sorry about the accident. But you can't take me because you don't have a car. The jolly bus is all I have left."

"But you can barely walk," objected Bryan. "Wait here

for me, Ivy." He turned and ran back up the path.

Ivy was on the pavement now, next to the road. Only one kilometre to the bus stop, she thought. Keep courage!

"Ivy, you're being obstinate," said Marc. "Why are you doing this?"

"You don't know the background," replied Ivy. "Marc, my little niece is having a miscarriage. But she's in the hands of a criminal who deals drugs and sacrifices children. There's a whole black magic ritual involved. He's with her right now, in the hospital. I want to prevent further damage."

"What damage?"

"I have no idea what's up his sleeve," said Ivy. "But he didn't go with her out of love, I can guarantee you that."

"Ivy, there's no such thing as black magic," said Marc with a smile.

She stopped in her tracks and stared scathingly at him, at his enigmatic dark-blue eyes under those heavy eyebrows. He could be anything. He could be a Master Mage. Powerful as hell. But he chose not to believe.

Well, neither did she, actually! But this wasn't about that pathetic little bit of magic being flung about by teenage witches.

"Marc, in principle I agree fully with you. But in practice, teenagers keep on trying even if they can't get it to work. And in the process they commit fiendish crimes. The babies that get killed, the cats that get slaughtered, those are real, Marc. It's genuine murder. Even if they can't get anything magical out of it."

Marc nodded and didn't try to hold her back when she retook her path to the bus stop. He did keep up with her though.

"Bryan is right, one of us must go with you," he said. "You're in no state to be up and walking. We thought you were comatose, for a while. You were out colder than a duck."

How cold is a duck, wondered Ivy.

There was a roar behind them, and Bryan's large bike drew up.

"Hop on," he said, handing her a helmet.

"You guys go carefully now," warned Marc.

"Sure we will," Bryan assured him as Ivy took the pillion seat, Peridot having hidden under her jersey.

As Ivy held onto Bryan, travelling up to Putney at a breakneck speed, she relaxed for the first time. She drew strength from his calm aura, and courage from the fact that he was there – no matter that he'd so far not demonstrated any magical skills more impressive than warding her amateurish lightning. Well, he'd taught her enough to avoid that cobra. And he had immobilized it... but the cobra itself had been an illusion! Scare tactics by Jake. So, add hypnosis to the list, she thought. But genuine magic? *Was* he an experienced mage? She was beginning to wonder. He was clued up, but that was knowledge. Not magic.

Still, his presence gave her what Jake's evil grit-ball had

robbed out of her: Hope. And Peridot purring in his spot by her collarbone, on the inside of her jersey, restored her joy for life. Blessed little cat!

What awaited them at Queen's? She didn't know. But she felt her strength returning, and with it, her courage to face up to anything and save her niece.

They didn't stop at Queen's first, though. To Ivy's surprise and annoyance, Bryan directed the Triumph Rocket III to Bex's house, and stalled it in her driveway.

"What's this?" asked Ivy angrily.

"Covering all the bases," said Bryan. "Bonnie is quite safe right now, we've been through this."

"She's *losing her baby,*" said Ivy. "She's going through hell. Why are we here and not at the hospital?"

"Follow me," said Bryan and led the way to the front door.

Ivy fumed but followed him. She didn't know how to hot-wire a motorcycle, or she'd have stolen the Rocket III that very moment.

Was this how Marc controlled Alison, she thought, then wondered about the connection. Marc had struck her as a very sensible, pragmatic man. A bit narrow-minded perhaps – well, he couldn't know that, after all he hadn't been the one flying through the air on a motorbike. Even though it was his bike!

Bryan undid the spell Ivy had cast, that kept the lock of the front door fused closed, and it popped open. He opened the door, and she followed him into the house, aware of Peridot's on-and-off purring against her collarbone.

There was a dank stench in the house, of mould, or something else Ivy couldn't really define. But she could feel Peridot's claws, and she could literally see how Bryan's hair in his neck stood on end.

"This isn't right," he whispered, turning to her. "Send out a light probe to show where she is!"

"A light probe?"

"Like you did in that warehouse."

Her athame was missing. Before she could voice this, Bryan stuck it into her hand. She understood. She must have let go of it in the Jeep, when they crashed. She lifted the small knife and closed her eyes, focused and sent a light ball out.

Lightning's searching fingers crackled all over the house, into every corner; but it fizzled and died.

"Didn't it work?" asked Ivy, disoriented.

"She's not in the house," said Bryan. "But I can *sense* her presence! Come, Ivy, help me find her."

They searched the whole house. It took them a good thirty minutes before they had to accept that she was not there – and the dank stench was worse in places.

"Let's go," said Bryan, and led the way out. Ivy grabbed a deep lungful of air as they emerged from that awful house with its weird smells.

They climbed back onto the Triumph and left for the hospital.

10

The sun was setting behind a thick cover of cloud as they drew up in the parking lot of Queen's Medical Centre in Richmond. Wet leaves were blown about in clumps in the chilly wind, but at least it was not raining.

Bryan shot a critical glance up at the cloud cover.

"Wonder if that's going to stop them."

"Bryan, she's lost the baby! That ought to stop them."

"So what do you think they'll think of sacrificing next, Ivy?"

She shivered. Bonnie herself was next down the list.

"If they can get one of us, they'll much rather kill us," said Bryan. "But she's a soft target, right now. Baba Yaga cannibalizes children, but she'll have to make do with tougher meat tonight. Not much tougher, I think."

"So why did you leave rescuing her so late?" challenged Ivy.

"Because I don't like surprises either," said Bryan. "I wanted to see what's coming our way from Bex's side. I'm afraid she's outsmarted us. There's one nasty surprise waiting for us."

"What was that awful smell in her house?"

"Decay," said Bryan. "Dead things. Wish I knew where she stashes them."

"You don't think Bex herself -"

"People don't smell like that until a good couple of days after they die," said Bryan. "Don't worry. Or maybe I should say: Be worried. She's most definitely alive."

"You're callous," said Ivy moodily.

Bryan said nothing and led the way to the reception, where he asked for Bonnie's whereabouts.

"She left," said the receptionist. "She was booked out around four."

"Did she leave alone?" demanded Ivy.

"No – her boyfriend was taking care of her. We would have kept her here if she'd had nobody."

"And the pregnancy?" asked Ivy.

"Lady, I'll have to look in the medical file," said the receptionist. "We don't do that for strangers. You'll have to ask her."

"I could strangle you," Ivy bit out when she and Bryan were back in the parking lot. "Why didn't we come here first?"

"You heard," he replied calmly. "We would have been too late. She was discharged at four."

"And you didn't think of checking on her after the accident?"

"We were more worried about *you,*" he pointed out. "Thought you were in a coma."

"Then why wasn't I in hospital too?"

"The hospital wouldn't have been able to help you," said Bryan. "What Jake flung at you there was a hellish pitch ball. It is shot into your solar chakra and robs you of all life energy. If it is left there, it destroys your organs."

"What?" Ivy shook her head, rejecting this. Voodoo!

Bryan levelled a long, searching gaze at her and then took his spot on his bike.

"Hop on. There's nothing we can do for now. We'll have to wait until they start their ritual on the Heath."

"There's one thing," said Ivy. "I need to buy something." She reached inside her jacket and stroked Peridot, who purred at her. The kitten must be exhausted. She was going to get back into carrying a bag for him.

"Do you have your purse on you then?" asked Bryan with a smile.

"Got some cash," she said and stuck a hand into the back pocket of her jeans. Right, there were a number of fifties in there. She'd armed herself with them before setting out to the warehouse this morning. "Think the party shop is still open? And I need a general retailer too, maybe Argon, that's just around the corner here."

"I know this place too," smiled Bryan. "Alright, I'll take you to Marks and Spencer, we've got a better chance catching them open." He turned his bike and they growled towards St John's road, Ivy clinging to his back again.

The temptation to reach for some sensitive spots on his chest and pinch really hard was overwhelming. Right now she could murder him – or more specifically, torture him really badly until he begged for mercy. How could he be so *laissez-faire* about the safety of her niece? Poor Bonnie, to have to go through a miscarriage alone! And worse, with that vulture hovering close!

They made it into the shop in the nick of time. Ivy collected a bottle of wine and found a nice little eye mask for Alison's party.

"I'm at least going to show my face there - well, part of it anyway," she commented as she trailed through the mops and buckets. And then she found it. She put her hand on it, and picked it from the peg on which it was hanging.

A telescoping mop.

"That won't fly," came Bryan's dry comment from behind her. She spun round.

"And *why* not, Mr Arcana?"

"Too light. Anyway it's metal, it will heat up with the friction..."

Ivy put it in her basket and found a small backpack and some kitty snacks for Peridot, and went to pay for it all.

"My place is a mess," she pointed out. "I need a few implements."

"Hardly the time to think about that," said Bryan.

"Bryan, it's *always* the right time to think about clean living," she informed him haughtily. "I wasn't raised with servants waiting on me hand and foot. I like my place comfy. Clean is part of that. Gracious, it's going to be complex to keep clean with all that antique stuff in it!" Suddenly she missed her bare bachelorette box.

He grinned. "Whatever, Ivy."

They returned to Alison's house. She welcomed them as they arrived in the driveway. She was already wearing full costume – a long black skirt, a pointy hat, a witchy grass broom. Even the boots she was wearing had pointy tips.

"I shall wear midnight!" she giggled and did a full spin. The skirt flared out.

"Impressive," said Ivy. "I'm not quite dressed yet. Give me five please?"

"Did you find Bonnie?" asked Alison.

Ivy shook her head. Bryan revved the Rocket III's engine. Alison waved, and the motorbike growled off towards Ivy's cottage.

"Come in," invited Ivy as he parked his bike on her lawn again. Across, in Alison's garden, Marc was lighting a bonfire. Ivy spotted quite a few guests; all dressed 'weird and wicked'.

She peered into the darkness beneath the trees. No white leopard tonight? But clearly the bonfire must frighten the beautiful creature.

Bryan put a hand on her shoulder.

"Ivy, about your bike."

"Alison told me," she said. "Haven't yet had time to insure it. Damn."

"It's written off," he said. "Beyond repair. I've ordered a replacement. Exactly the same model, make – brand new, you know, back stock from the factory... got it through contacts... but there's no guarantee that it will fly."

She shook her head. "Bryan, you don't have to! It was an accident. You've got plenty of cost with your own repairs."

"Then again my car and contents *are* properly insured," he replied with a small smile.

She nodded.

"At least you'll have your transport back," he said. Ivy sighed.

"Make yourself some coffee," she invited and took Peridot out of his bag. The kitten staggered around on the floor, stiff from the long drive. She gave him some food, then ran a hot bath, took the clothes she was planning to wear into the bathroom and closed the door.

It was some comfort knowing Bryan was in her front room. Should any police or other horrors come in, at least he could warn her.

Her energy deserted her while she was in the bath, and

she simply lay there, her eyes closed, soaking until there was a knock on the door.

"Come in," she called reflexively.

There was a low laugh. "I don't really think you mean that," said Bryan through the closed door. "I wanted to check that you haven't drowned in the bath. It's been three quarters of an hour."

"Gosh!" She sat up, oriented herself and got out of the bath that had cooled down significantly. Her fingers and toes were wrinkled. She'd last bathed that long when she was a child. In flying haste she dried herself and got into her outfit: after all, her black, tight skirt with subtle pinstripes – above the knee, kicking out a bit as was her favourite office style. Warm black silk stockings; her black boots with heels; her black polar neck and the jacket that went with the skirt. She emerged from the bathroom, her hair in a towel, and saw Bryan sitting on the bed, paging through the Arcana.

"When all this is over you are welcome to have your book back," she said with a smile.

"Oh no," he said and closed it hastily. "It's yours! I must find you more."

She pulled a face and found her hair dryer, plugged it into a functional socket – to her mild vexation she had discovered by now that she'd have to replace some of the electric boxes in the cottage – and blew her hair dry. As she pulled her fingers through it she mused how this wasn't half the battle it used to be. Her hair was well-mannered these days. She hoped it wasn't thinning.

Peridot came strolling into the room like a real adult cat, his tiny fluffy tail held high with the tip twitching. She smiled at him and he leaped up on her lap.

"You're going as office fairy?" asked Bryan.

"Just about," she said. "Face it, Bryan, I don't exactly have a wardrobe full of fancy dress costumes."

He handed her the mask that was to go over her eyes.

"And you?" she asked. "Are you actually going too?"

"Sure. Can't leave Marc to fend for himself with all those beers."

She flashed a grin. "So what are you going as?"

"Myself," he said. "I'm always a plain-clothes operation."

"Like Marc," she grinned. Bryan left it at that.

When she and Bryan locked the door behind them and walked over to Alison's party, with Peridot perching on her shoulder again, Ivy saw what Alison had meant with 'skyclad'. There were actually a few guests in their birthday suits, sticking close to the fire cradling drinks.

"Are they not cold?" she asked incredulously.

"They will be soon," said Bryan. "But then they put on their cloaks and cowls and all that."

"This really looks like a proper witches' coven," remarked Ivy. Bryan gave her an odd glance.

Alison came dancing towards them and welcomed Ivy.

She approved of the sophisticated joke of the girl coming dressed as herself ("how sinister!"), but commented that probably not every CA had a cat on her shoulder. Ivy grinned. Alison welcomed Bryan with a peck on his cheek, giggled and grabbed Ivy's arm to lead her to the fire. She proceeded to introduce her to every last party guest until Ivy's head swam.

"Now, Bryan, I want your opinion with something," she chirped and grabbed Bryan by the arm and led him away from the crowd, leaving Ivy surrounded by all these witches, warlocks, monsters and ghouls... and of course the happy skyclad people.

She peered through the crowd. Marc was in a corner, pouring drinks for everyone and every so often knocking one back himself.

Too young and handsome to be looking that lost! Her heart ached for him. She could see clearly what Alison was playing; but hell!

Alison and Marc were mismatched, she decided. Young, married and not suited to each other. Alison had found someone much closer to what she wanted. Where did that leave Marc?

Why didn't he get involved in the Craft and wow the socks off his errant wife? It ought to be easy for him, with his latent power! She decided to chat to him and made her way there.

"So," he asked her, "has Bryan got under your skin as well now?"

"What?"

"Like he does with every last girl in this – what Allie calls a coven."

She blinked. "This *is* actually a Wiccan gathering?"

"You didn't know?" He poured something into a glass for her. She realized that he was already quite inebriated. Still, she accepted the glass and noticed with surprise that it was hot to the touch.

"Mulled wine," he said with a smile. "These Wiccan festivities have their perks. Luckily you're wearing black, one doesn't see spills as easily on that."

She peered at the 'coven'. Sensible adults dressed up like kids. Dancing a-skyclad around the bonfire chanting along with the music – which rather reminded of Gregorian chants.

Did she want to participate in that? She thought not!

"Marc," she said, "about the bike you sold me..."

"I know," he said gruffly. "Damn Bryan for driving like an idiot!"

"I'm sorry."

"No, I'm sorry for *you*," replied Marc. "Now you don't have transport."

"He's replacing it," she said. "He was insured."

"Insured, Bryan?" Marc snorted.

"Apparently. Marc, I wanted to ask you. I don't want to cause any friction between you and Allie. But I can see that you guys are battling with finances. We need a receptionist at work and I think she'll be great."

Marc cocked his head and eyed her. "What's the set-up at your workplace?"

"There's just me, Biljana and Mr Oates. He's the boss."

"Tall, dark and handsome... what the hell, maybe at least he'll break her fixation with Bryan."

Ivy smiled. "No, Marc. Mr Oates is near retirement. And he's totally devoted to his wife. They never had children, so probably Oates & Son will be sold when he retires."

Marc nodded thoughtfully. "It might do her good. How's the pay?"

"Entry-level, I suppose," said Ivy. "We can't afford much at this point, things have gone bad with this whole Bex story. I have a plan but who knows if it will pan out. If it does, we can look at more, but if it doesn't, it all very much hangs in the balance."

Marc shrugged. "Damn that Bryan. All that luxury in his house to wow a girl with, and here I am, a fully qualified architect, doing the job of a bricklayer."

"What does he actually do?"

Marc shrugged. "Who knows? Listen, Ivy. If you really want to do me and Allie a favour, keep Bryan busy. But it's not fair to you."

"Keeping him busy is the easy part," growled Ivy. "Surviving the bloody gig is another story. I nearly got killed today, by some bastard little devil-worshipper." She sighed. "Marc, how much has Bryan told you?"

"Bonnie was already out of the hospital when you

arrived, and Bex has gone missing," he summarized.

"Yup, that pretty much says it all." She downed her wine. "Happy Halloween, Marc. I have to go sort out my niece. If I find her in one piece, can I bring her?"

"Of course," said Marc. And he knocked back another glass of something. Not mulled wine. It was the wrong colour for that.

"Marc," said Ivy, "I'll put my feelers out for you too. See if I can't find you an appointment in your actual line."

"That would be great," he said.

"I'm going to find my niece now," added Ivy. "Please make my excuses to Allie. I know she'll understand."

"Of course. Taking Bryan with you?"

"I think not," said Ivy. She excused herself and marched back to her cottage.

Taking Bryan with you? Hah, she thought. If damned Bryan had played by the rules today she wouldn't have to go anywhere right now! She'd be nursing a sore and sad but alive Bonnie in her cottage.

Ivy took her spiky heels off and put on her pumps. There might be running involved. She switched off the lights in the cottage, took her telescoping mop and made sure that Peridot was on her shoulder, and locked the cottage door behind her.

And she paused, taken aback. Bryan had come rushing past her towards his garden gate; she couldn't see his expression in the dark but from his body posture she could tell he was very upset. He stormed through the gate, not bothering to close it. And there, between the trees, was the white leopard, following him.

She caught the eyes of the leopard. The great feline stared at her with its intense gaze; then it loped after Bryan through the gate.

Whatever had upset the man and his familiar would have to wait. She couldn't afford to lose more time. She picked Peridot off her shoulder and stuck him into the small backpack she had by now shouldered, and extended the telescopic mop. To make that thing fly? In the first place, how did one ride on something like this? She laid it on the floor and tried to sit down on it. Impossible. She lifted its front end, meaning to pick it up as she was getting up -

there was that weird little shift, as though her Flymo were going over a bump, and the jolly thing was up in the air, hovering about at hip-height, and she understood suddenly how damned uncomfortable a broomstick was and why witches travelled side-saddle. But she didn't trust herself to be able to steer it side-saddle. She'd at least get a bicycle saddle for it, she promised herself. She imagined that the stick was an aeroplane's yoke, and pulled it upwards. The mop-stick started moving forward. She grasped it firmly with both hands and flew off.

It was in fact a lot easier to steer than her Flymo. But she hated the feeling. Her Flymo was comfortable and solid beneath her. This blooming piece of metal was nothing at all.

She was sorely tempted to steal Bryan's Triumph – what a bike! Comfortable, spacious, and above all, immensely powerful. And with a name like 'Rocket III', of course it would fly. After all, he'd said that it was she doing it, not the bike.

Which meant that her Flymo replacement would also fly. If she lived to tell the story. She directed the weird broomstick towards Putney Heath.

The circle of lights greeted her while she was still high up. Small candles placed on the outside of the ritual space. Tonight there was a large stone slab in the centre; a sacrificial altar, she understood instantly.

Bonnie was part of the ring of young gangsters standing in ceremonial garb around the altar. She didn't look as though she were going to be sacrificed; she didn't look scared; on the contrary she looked as though she were very much part of this, chanting and invoking with the others.

The altar was empty.

Ivy tried to spot any kitty, or human child and couldn't see any. She tried to assimilate what Bryan had said. Baba Yaga was a cannibalistic evil spirit who ate children. They had to feed her a child to invoke her. There were no children or pets anywhere to be seen. Maybe they had given up on Baba Yaga and were trying to invoke someone else?

Ivy firmly refused to believe in demons and evil spirits. Whatever these youngsters tried down there, it would fall flat, because there were no such spirits. But if they weren't sacrificing anyone, human or otherwise, then what they were doing could be regarded merely as an elaborate game. If it didn't harm anyone, how were they different from the Wiccan party over at Allie's? Prancing around naked in the middle of autumn, just to prove a point by freezing their gahoolies off? She was tempted to turn around and buzz off, and leave them in peace, and go back to her own Halloween party.

Jake stood next to the sacrificial altar by now.

"My friends," he said gravely – she heard his voice clearly as the cold wind carried it up to her where she was getting a numb fanny from sitting on a cold stick - "you all know what's happened. Due to that interfering lightning witch, we now don't have our sacrificial offerings. And we can only invoke Her if we sacrifice to Her."

"Baba Yaga, Baba Yaga," chanted the whole group.

"So I am asking you: Is there anyone in our number tonight who wishes to come forward voluntarily and sacrifice him- or herself?"

The "Baba Yaga" chanting carried on for a while, then faded away. There was a breathless silence.

Then Bonnie moved forward, her movements jerky and uncontrolled, as though she were on heavy drugs. She laid herself down on the stone slab.

"Bonnie, my love," said Jake fondly. "You are the truest follower I've ever had. May you reap the rewards in the world of the Dead."

He unbuttoned her jersey, then carefully cut her T-shirt, from neck to waist, with the tip of his ceremonial dagger without as much as nicking her skin. That knife was sharp!

Ivy panicked and directed the mop-stick downwards, meaning to swoop in and pick Bonnie off the altar. Something about that movement drew Jake's attention and he looked up, and laughed aloud.

"The Lightning Witch is here!" he crowed in delight. A heavy black wind blew Ivy back. She focused and tried to push through it; it intensified as Jake looked up at her with the whole coven and laughed.

She saw now that tears were streaming down Bonnie's face; but the girl didn't utter a sound.

"Take this, Lightning Witch," yelled Jake and launched a handful of black muck at Ivy. The blob cut through the barrier, and through her warding spell, and hit her squarely in the solar plexus. Her breath was knocked out, all energy drained from her and she plummeted, mop-stick and all, down into the circle.

Peridot crawled out of his backpack and pawed her face, vigorously licking her nose. She picked him up, and then herself, just in time to see something lurching towards her -

It was Bex! Jake raised his knife over Bonnie, chanting,

"Baba Yaga, come and take what is due to you! Baba Yaga, come and feast on human flesh!"

Ivy lifted the mop-stick off the floor and pointed it at him.

"Khazam!"

Lightning crackled; amplified by the metal, it picked up power and punched into Jake, flinging him and his knife far away from the altar. Ivy crawled between Bonnie and Bex, and pointed the stick at Bex.

"Receive your sanity back, Bex!" she yelled. "Remember who you are! This is your child they're trying to feed to Baba Yaga!"

Bex stopped, disoriented. Ivy kept pointing the mop-stick at her.

"I release you from all spells and curses that were placed on you," she yelled. *"Khazam!"*

It was as though years fell away from Bex. She straightened out; her hair was dark again; her skin, young and smooth. She looked her physical thirty-six, and not sixty any longer. And she looked as though she had just come awake out of a nightmare, only to find herself in a worse one. She stared at Ivy, terrified.

"Bex, is that you in there?" asked Ivy.

"My God, Ivy, what is going on?"

Ivy breathed a sigh of relief. "Bex, take your little girl and walk with her, out of the Heath, and to where there are people. Take her to safety. Bonnie..." She turned to look at her niece who was crying uncontrollably. She pointed the mop-stick at her too. "I release you too from all magic working on you!"

Bonnie sat up, and staggered to her feet. Her mother put her arm around her and stumbled with her out of the circle of gangsters, who merely watched and took no action. They were waiting for cues from their leader.

"Bye, Bonnie," called Jake. "See you in class tomorrow!"

"Not if I have a say in it!" exclaimed Ivy, incensed, and raised her lightning stick at him.

With a flick of his ceremonial knife he blasted it out of her hand and sent another black ball of filth into her innards. Already on her knees, she dropped down to all fours, cringing in pain.

Organ damage, Bryan had said. Yes: It did feel like that. The burning, stabbing pain in her innards was nearly unbearable.

"Thank you, Lightning Witch, for volunteering to be our sacrificial offering to Baba Yaga!" said Jake gleefully as he and eleven others grabbed her and laid her down on the altar. "I believe we even have a cat! What a bonus! Where is the little pest?"

Peridot had disappeared.

"It will have to be good enough without cat," said Jake. "Oh well!" He lifted his knife. Ivy couldn't move; deathly lethargy had taken hold of her, seeping all will to live out of her limbs as the dark masses inside her worked their evil. She tried to rally a lightning ball but couldn't even lift a finger.

"Baba Yaga, Baba Yaga," chanted the crowd. It became like a faraway backdrop in Ivy's ears. A huge figure loomed up overhead, just behind Jake's sacrificial knife – a black demon with the face of an old woman, but a huge mouth full of sharp teeth, and a greedy, hungry look in her eyes. Waiting for her food.

"Baba Yaga, Baba Yaga..."

"So now, miserable human, I sacrifice you and your electric powers to the mighty Spirit of Night, Baba Yaga," announced Jake and lifted his knife.

"Wait," said Ivy.

Jake hesitated quite deliberately. "Any last words?"

A vestige of anger reared up in Ivy.

"You all have no future," she told the gathered teenagers, rasping out the words past the pain in her innards. "England is in crisis. There is no money left. There are no jobs, and the dole is dead. You will be sitting on the street!"

She could feel the chill running through the youngsters. This was good. She was playing for time, hoping that Bex could reach civilization before they were done with her. She had no idea that her eyes were actually sparkling lightning as she spoke.

"Your parents will need your help to support them. But you won't have jobs, so how will you do this?" Her voice was strengthening; she was winning the battle against this infernal weakness.

They stared at her, even forgetting to chant "Baba Yaga". The black demon wavered; even Jake was losing his grin.

"What will you do when you are grown up?" she challenged. "I can tell you now, there is only one kind of job that's floating: The financial job. So, how good are all of you in Math?"

Shocked silence.

"I'll say one word: Austerity!" she said ominously.

"Jobs?" Jake's laughter seemed incongruous. "You're so deluding yourself, lady! Who wants a job? We're *suppliers!* There's always a space for us as long as people need their stash!" He raised the knife. "Silly little woman! In the end you were not so smart, were you? Die, Lightning Witch!" He brought the knife down forcefully, stabbing it – at the rock slab, because she'd rolled aside and grabbed his legs.

The young hooligan stumbled backwards. She clung to his legs, forcing her flagging resources into her hands, making the lightning flicker from her palms, burning him. He screamed. Ivy felt her powers running out, and released him. He lunged for the knife he'd let go of. He raised it over her and brought it down again.

And suddenly the place was as bright as day. Light flooded the gathering. There was a howl of sirens; men in uniform rushed in to arrest every last one of the youngsters. In the midst of the noise and motion, Ivy felt Peridot lick her nose, and grabbed him and held him close to her heart. Darling little cat! He purred like the Flymo. That was the last thing she registered.

11

Bryan stalked through the site where teenagers were being handcuffed and taken away by the police. Where Ivy's lightning had fallen, the grass was charred and in places, burning. Jake lay on the ground writhing; the lightning that Bryan had seen Ivy discharge directly from her hands had burned right through the boy's jeans and left big burnt welts on his thighs, where she had clung to him. Police picked him up on a stretcher and carried him to the paramedic van. He jumped off the stretcher at the last moment and bolted into the woods. Some policemen charged after him.

Bryan knelt down at the still figure of Ivy, under the soft shield of invisibility he'd cast over her. The ceremonial dagger stuck in her side. She must have managed to roll at the last moment; because the steel wasn't sticking in her heart, as Jake had intended. It had cut through skin and soft tissue and the blood was seeping out of her in an endless stream. He pulled the knife out and staunched with both hands, lifting the invisibility spell and calling for the paramedics. And looking down at her...

A small shadow crept out of her hand and sought refuge

in his lap. Peridot. The hand dropped lifelessly to the ground.

Bryan called again for the paramedics, cursing that they weren't there yet. *Here* was the emergency; sorting out drug-related daze did not constitute an emergency. Why didn't they come?

Her body was beginning to cool under his hands. He looked into her still face. Damn, Ivy, he thought. Why couldn't you have called me?

He'd had to cast a Subdue on the group in any case, after the police had made their presence known, because these crazed teens had all picked up sharp implements and fought off the police with all the teenage rebellion that was in them. They didn't know yet that resisting arrest aggravated your case. Attempted murder, and accessory to same... he gazed down at the still shape that had been Ivy. She had stood in for her niece, taken the brunt of the teen insanity. He had to admire her courage. *Attempted* murder?

The paramedics arrived at last. Bryan helped them staunch the blood flow, first of all; then helped lift Ivy onto their stretcher. He walked with them to the ambulance; got into it, asked one of the officers to bring his motorbike.

The paramedics hadn't covered her face. They were trying to resuscitate her while not causing too much extra damage. Relentlessly they took turns, working at a fever pace as the ambulance rushed towards Queen's, sirens howling.

Damn Alison! She'd taken him aside, given him some mulled wine, and asked his opinion over some highly technical

Wiccan question, all the while finding ways to lure him to her bedroom. And that with her husband right outside, having seen him follow her into the house! Talking his way out of her tender care and then, on the way out, defending himself against Marc's massively vicious assault, half-verbal and half-physical and probably fully deserved for his stupidity of following Alison into the house, had taken him that critical bit of time that was now missing.

He had no issue with Alison. She should back off. She was a married woman, for crying out loud, and he had considered Marc a friend – until tonight, being shoved around like that, and not defending himself because he had a more urgent mission. In fact he had no issue with any women, at all. He'd never particularly understood how anyone could throw away his freedom to become emotionally dependent on anyone else. Until recently, when this fiercely independent young professional with her flippant skirt and her cat-green eyes had walked into his favourite bookshop muttering curses under her breath.

He had been captivated. And he'd given her the most valuable thing he had on him at that moment – the Arcana. To stake his claim, in a way. She had something of his. He had a right to find her and tell her more. He'd laughed at himself and his own underhanded tactics. And she – had seen straight through him, and was not biting. She'd moved right into his neighbour's backyard; so close, nearly touching distance. She'd spent a night right in his house – properly in his guest room. Heaping love and care on her kitten, which, he did have to admit, was a pretty amazing creature. And she had clung to him, in a way he'd want her to cling always, riding pillion on his bike. And she felt nothing?

The more he pursued her, the more she became – comfortable in his company. Ha – she'd even invited him into her bathroom, but that had been accidental. She was like Peridot in many ways. And she hadn't flinched or blushed at the naked party-goers at Alison's – merely been mildly surprised and asked if they didn't feel cold.

But she had risked her life repeatedly for her niece, whom she obviously loved even though the girl had betrayed her horribly. She'd cried for the unknown baby she'd never meet because her niece had miscarried. And she had unhesitatingly rescued her niece and her antagonistic sister-in-law and sacrificed herself instead, knowing that the dirty powers of Jake were more than she could handle.

He sat there next to her in the ambulance, his hand on her ankle because the paramedics were still frantically busy working to revive her. Peridot had gone into hiding inside his leather jacket that he usually wore when going by motorcycle. Damn Bex, damn Bonnie. The police had taken both into custody along with eleven of the twelve young gangsters. But number twelve, Jake himself, had on last count not been caught.

Baba Yaga's face grinned at him through the window of the ambulance. He cast a protective golden shield around Ivy's body and threw a fistful of white light into the monster's face. She retreated from the window, but he knew she was still lurking in the background. He'd better keep watch over Ivy. And as the paramedics hadn't covered her face yet, he wasn't going to believe that she was dead.

They arrived at Queen's. Ivy was rushed into surgery, from where the medical personnel blocked him. He cast a protective shield around her once more and went to the front desk to book her in.

He had meant to stay there and not budge from her side; but while he was waiting for the operation to finish, the call reached him. Bex, from the police station, implored him to check on her house.

Right. There was something seriously wrong there. He called the police back and asked for two officers to take along. They met him at Queen's and followed him and his motorcycle to Bex's house.

The front door was unlocked. Whether this had been Bex herself, was hard to tell. The police apparently had got no proper statement out of her.

The two officers both recognized the stench instantly, as he had. They followed it until they were in the kitchen. It was hard to pinpoint; until one of the officers went down on hands and knees and sniffed at the floor.

"It's coming through the floorboards."

They knocked and hammered until they had found the trapdoor. The stench hit them like a wall. They followed the steps down into a dark cellar. One officer shone with a torch until he'd located a light switch, and threw on the light.

What awaited, was grotesque. In the middle of the room lay a large stone altar. On it there were remains of a dog; entrails and so on. A circle of black half-burnt candles on the floor marked the area as a chamber of spells. Shelves upon shelves were lined with, amongst all sorts of magical bric-a-brac, bottles with animal parts in formalin. They fine-combed for human parts, and found them – in the form of dead, bottled foetuses. All around twelve weeks. There were four in total. The bottles even had names on.

Bottomless sadness gripped Bryan as he looked at those would-have-been children, and thought of what had been done to Bonnie. How callous did Bex have to be to bottle up and keep the grandchildren that Bonnie had produced and sacrificed for the Dark Craft? He thought of Ivy's experiences in that 'mercy' clinic and was thankful that she was being spared this – whatever else she was going through right now. The younger one of the two police officers excused himself and ran upstairs, where they heard him throw up noisily.

What madness was it that possessed people to commit such crimes? To want such power as only dark magic could provide, and at what a price? And he thought of Ivy, who'd made a motorbike fly through the air quite by accident; who'd discovered her lightning gift without any tuition; who'd turned her curses into blessings without hesitation, first out of compassion and then to profit her boss's failing shop.

Had she asked for those powers? No. Her line was clean, honest accountancy, doing a job that for most people was difficult to understand and tedious to carry through. Because she liked the sleek, lean honesty of it. Was she some arty diva, full of herself, or some little snob who believed money made her more important? No. She thought in goals, problem solving, and serving others. Her focus was not on herself at all. The ideal Wiccan – if she were in any way interested in Wicca. Or any other religion for that matter. But there too she had no preferences, half refusing to believe all the supernatural stuff happening around her. While opportunistically exploiting it. As though she were a child who'd found a bag of sweeties in the street, couldn't believe her luck and was now quickly eating them all before someone could take them away. Knowing there was an end to them.

"When this is all over," he'd heard her say.

Well, it was all over. Particularly for her. She really hadn't stood a chance against the real Satanists in the first place.

Jake had come out of his hiding place. He was a dog with a scent now: He needed to trace that scent until he'd found the owner. And then maul her.

The police weren't going to catch him that easily! Just in case, he had gone back after they'd all left, and had retrieved his ceremonial dagger and looked at the Witch's lightning staff.

She'd been riding on it, that crazy coot. When he found it, he couldn't believe his eyes. It was a plain old mop with a telescopic handle.

Clever! He had to give her that. She was smart, and she was a fast learner. But nobody tangled with him who had the Forces of Darkness on his side. And at this point, Baba Yaga, that forest horror from Russia.

He had looked forward to watching that mauling. In fact, it would have been nice to see her eat that child they had kidnapped. Jake hated little children. It was his little sister who'd killed his mother, simply by being born. How unfair: The little brat had lived, and Mommy had died. And since that moment, the little sister had been everyone's focus, and he'd simply had to adjust, and that in a year when he was starting school.

Jake had battled his way through school, barely passing most years, flunking twice; he was in fact two years older than Bonnie. He had given abuse and bullying as good as he got. And two years back his father had remarried; his little sister, eleven by now, had been sent off to a convent school. But his stepmother didn't think convent was a good idea for him. His marks didn't support it. He knew that she knew he was taking drugs; she'd tried keeping him under control, but he'd shown her! Ha! By now he was seventeen and she was weary of battling. So she left him to roam the streets with his friends, only occasionally calling one of his friends' parents – he was very selective whose numbers he let her have, as he knew the parents would cover for him and his friends, gullible as they were. "They've gone to the mall," and "they've gone to the cinema," - well, his friends' parents believed they were telling the truth.

What had made Bonnie fall for him, he had no idea. But it had been handy. He'd used girls before – and boys, mind. In fact he seemed to be quite a hit with younger boys. They too liked the 'bad-boy' image he wore proudly like a badge. He didn't have to; his stepmother saw to it that he had a wardrobe full of goodie-two-shoes neat clothes, even with yuppie little labels on them. He traded them, asked his friends for their oldest, most worn clothes in exchange for new Levis, Nikes and Calvin Kleins.

So he was disappointed along with Baba Yaga that she had been cheated out of a small child. But the Witch would have satisfied him fully. She was the one who'd taken the child away; then caused the loss of the pregnancy and lastly, ripped his 'volunteer' from the altar.

Baba Yaga had an issue with her too by now. Not only was she hungry; but her human vessel, Bex, had been removed. She was one angry spirit right now. He wasn't sure that it was safe dealing with her. But it made her immensely more powerful, and he liked that.

The forest witch took the lead, showing him where the ambulance had gone. He followed the dark spirit to Queen's, where she led the way along the passages to where the restricted areas started. He slipped into the place; it was unguarded. He hid in a chamber with a lot of doctors' uniforms, and slipped into one of those, including mask, cap and huge socks over his yawning sneakers. This was great stuff; he could pretend to be a doctor.

He followed the wood witch further through the inner passages, to right outside the theatre. He should go in. But something blocked Baba Yaga. She couldn't pass. It was that other man, he thought angrily. That boyfriend of the Lightning Witch. He'd placed a ward of sorts. Jake stayed outside with the monster spirit, trying to think of a way of getting her into the theatre past the safeguards.

Bryan got the call.

"Will be right there," he said and left that haunted house. He mounted his motorbike and stormed off back to the hospital. The theatre nurse who was his contact, had sounded pretty desperate.

Ivy's organs were failing; in theatre, as they were stitching up the fairly superficial wound, she was going into crisis. He was glad that she was still alive enough to have a crisis; but whether he'd be in time, he didn't know. He drove like a madman, dodging trick-or-treating groups of youngsters, barely avoiding two accidents. He couldn't go missing now.

He arrived, and another nurse – colleague of his contact – led him through the passages to the anteroom. She showed him how to scrub down, made him put on theatre greens.

"Hurry, Dr Woodwright!"

She gave him directions to the theatre, but then she had to heed a call on her pager. This suited him. He followed her directions. As he turned the last corner, he saw a young intern standing outside the theatre's door... wait a second!

Bryan raised his hands, latex gloves and all, to cast the immobilizing spell that had failed to get a hold on Jake earlier. Jake gave him a wide-eyed stare and ran, taking his filthy demon with him. Bryan sent a massive ball of white light after the demon. Baba Yaga let out a wail like a banshee as the light hit her. She cringed in pain and thinned out like smoke before disappearing. Jake didn't wait, but ran as fast as his yawning old shoes would allow him. Maybe there was something to be said for a brand-new pair of Nikes.

Bryan focused on the theatre. He couldn't well walk in there and do what he needed to; they would know instantly that he wasn't a surgeon and had no theatre clearance. So he stood in the passageway, closed his eyes and sent white light into the theatre in as massive a torrent as he could manage. He felt like a funnel, channelling the cosmic energy straight from the divine into that place of darkness.

When they wheeled her out half an hour later, he was there by her stretcher.

"Dr Woodwright," he introduced himself to the surgeon and the internist that had been called in, both of whom looked fairly beat. "How's the patient?"

"Hanging in there," said the surgeon. "We thought we

were losing her. Systemic inflammatory response syndrome. But we got her stabilized. This is no simple wound. She's a healthy young woman, there should have been no cause for this. We're suspecting poison."

"Quite possible," said Dr Woodwright, nodding sagely. He followed them to the prep room where they tried to bring her back to consciousness. They battled for two hours, with him standing by, assisting, and when he wasn't doing anything to help the doctors, sending more white light.

He could feel the vile missiles that had been shot into her. Three pitch balls, all hitting their mark perfectly in her solar plexus. Aimed to rob her of her strength and life energy. Her solar chakra was all but destroyed. If she lived, it would take months or years to rebuild her strength. And he'd be there. He'd be by her side to put her back on her feet. If he was lucky enough that she survived.

He could only keep up the pretence of Dr Woodwright while wearing his greens. Woodwright he was, but no doctor. He'd have to devise another plan, he thought when they finally gave up trying to bring her back to consciousness and wheeled her into the ICU. He stayed and observed how the ward sister took over, hitching all sorts of machines to Ivy.

"Doctor, don't you want to change?"

He smiled at her behind his sterile theatre mask. "In a moment, sister. Thanks." He waited for her to finish connecting all those tubes to Ivy. When she returned to her desk, he cast a protective shield around the still body on that hospital bed. He did this without gesturing; mainly with his mind. Then he went back to the anterooms of the theatre and changed back, retrieving his leather jacket.

Surprising that that little beast hadn't stolen it! Peridot was sleeping in the inside pocket. The kitten seemed exhausted.

Right. He needed to go home and change. A leather jacket would never do it. But he wasn't about to leave the hospital, and abandon Ivy to the devices of that little criminal who was still hiding out somewhere in these passages. He called Alison.

Half an hour later she arrived with a friend who had offered her a lift. She took his jacket and brought him the clothes he had specified. Then she pecked him on the cheek – to his annoyance; she should stop doing that, dammit! She was upsetting her husband! Any overwrought control Marc was exercising over Alison – she had asked for it by her blatant flirting with him, Bryan.

He gave her instructions to look after Ivy's cottage, thanked her for the clothes and went back into the hospital. She'd asked to see Ivy. But they didn't let visitors into the ICU. 'Dr' Woodwright would have to tread carefully now, without any outward signs of indeed belonging to the profession.

He changed into the clothes she had brought – a warm jacket that was not of leather, that had an inner pocket large enough for the kitten, and a few other items, and put the clothes that were so drenched in bad luck, in a plastic bag. He wove an invisibility spell around himself and the cat and returned to the ICU, this time completely unseen. He drew up an invisible chair and sat down, placing his hands over Ivy's solar plexus.

The surgeon had done a great job. Now it was the turn of the psychic surgeon.

It was late afternoon, the first November. Jake was spending the day hiding in the warehouse. He was not in the mood for going home and listening to his stepmother – the Hag – nagging at him about going to school. He was making a pretty good living altogether without any of that. Mammon, whom he invoked regularly, was gracing him with a fine trade. Even today, after the exhausting events of last night, every half-hour or so a customer pinged into the warehouse to buy some stash. Money was flowing in freely.

As he turned his ceremonial dagger and examined it from all sides – a knife deprived of its prey, last night – he contemplated that he'd actually consider a career in something larger than only drugs. He was savvy and fast enough to become a professional assassin. Take orders from people to satisfy what he proudly defined as his blood lust. Sacrifice his victims to the great forces that were permanently backing him up; get a kick out of it himself, feed the demons and still get paid! It sounded like a bargain to him.

For that he'd probably have to contact some

organizations. He wanted to reach high. Killing a president, or the Queen, that ought to be a first-rate experience. Getting past all their security – more sacrificial lambs, he thought indulgently, nearly drooling. Poison darts, garrottes... thoughts of the equipment alone turned him on. He dreamed of how many common items could be turned into something lethal that could be used for strangling. And the feeling of that victim, jerking in his arms... he nearly climaxed.

But he had to make it clear from the outset that he was not game for any suicide missions. He wasn't lethally depressed. He merely enjoyed making others die. The fantasy spun on in his mind, an orgy of blood and gore providing plenty of fodder for his masturbation.

And then there were eyes. In the dark, watching him. He paused. As worry reared its head, so his sexual excitement ebbed out of him.

"Who's there?" he asked.

No answer; but the eyes – several pairs now – watched him intently.

He knew who was there. It was a bit disconcerting.

"I feed you guys," he said. "So what do you want now?"

They didn't respond; but they moved a bit closer. He could feel something like a cold fog rising from the floor.

"They haven't turned this place into a fridge, have they," he said aloud. He could call each one of them by name.

Once again the eyes shuffled a little closer. This was freaky.

"Okay guys," he said jovially, "I know it's Halloween. Trick or treat. I've always given you treats. Be nice and give me a treat as well."

No reply; the demons crept closer still, homing in on him. He raised his dagger.

"Okay, fellows, game's over. Go home. It's broad daylight. Go!" He was scared now. "You can't be out in the day, you know this. Go back to your realms. I'll call you soon enough, and then we'll feast."

There was no reply.

It was Halloween. The gates were open, it occurred to him.

"Yeah, fine, so the gates are open. You know where to take yourselves," he said. "Go now! Go home! I'll play with you later! Promise."

But these were no child's playthings. He knew. One of them advanced on him, suddenly. Jake lunged forward, warding the demon off with his ceremonial blade; slicing through the black fog. A hissing sound as the demon reshaped itself.

This was not working. For the first time Jake was really afraid of the forces he had invoked.

Baba Yaga had been destroyed, last night – or the demon that had borne her name. Baba Yaga was probably alive and well; she couldn't die, because she was merely a concept. A persona to slip into like a costume, by any evil entity that fancied a snack of human child. Many of the great demonic figures were like that. They had been killed many times, by those hated light-workers; but every time, merely a new demon slid into the skin of the legend and wore it, and became it.

Those eyes were too close now, within arm's reach. He could feel their icy breath in his neck, and he shivered. Cold like interstellar space. It leached the life energy from a person's body.

He understood at last. It was his life energy they were after. Coming to drink his blood, as they had so many of his victims. And they didn't need his permission.

"Get away," he yelled. "Go back to the depths of the pit where you emerged from, foul spirits!" He brandished his blade, cut once around himself, slashed through the fog – they merely reformed, and pressed in on him, their hands – long cold fog-fingers – on his throat, feeling for that life force. He choked and swatted at them with his dagger. And he felt them release him.

He wiped across his brow, feeling weak. The scant light that still fell in, showed something red on his dagger. He'd cut himself. He felt dizzy. The demons gave him a little space, watching, waiting.

"That's right," he choked and wondered why he couldn't use his full voice, "you go. Go away."

His voice faded out under him. The dark lightened a bit; turned into a strange grey. He could see them clearly now, every hairy, scaly, monstrous detail outlined as they sat there, watching him.

"So go," he whispered. "What's keeping you?" He realised that he didn't have a voice at all anymore, and reached for his throat in surprise. There was nothing. He glanced down and saw his body lying crumpled on the cold cement.

The evil ones only waited for that dawning of comprehension. Then they descended on him, all of them, slurping him up while he was still screaming, silently; sucking his spirit away until nothing remained except the silent scream.

Then they settled down to devour the body. The rats of the warehouse came and helped them.

12

Alison opened the cottage for Bryan. He entered and took a look around, then switched Ivy's laptop on. Peridot climbed out of his jacket pocket and jumped to the floor, investigating whether his home still stood, and using his litter box.

It was cold outside now. Wind and rain, on a constant basis; no snow though. Just standard London winter weather.

"How's she doing?" asked Alison.

"Same," said Bryan. "I don't understand. It's an uphill battle."

"It's been two weeks," said Alison gravely. "She hasn't surfaced, has she?"

Bryan shook his head. "She's fighting for her life. The blooming doctors are trying to force me into a decision."

Alison looked unenlightened.

"To take everything off her," he said. "Switch her off, if she were on any equipment. Take her drip off. Withdraw medical care. Let her die."

"That's horrible!" exclaimed Alison. "Why?"

"They don't have any hope that she'll surface," he said. "Her organs are in too bad a state, and her brain patterns are classic for long-term coma. The type that passes on without ever waking up."

"Poor Ivy!" Alison sighed. "But she's not on breathing machines, right? What can they switch off?"

"If they take off her intravenous drip, she'll die from thirst and fever," said Bryan. "And kidney failure. There's still a lot of rubbish being cleared out of her system."

"What a horrible death!" exclaimed Alison. She narrowed her eyes at him. "Why do they ask you? Isn't it normally the family who takes that decision?"

"What do you think *her* family will decide?" Bryan asked caustically. "No, Allie. *We* are her family now. She has no-one else. Not a damn will I let them. Not a damn! She is *not* dead! Her brain activity is what it is because she's not in there. But she'll be back!"

Alison nodded gravely.

"I'm with you, Bryan," she said with feeling. "She's a lovely girl, and she seemed to fit in here like – like one of us."

"She *is* one of us, Alison," he replied. "She's a born witch."

"With impressive powers," added Alison with a smile.

"How is your Wicca doing?" asked Bryan.

"Still the same," she shrugged. "I try. But it doesn't really work, you know."

"It does," he smiled. "Your mindset is wrong. Are you practising your meditations?"

"Oh, those are just – window dressing, you know? Feel-good factors."

"They're not, Allie," said Bryan with a smile. "They are the key."

"I've been trying to witch an architecture job for Marc for months now," she said with frustration. "Nothing! Not even as much as a call."

"You are waiting for them to *head-hunt* him?" asked Bryan incredulously.

"No! Of course not! We look at ads and reply, the perfectly mundane route. And *then* I witch. But... nothing."

"Got Marc to participate yet?"

Alison shook her head. "He doesn't want to," she said. "He says it's all childish games. Meanwhile I'm sure he could be a phenomenal mind mage..."

"Alison," said Bryan intently, "you need to do something about him. Keep a close eye on him! He is getting more negative by the day, and while he disbelieves all of it his negative energy is being strewed around in a random way. I can feel the influence of his black moods every time I try to work anything. They're extremely disruptive."

"Yes, he's very negative," she agreed. "What should I do about it? It's the money situation. Say, Bryan, has Mr Oates said anything about a job for me?" There was urgency in her voice. "You understand... we really need the money."

"I'm going to swing round to Oates later today," promised Bryan. "But -"

"Take me along," Allie suggested.

"My car isn't yet repaired."

"But your bike takes two," she said.

Bryan laughed. "No, Allie! If you fall off, what do I tell Marc?"

"Oh Bryan!" She put a placating hand on the collar of his jacket. "Having one accident doesn't mean you'll have one every day now!"

He cast her a critical glance. "What I was going to say," he said, "it's not only the money, Allie. It's his marriage. He feels that he's failing on every level. You can take him out of that. I think you ought to do something sweet for him every day."

"I do," said Allie. "I cook, I clean, I keep the house... I fold his clothes while he is out working..."

Bryan rolled his eyes. "Something *sweet,*" he said. "Not something humdrum."

"Something sweet like *this?*" asked Alison and stood on tiptoe, took his head in both hands and kissed him tenderly on the mouth.

Bryan was so surprised that it took him several moments before he could react. And her kisses were sweet! For a moment, he was drawn into their wildness, their raw emotion...

He must be insane! He pushed her away, rather a bit more roughly than he'd meant – and caught sight of Marc in the doorway.

Oh Alison, Alison!

"I'll kill you!" exploded the architect. He stormed at Bryan. That first fist landed against Bryan's left temple like a sledgehammer and left him reeling.

"Ward," he muttered reflexively, raising his hand. Marc froze in mid-motion.

He was marginally taller than Bryan, who was no midget himself; but Marc's muscles were honed from months upon months of bricklaying, and his mind dulled by the frustration of having to do a menial job when he'd trained for so much more, and not being able to pay his own way. Bryan waited until the stars passed from that impressive blow.

Alison stood back in shock; then she took herself off to the main house. Bryan wasn't sure whether she was gleeful. He was livid; but not with Marc, whose righteous fury he could understand.

"Let me out of this ridiculous spell," screamed Marc, livid.

"Marc," said Bryan, recovering his senses. "you're misreading this."

"Sure I am!" bellowed Marc. "I saw it with my own eyes, after all! Release me from this wussy spell of yours! Can't you even fight like a man? What is all this fay dabbling in magic, like a half-baked..."

"Shut up, Marc," snapped Bryan. "I didn't ask for this. You take care of your wife so she doesn't get so – depraved. Go and dominate her a bit. I've got to go check on Ivy."

Marc, still stuck in the immobility spell, was flashing eye-daggers.

"Ivy," he scoffed. "You like her, don't you? Pull into

every woman you can lay your hands on! Must be nice to be a 'mage'. Can't believe they all fall for it."

Bryan fought hard to control his own irrational anger. He was in the mood for sending curses at both Marc and his wanton little woman, Alison. But he must never curse. Never.

"I'll see to it that you can never have Ivy," Marc yelled at him. Bryan released the man from the immobility spell, adding a psychic shove that sent Marc flying out of the door. He scooped up Peridot and exited the cottage, turning to lock the door when the second fist landed – this time in his neck. It brought him to his knees, ears ringing, stars circling before his eyes. Marc was angry enough to kill him.

Ward, he thought, too dizzy to actually speak the spell. Too late to stop one massive kick from Marc's heavy boot. But in time to block the rest. He could feel Marc psychically straining against the immobility spell. The man's powers were awakening.

May he use those blasted powers on Alison, thought Bryan angrily, and then immediately, *ward!*. He didn't want Alison to be beaten up. Though she deserved a good hiding! *Invading* him like that to draw a reaction out of her own unromantic male.

Marc didn't know this, but Bryan's biggest problem right now was self-restraint. He had a few blows up his sleeve that could render a strong man unconscious, even kill him. But he didn't want to damage his friend.

He came back to his feet, turned and looked at Marc who

was raging inside that blue immobilizing bubble.

Bryan knew that he wouldn't tolerate one more blow or kick from the man who used to be his best friend. He knew his restraint was at its limit. He'd been the Best Man at Marc and Alison's wedding – not all that long ago. They all had studied together; Marc doing architecture and Alison, arts. And he had been taking some courses in psychology to brush up on what he was already doing – perhaps to understand himself a bit better, though the course had failed him in that.

Leaving Marc in the immobility spell, to break out of it himself, was a risk. It could be that the man would stay stuck in this spell for a couple of hours, until he had time to come and check. But the larger risk was that Marc would figure it out – which would mean that he'd have an enormously powerful untrained dark mage running amok.

Bryan decided to take that risk, rather than to break his own karma by hitting back at his friend. He got on his motorbike, still shaking with anger, and rode off to the hospital.

The doctors were pushing him for a decision. They wanted to switch off the monitors and the IV drip. Ivy was breathing by herself; but the IV drip contained her nutrients and medication, and if they took that off, she would die of thirst and fever before she could wake up.

Bryan walked into the ward where she lay sleeping and glanced at her still face. No, she was not dead. Not brain-dead either as the nurses wanted to imply. She was somewhere...

and fighting for her life.

Marc's angry threat came back to him. Just words, spoken in anger. If the agnostic only knew what damage words could do!

Her condition had once again reversed a bit from when he'd left her, before lunch. He got to work, cleaning more sticky, hellish pitch out of her innards where it had started spreading again. Like a fungus.

The black parasitic goo had woven its way into her internal organs. After days of intense psychic surgery, her kidneys were again free of it; her liver, recovering. Her lungs had, thank heavens, not been affected. Her heart, her spleen – her entire lymph system – he cleaned it out daily until there was no goo left, but somehow, the moment he turned his back, went for lunch or something, the progress she had been making was lost and she relapsed.

As though there were no answering spark. Her chakras were glowing dimly, like flames about to be snuffed out. Her solar chakra was non-existent, a black hole in the place where her energy generator was supposed to be. It had been utterly destroyed. And that was the core of the problem.

It was draining the life energy out of both him and Peridot by now, even though he was only a conduit for the limitless White Light. He needed her to wake up so he could instruct her how to regenerate the solar chakra; if she wouldn't do it naturally. But she didn't have the energy to wake up!

He needed help.

"Peridot," he said as he eventually sat down on the chair next to her bed, the kitten on his lap under an invisibility spell as usual, "what's going on here?"

Bex looked up from behind the bars. She had a cell to herself. And for good behaviour, they were talking of letting her out on parole, and replacing her prison sentence with community service.

"Bryan. Coming to gloat?" She pulled a face. "I guess you have every right."

"I'd have come earlier," he said. "But I was reluctant to leave Ivy while she's in hospital. Anything might happen."

"Ivy is alive?" asked Bex, evidently surprised.

"Yes," replied Bryan angrily, "no thanks to you! She's in a bad state, the chances are that she'll still be in hospital for a while."

"Poor Ivy," said Bex. Bryan couldn't tell if she was sincere. "Oh my god. She sacrificed herself for us. You should have seen it, Bryan. I've rarely seen such courage. And she freed me from that – ugh – drugged state. With a flick of her wand."

"And she made you young and beautiful again," completed Bryan. "Released you from any and all magic that had a hold on you, including her own."

"I feel so horrible about all that," said Bex. "You know, when one's so deeply in some negative spiral like that..."

"You're going to do community work, I hear?" probed

Bryan.

"Yes. In a convent school. A bit of gardening, admin, they might give me the choir to lead if I don't give them reason to throw me out. So I'll have to get used to the whole Catholic gig."

"It's not a bad gig," commented Bryan. "You may like it."

"I think so. I love looking at the image of the Virgin Mary with her little baby, and thinking, that is mother love. Where did I go wrong with Bonnie?"

"Where did you go wrong with yourself?" he replied. "Figure that out and you have the answer."

Bex nodded gravely.

"I have to go," Bryan told her. "I want to check on Bonnie, too."

"Tell her that I love her," Bex said. "If she laughs, tell her that I mean it."

"That should shut her up," grinned Bryan, and left.

Bex? Well, it wasn't impossible that she was still sending evil vibes after Ivy, but it wasn't too likely. Bex was not powerful enough to work with pure energy, let alone interfere with the workings of a White Mage. In her incarcerated state, she didn't have her equipment. Nothing to sacrifice either – perhaps a roach or two – did that count? Who knew!

But if she were practising voodoo on the other hand, all it took was an effigy and some sharp object. An effigy could be fashioned out of all sorts of things. And voodoo was pretty effective, even if a less powerful witch used it. Still, it would take quite some power to penetrate the golden shields he'd layered around Ivy like onion skins. To break through *those*...

He should search her cell. But it was a lot more likely that Jake was still at it, interfering with the healing, trying to get one last shot at "his" sacrifice for Baba Yaga.

"Bonnie has been asking for you," the receptionist at the nerve clinic told Bryan. "Are you her uncle?"

Bryan glanced at her, then nodded. He'd already bought himself all that visiting time at the hospital by claiming to be Ivy's husband, because he was tired of permanently keeping up the invisibility spell. That would logically make him Bonnie's uncle.

"She said you'd come check in today," volunteered the receptionist as she wrote down his details and handed him the key. "Down the passage and fifth door to the left," she said. "She's not aggressive, you won't need an aide to go with you."

Then why are you keeping her locked up, thought Bryan, and, *cancel that thought!* Bonnie was locked up because she'd been caught in the midst of a murderous circle of cannibalistic demon-worshippers and had been part of the gang. She was in here and not in prison like her mother, because she'd had a nervous breakdown.

He buttonholed an aide who came down the passage. "Pardon, can you tell me – the girl that's in number five."

"Bonnie Pennington?"

Bryan jolted on hearing Ivy's surname. "Yes, yes of course," he said, catching himself. "That's her name, she's Ivy's niece. People tell me that she chants. Do you ever hear her?"

The aide smiled.

"She doesn't chant," he said. "She sings. Hymns upon hymns upon more hymns. And Christmas carols. She has the sweetest, most enchanting voice. I'm so glad she does this. Music heals people, you know that?"

Bryan smiled. Hymns! Gosh! He was instantly suspicious. The girl was putting on an act as only a salted witch could. She had long since recovered from her nervous breakdown. He had to be on his guard.

When he opened her door, she looked up from the chair that she'd pulled up to the window, watching the endless rain.

"I'd like to stay here," she said. "It's so peaceful."

"Glad you think so," said Bryan. "Your mother sends her love."

Bonnie smiled. "She's lying. She never loved me. She used me to get married to my dad, that's what she told me often enough. But I've forgiven her."

"That's another lie," smiled Bryan. "You two are a pair! Do you know they're talking of letting your mom work off her sentence in community service?"

"She mustn't be let out," said Bonnie, alarmed. "You did see what's in the bottom of our house, didn't you? That's *her* altar, Bryan. She does horrible things there."

"I saw," said Bryan gravely.

"The hospital said I'm sterile now," said Bonnie with a brave little smile. It wavered.

Bryan sat down on the bed, facing her.

"See, Bonnie," he said, "it's like this. You were born with the most precious gift. The gift to create new life. How many times did you have abortions?"

"Seven," she whispered, and averted her eyes. Tears started down her cheeks. She turned away, wiped her face, gathered herself and looked back at Bryan.

"You see," he said. "You misused your gift, and instead of creating life you created death. So it was taken away from you."

"I'd have loved to have this baby," she said. And her composure suddenly cracked; her voice wobbled, and then she was crying openly. "I thought I felt him move. Like a – little butterfly." She covered her face in her hands as she sobbed.

Bryan watched this with a critical eye. It didn't look like the act of a versed little witch any longer. It looked like a young girl genuinely distraught about her loss.

"Then suddenly it all was so real," she wailed. "It was as if he'd looked up at me and said, 'everything will be fine, won't it, mommy?' And here was I, lying to my baby, saying, 'yeah, baby, you'll be fine, don't worry'. Just like bloody Bex!"

Bryan nodded, observing.

"I didn't want to play Jake's game anymore," Bonnie

choked out. "And Bex's. So I tried running away, but Jake followed me to Ivy's place. The next thing, he seduced me again, and then Ivy came in and threw me out." She fought for composure, and her voice steadied a bit. "I was trying to convince Jake to let me keep this baby. I think I almost had him talked round, but then you guys came and stole that other child -"

"Bonnie," said Bryan intently, "if that had been your little girl? And some group of kids had wanted to kill her?"

"I know," she wailed. "I didn't want them to do that, but you know, once such a ritual is going it's very hard to stop. The forces come and take revenge." Her voice dropped to a whisper. "They got Jake. You know, don't you?"

"They caught him?" he asked, surprised.

"The demons caught up with him," she stated flatly, wiping over her eyes with the back of her hand. "They found him and ate him up. I *saw* it!"

"That was just a nightmare," said Bryan gently. Ivy had been right. Bonnie was one confused kid. Under the right guidance she might recover.

"No, Bryan. Go look. In the warehouse. You'll find him."

It's a trap, thought Bryan.

"Take the police with you," said Bonnie. "Otherwise they'll say you did it."

He nodded. That was the least of his worries.

Once again when Bryan returned to the hospital, Ivy's condition had weakened. And this morning she'd seemed so much better! So much nearer to waking up. But perhaps her mind was shying away from waking up, thought Bryan. He wouldn't want to be inside that body while it was still so damaged. It had to be painful.

Damn Jake! Bryan took out his cellphone and tipped off the police. He didn't have to be present in person; whatever they found relating to Jake, who was basically an escaped convict – they didn't need Bryan Woodwright there.

Half an hour later the call-back came from his contact in the police.

"Bryan, this is Joe. You won't believe this. They found him."

"Yes?"

"Dead. Already for a few days. Probably the first November. The rats have been at him. Ugh! Apparently he slit his own throat with his huge occult knife."

Bryan shuddered. Slitting one's wrists was a common teen suicide habit. But the throat?

"Please," he said, "Joe. Won't you inform his parents? I have my hands full."

"Sure," promised Joe and rang off.

Bonnie had been right.

Bryan gathered up Peridot who had been chasing

shadows under Ivy's hospital bed under his invisibility shield, and got up.

"Don't you dare deteriorate further," he said quietly to Ivy's sleeping face. And he left for the nerve clinic, visiting Bonnie a second time that same day.

"You see?" she asked. "I knew it. The wheel turns, Bryan."

He nodded.

"It will turn for me too," she added, frightened.

"I think it already did," commented Bryan. "And your auntie took the punch for you."

"How is she?"

"You *know* how she is," he snapped, angry. "Every time I leave the hospital, she backslides. It's as though someone is still attacking her! And it's clearly not Jake, he's been gone for fourteen days."

"Baba Yaga," she whispered fearfully.

"I destroyed Baba Yaga, or whatever that demon was," said Bryan impatiently. "Bonnie, show me that voodoo doll. Or I'll find it with my psychic magic detector."

She shook her head, frightened.

"I haven't been practising voodoo. I wouldn't dare go up against you! Honest! I'm trying to get out of this cycle! I swear, by the ..." she stopped herself. "I'm not allowed to swear by Her yet."

"Whom?"

"Holy Mother Mary," she whispered.

"Catholic?" asked Bryan, puzzled. "You're converting?"

"Bryan, face it, they are the only ones who can save me now," said Bonnie. The desperation in her eyes was pretty real. "Mother Mary and her holy Baby Jesus. He washed all our sins away, with his blood..."

Bryan bit his tongue. He'd thought she'd have enough of being bathed in blood!

"But Bryan, you don't understand!" she insisted. "I know what you're thinking. Jesus' blood is *spirit* blood. It washes clean. It's life force. That which the enemy – I mean, that was the White Wiccans – call the White Light. They're not the enemy anymore, Bryan, true Christians only have one enemy... you know, at night the shadows come crawling closer, they want to eat me up like they ate up Jake... and then I pray to the Holy Mother and Child... and they back off. It's the only thing that works."

He nodded, swallowing more comments. White Light. It would indeed protect this poor confused child. It was what he had been channelling, non-stop, into Ivy when he wasn't busy clearing dead matter out of her chakras. The White Light was limitless, and it was all-powerful, and the only reason she hadn't yet died and he and Peridot hadn't yet burnt out in their healing efforts. But he felt as smooth-licked as the rocks a waterfall thunders over. The White Light was taking all his discernible quirks off his character, he thought with irony.

Bonnie was right. The only thing that could really save a recovering black magician from themselves and their own karma was the Christ force. And Catholicism was quite a palatable form, replete with saints and apostles, and of course the Great Mother. Plenty of good spirits. And rituals. Candles, chants, rosaries... Hmm. She needed this conversion.

"As long as you are dead serious about this, and don't treat it like yet another game," he warned.

"No, I won't," she said earnestly. "I don't want to end up like Jake. I want to change schools, if they ever let me out of here," she added. "I've picked a convent school I'd like to attend."

"Think your mother will let you?"

"Bex has no say in the matter," said Bonnie. "I'll find out who administrates my father's estate, and ask them straight. My father would have wanted me to."

Bryan agreed. "Your father was a good man, Bonnie."

"You knew him?"

"Remotely," he said with a smile. "Honour his memory, girl. Save his little sister."

"Bryan, I swear, I'm not cursing her. How could I? She saved my life, and my soul, and she even tried to save my little baby when I didn't mean to..." Those tears were streaming. Bryan put his hand on her shoulder; then he got up and left without a further word.

A convent school? He'd better investigate before he helped her with this goal.

It was true. He'd known Ivy's brother. But he had never made the connection between gentle Dennis and Ivy the red-headed witch. He'd never met her, before that day in the bookshop. It came as a surprise, prying into her family history and peering at photos she had on her laptop as a screen saver, to discover an old friend. And of course – Pennington. There weren't that many Penningtons about.

But thinking about Dennis had set Bryan's mind on a track. This looked very strange. He was tricked into early marriage by some wild woman; landed with a baby before he was even twenty; then went on to a highly successful career in law, but died at thirty-one, just when his practice was starting to pick up and he was in junior partnership with some legal heavyweights. Not only that, but he insured himself to the eyelids, then had a lethal accident...

And the way the estate was set up, was weird too. Bex had no direct access to the money, beyond the comfortable figure that appeared in her bank account month after month. The lion's share of the fortune, the part that was in the hands of a competent investor, was kept in trust for Bonnie. Clearly Dennis hadn't trusted his wife as much as would have been normal.

And how much of it had been left to Ivy? He'd have to investigate. Bonnie was right: It was a bad idea to get Bex out of jail too soon. It had to be Bex, trying to break Ivy. She had a motive, the opportunity, but – not the means, and that was what floored him. How was she going about it?

13

"Where's Peridot?"

Bryan's clear-blue eyes hovering above her face as she peered through slitted lashes.

"He's the first thing you ask after?" he enquired quizzically. "Welcome back to the living, Ivy. Welcome back!" He smiled at her.

She looked at him, puzzled. Were those... tears in the corners of his eyes?

"Bryan? I'm alright, man! Don't stress so! I'm pretty tough, you know. Pests don't perish all that easily."

"You, my girl," he said seriously, "have no idea."

She shrugged. She felt stiff, as though she'd been lying still too long. She tried to sit up and found that she was weak. Awfully weak.

"So that little rat shot me down," she said. "With those disgusting pitch balls. Bryan, I'm convinced they contain poison. They burn like hell when they eat away inside of you."

"Do you have pain right now?"

She shook her head.

"Great," said Bryan. "Then we can get you home. Save some hospital bills."

She grinned. "Really!"

He called the nurse, who stared at her with wide eyes. "She's awake!"

"Doctor said, the moment she is awake, she can go home," said Bryan with no small amount of glee. He'd fought battle after battle with the blooming doctors to keep the drip going, keep her in that hospital bed. He'd even cast spells of hypnosis to make the doctors more amenable. They didn't want to deal with a comatose patient who dipped a few times per day as though she'd die, and spent the rest of the time recovering from the dips. And her obnoxious husband who saw to it that every protocol was fulfilled. She was a dead patient waiting to die, in their opinion. Waking up wasn't part of that equation.

Of course, as long as she'd been comatose, the drips were there to keep her hydrated and medicated. Without them she'd have suffered kidney failure within six hours, at the outset. But her kidney functions were completely recovered, and now that she was awake there was no reason...

"If you can provide her with the right diet," said the nurse. "I'll print it for you. Remember, the times and quantities are terribly important. She's like a baby now, so look after her well."

Ivy laughed. "So I'm a baby?"

"You must just lie still and get well, Mrs Woodwright," said the nurse.

"But..." They've got the wrong patient, thought Ivy. "Alright, sister."

"And don't you sister me," said the nurse fiercely. "I'm the head matron of this whole division!"

"Sorry, Matron," said Ivy meekly. Bryan saw those naughty flashes in her eyes and set another of his worries free.

The pitch balls had not eaten her brain, or her character. She was still Ivy.

"Why did they have me booked in as Mrs Woodwright?" asked Ivy quizzically when she was on the passenger seat of Bryan's newly repaired Jeep.

He laughed. "It was easier to book you in as my wife and plead chaos than try to find your birth certificate and proof of residence."

Ivy nodded, and watched the landscape slide by. She was feeling very lethargic. Even getting into and out of the wheelchair they insisted on her using had exhausted her. Jake had really done a very thorough job poisoning her system.

But... wait a minute...

"Say – I imagined that little horror actually stuck his dirty knife into my side," she said. "He tried for my heart but I rolled..."

"Have a look," said Bryan.

Gingerly Ivy lifted her pullover, that the nurse had helped her put on with Bryan *not* watching, and looked where she'd been stabbed.

She had expected a huge bandage, and some significant pain and stiffness. But instead a nasty red scar and some fairly recent stitch marks marred her smooth white skin.

"What -?" How the hell could that have healed overnight?

"It's the twenty-first of November, my girl," said Bryan gently. "You lost three weeks from this."

"I was in hospital for *three weeks?* Why so long?"

"Well, were you awake before now?"

She shook her head. Coma? She'd been in a coma? Ugh, this was disorienting.

"No wonder they were tired of me."

Bryan laughed aloud. "They were a lot more tired of *me!*"

"You visited a lot?" she asked. This was fascinating!

"Yeah..." He grew vague. "I checked in every so often. When I did, I kept asking questions. You see."

She smiled. "So you're a difficult customer."

"You have no idea."

Alison had cleaned Ivy's cottage, the moment she got the news from Bryan that he was bringing her home. Both Marc and Alison were there to welcome her home. She smiled broadly. An advantage of being in hospital long: People actually welcomed one home.

It was wonderful to be pampered and spoilt by her friends. Ivy hung in the armchair that she thought of as Bryan's by now. It had a marvellously calming feel to it. Alison had cooked some soup for her; she was forced to eat this while the others watched indulgently.

"We missed you, girl," said Marc with feeling. "In the two days you lived here we got so used to you..."

She laughed. Really!

They sat for an hour catching up on gossip. Bryan was surprisingly quiet; once again Ivy noted the terrible love triangle going on between her neighbours. And she wondered what to do about it. Marc simply heaped his attentions on her; but always with Allie in the corner of his eye, as though he were doing it for effect. And Allie was flirting outrageously in Bryan's direction, who sat and scowled and said nothing.

Caught between a rock and a hard place, thought Ivy. He couldn't date Allie because she was married, and he didn't want to walk in on her marriage, break it and upset his friend and neighbour. How long those two were going to remain friends, was a riddle. Their interaction looked uneasy, at best.

At some point Ivy yawned. It would take a while to get rid of Jake's poison, she thought – and then she shivered, remembering that it had already taken three weeks.

"Alright, Allie, Marc," said Bryan, "Ivy's tired. I think she should go to sleep now. Let's all leave her to it. I'll stay here and guard."

Marc grinned indecently. Bryan proceeded to chase the couple out. He locked the door. Peridot zipped around the floor, skidding on the smooth parquet where it was intact. And he tripped on a loose piece and fell on his nose, and got up indignantly, sat down and washed himself.

"His fur is getting so smooth now," said Ivy with a smile.

"He's not all that tiny anymore," agreed Bryan. "Come, girl. Let's get you into your bed."

"By *myself*," she emphasized with a grin.

"Oh for heavens' sakes, Ivy," laughed Bryan. "Fine. Second invitation declined. I'm warning you, girls only get three chances with me."

She grinned broadly. "And most accept your invitation at how many attempts?"

Bryan snorted and refrained from answering. He went and poured her a bath, adding a couple of glugs of bubbles out of the bottle. Then he left her to it and closed the door between the bedroom and the lounge.

"Let me know if you need something," he called from the lounge.

"Thanks," she called back and sank into myriads of bubbles. She really had to search to find the water under all these bubbles. And she closed her eyes.

Instantly fear clamped around her heart. She ripped her eyes open, hyperventilating. There was nothing.

This was uncanny. Was Baba Yaga still out there stalking her? She had never believed in evil spirits; but she knew better now. She knew to be very, very afraid.

She washed herself fairly quickly, glancing fearfully into the corners and at the darkened windowpane. Outside rain was stroking, stroking down and the trees were blowing, some branches scratching at the roof and windows. In the morning she'd trim those back, she promised herself. If this was what drove people from this 'haunted' cottage, she had to laugh.

She got out and found warm pyjamas, put them on and was about to crawl into her bed -

That wasn't her duvet! It was one of those really fluffy ones from Bryan's guest room. She smiled. That was thoughtful of him. And she crawled in.

"Come and chat," she invited Bryan. For some reason she didn't want to be alone tonight. The irrational fear that had grabbed her a moment back was enough. She wasn't up to this.

Bryan pulled up a chair.

"You're tired," he observed. "Do you really want to chat?"

"I have to find out what happened," she said seriously. "Bryan, I don't know, I don't seem to have any friends or family anymore. Didn't have many friends to begin with, and well – Bex and Bonnie, they were my only family. I can't call them that now, can I?"

"You're feeling a bit desolate," he diagnosed. "Don't throw Bonnie away, Ivy. Remember why you were prepared to defend her with your life. And you did! But Bex... well... I don't trust her." He told her in detail everything that had happened since the police descended on that circle.

As he talked, her eyelids drooped.

"Bryan," she said, "please, don't leave yet..." And she felt horribly selfish. "I can't even offer you a guest bed! There's an air mattress in the wardrobe, I bought that for

Bonnie when I thought she'd be bunking down with me... aw hell, Bryan, sorry, I'm inconveniencing you..."

He held up a hand and smiled. "Shoosh, Ivy. I'll sleep on the *chaise longue*. Stop carrying on. You were still supposed to be under hospital care tonight, the only reason they allowed me to take you home was that I promised to take care of you like a ward sister."

"But, Bryan – you really don't have to!"

"Shoosh, Ivy, I really have to. I made a promise."

She sighed.

"Alright, but it would be a lot more comfy for you in your own home, am I right?"

"But this is *your* comfort zone," insisted Bryan. "Ivy, now stop resisting. I'll camp out here until *I'm* satisfied that you don't need a ward nurse anymore. Understood? Now accept it – resistance is futile."

"Okay, Dr Woodwright." She scowled. "You shooshed me! Twice!"

"Yes. Now relax. It's what friends are for."

Over the next few days things settled into a gentle routine. Bryan woke Ivy up with a tray of breakfast in the morning; they chatted and laughed, and then he got his computer out and got stuck into whatever he was doing. Ivy had no idea; he didn't give her any, either.

She pottered around the house some more as she stared feeling better; even around the garden a little, but that was still very draining. On one such occasion she saw the gorgeous little Honda that was parked behind her cottage. It looked just like the Flymo.

"You replaced my Flymo!" she squealed in delight.

"Insurance did," said Bryan matter-of-factly.

She ran her hands along the lovely machine. It didn't matter if it didn't fly. She didn't want to dabble in magic anymore anyway. She'd had her dosage.

"Flymo II," she dubbed it. But she didn't yet feel strong enough to take it for a spin.

Some days Bryan would drive out on his motorbike, leaving her in Peridot's care, and sometimes with Alison visiting. He was usually back within two hours though. Ivy felt slightly policed.

Alison became a dear friend. Ivy spotted some extra bubbliness in the young woman these days, as though something exciting were happening. She asked about this but only got a mysterious smile. She suspected that her friend was actually pregnant; but didn't ask this directly.

Things began to look up as she slowly recovered her energy. There were times she only lay on her bed drowsing, envisioning a golden ball of light spinning right in the central part of her body, just underneath her ribcage but well above her navel, as Bryan had instructed her. These meditations left her feeling rested and centred, even if they didn't significantly raise her energy levels; Bryan had said it would take time and she should be patient. So she was cultivating something she'd never had much of before: Patience.

During such times Bryan would sit and hack away at his computer; the quiet clicking of his fingers on the keys a soft reminder that she was not alone. This got a bit straining at times.

Still, when night fell she was thankful that he was there. She had developed a horror for the night, ever since Halloween. Irrational fears would clench at her at intervals, when she was alone. After those she always felt extremely tired and drained, and usually went to sleep within a little while. And sometimes Bryan couldn't be there at night; during which times he put Alison in charge of her, because he didn't want her to be alone at all. He cited medical reasons; but she suspected he did it to help her with her fear.

He always returned at some point though, waking up Alison, seeing her safely to her own back door, and taking over from her. And unwittingly waking up Ivy in the process; but she was thankful for it.

About a week after Ivy had come home, Bryan was sitting reading in the comfort chair he'd put into her bedroom on a permanent basis; she was in bed, reading too, propped up comfortably with pillows.

And that icy hand of fear gripped her neck, and reached into her innards, and made her feel cold, so cold... she gasped and shivered a bit, and waited for it to pass.

Bryan glanced up and scowled.

"You've gone grey," he said and got up from his chair.

The panic passed and she lay there staring at him with huge worried eyes.

"It's nothing," she said. "Just a bit of nictophobia."

"You were never nictophobic," he contradicted her and put down his book, and placed his hands, palms down, about ten centimetres above her duvet as though he were scanning for something. "Sorry, Ivy," he said and removed the duvet, and 'scanned' her whole abdomen and her chest like that, without touching her pyjamas. He was looking at zero dimension, not at her or his hands, either. Just focusing.

"What do you find?" she asked in a hushed voice.

"Shhh." He continued the scan, then pulled up the other chair right to her bedside. "Ivy, how often does this happen?"

"Two, maybe three times a day – more often at night," she said. "It's nothing – a bit of residual fear from that horrible rite, I think."

"Don't self-diagnose," said Bryan. "You're too rational. You're missing it."

She smiled at him, a wan little smile.

"Psychological trauma can do all sorts of weird things," he informed her. "But that's not what this is." He placed his right hand over her solar plexus again. Even though the hand wasn't touching, she could feel heat radiating from it. It felt wonderful. "This," he said, "is a psychic attack. Someone is playing voodoo doll or sending you evil vibes."

"I think we're all a bit paranoid after those pitch balls," said Ivy logically, basking in the warmth coming from his hand. His left hand joined his right and now both were radiating heat at her middle.

He smiled. "You like that?"

"Mmm!"

"Good. Because if you didn't I'd just have to say, suck it up, lady!" His smile had disappeared. He looked nearly angry. "This stuff that I'm giving you is called 'chi', or life energy. This discipline of hands-healing is called Reiki in the Eastern tradition, for simplicity's sake. Mine is at a very high level because I needed it to be. So I educated myself and got the relevant training. We're working with energy, electricity, heat. Life force. You don't ask, understood?"

She nodded, unsure how she had managed to upset him. She'd heard about Reiki before. It was offered at various beauty salons she frequented for haircuts and depilatory manoeuvres. It was usually dainty ladies with long, carefully manicured nails offering this treatment, with soft music as a backdrop. She'd always thought of it as relaxation therapy; never bothered to go for a session. Never would she have expected a man to give Reiki – and then, that it was *this*.

"Nice seduction tool," she grinned.

"Shut up!" he snapped, his sense of humour gone. "Close your eyes and stop thinking of sex all the time. I'm working on saving your life here. I have no *interest* in getting romantic with you! Get it?"

Ivy stared at him, taken aback. And she remembered his predicament regarding Alison.

"That was just banter," she said quietly. "Sorry if I upset you. Didn't mean to."

"Yeah, well," he growled. Obediently Ivy closed her eyes.

The coldness was beamed away systematically by the radiant heat of Bryan's hands. Peridot jumped up onto the pillow and purred against her cheek, and she cuddled him, suddenly feeling miserable.

Well, that was shot through the roof! What had happened to three invitations? Damn! She'd touched a raw nerve, somehow, and managed to stuff up what could have developed... she'd had some hopes, she admitted to herself. He was a hell of a nice guy; and she'd quietly hoped that the relentless care and supervision he was extending to her meant more than just the duty of a mage on his path. Well, she knew better now!

She recalled his impossible entanglement with the neighbour. She bested Allie in everything without meaning to; save perhaps looks. Those were completely a matter of personal taste, and Allie was indeed gorgeous. Raven-black hair down to her bum, those green eyes that reminded of yet another kitten... a disinterested husband and a crush on Bryan, and she'd caught him hook, line and sinker, but he could not move, because his ethics forbade him to hit on the wife of his friend. This was not okay! This was... dammit.

"You're crying," observed Bryan.

She sniffed and wiped her eyes and shook her head.

"Just tired."

"No, you're not," he replied. "Keep your eyes closed, will you!" She'd been peering at him.

Ivy relaxed and let him do whatever it was he was doing. At some point it felt to her as though he reached into her intestines with long fingers and removed a lot of black muck. He took her internal organs out one by one, cleaned them and put them back. Then he beamed some purple hot water through her system, flushing out the bad stuff.

She was quite sure that real surgery never got quite that rough. But it didn't hurt; none of it did. It felt good, like an internal clean-up.

At some point she felt him zip her back up like a bag of potatoes, beam some light on her, and leave her side. She peered carefully; he'd gone to the bathroom to wash his hands. He hadn't physically touched her, not once; but after handling all that black muck, she'd want to wash her hands too.

Bryan returned to the chair at her bedside.

"How do you feel now?"

He looked grey and drawn. His eyes looked tired and without sparkle; his skin pale; she almost thought she could detect some grey hairs in his sandy-brown, unruly mane. Short, but not... tidy short. In school he'd get a demerit for needing a haircut. It made him look mischievous – usually. Right now he only looked worn out.

She reached out to touch his wrist.

"I'm sorry, Bryan."

"*You're* not supposed to be sorry," he informed her. "If I get my hands on -" He paused, getting dead serious. "Ivy, give me a minute. I have to check on something!" And he got up, left the cottage and locked the door.

Ivy waited. Peridot climbed around her neck and shoulders, licking her ear and then nibbling it. When she still lay listening intently instead of giving him attention, he bit her earlobe.

"Ouch!" laughed Ivy. "You little brute! Alright, alright!" She got up, a bit dizzy and wobbly from all the energy that had been pumped through her, and poured him a saucer of milk.

It was half an hour later when Bryan returned.

"Had to check," he said.

"Check what?"

He told her about Marc and his sinister promise.

"*Marc?*" she repeated, baffled. But Marc had been nothing but nice to her, and, on the contrary, he seemed to keep her in line as an option if his marriage failed. Well, that, or he was merely using her as a way to try and make Alison jealous. As though that would work! "Why the hell would *Marc* want me out of the way?"

"The man has found his psychic power. He broke out of my immobilizing spell."

"Why was he in a spell?" asked Ivy, too surprised to realize Bryan had evaded her question.

"He was attacking me."

"Why on Earth?" She peered suspiciously at him.

"...Bryan?"

"Leave it," he snapped. "At least, if it's Marc attacking you, he denies it. He nearly got violent with me for insinuating it, but then he has this uncontrollable temper..."

She shook her head, smiling. She knew now what had happened. Ha! Well, she was surprised it hadn't happened sooner. In fact – how should she know if it hadn't? And if the baby Alison was probably expecting...

Damn that, it was none of her business. She deliberately looked away, then asked Bryan to pass her the Arcana.

"Why the Arcana?" he asked suspiciously.

"Or rather, pass me 'The Millionaire Next Door'," she requested. "I was reading it before all this started. It's in the bottom of my bookshelf." The Arcana was a huge tome stack-full of an information overload on everything magical. Actually Ivy was quite sick of it.

"Why *not* the Arcana, suddenly?" probed Bryan.

She was finally tired of it all.

"Look here, Bryan. Marc is *not* hexing me! The man's a realist! In fact, if he weren't married I'd very much fancy him, he thinks very much like me. Then you could have Alison," she added with a slightly bitter aftertaste. "That effect of me losing my energy is metabolic. There was some sort of poison on Jake's dagger. It hasn't finished working itself out of my system, probably messed up some or other essential gland. That's all there is to it, finished!"

He glared at her. "So now you'll also deny that I've just

restored your energy using the White Light?"

"Marc," she said, and corrected herself, "Bryan, I mean. What the heck, you men are all interchangeable. Your Reiki feels fantastic, it really does. But it's relaxation therapy. How would you explain that I've been recovering from five to ten such dips every day completely without any Reiki?" She got out of bed and paced to the kitchen, to make herself some coffee, and made some for Bryan too, *en route*. "There. Drink this. It will calm you down and remove the cobwebs. I can really recommend 'The Millionaire Next Door', it's a relevant book for the real world."

Brian nearly threw down the mug she was holding out to him. He took it and placed it on the antique coffee table.

"Ivy, you have no clue," he retorted, furious. "*This* – these metabolic dips, as you call them – this is what took us three weeks to get you out of your coma. The medical staff wanted to let you go, they had no hope that you would survive. In their books you were already dead. But I wouldn't allow them. I booked you in under my name so that I could force them to do their duty. I was in there, day and bloody night, fishing more of that rubbish out of your insides. Every time I can see you improving, here comes the next missile, and bam! - back to square one."

She stared at him with her eyes wide in shock. "You were *in the hospital the whole time,* to save my life?"

"That sums it up," he said curtly. "That was me. Don't worry, I could fit my work schedule around it. I was due some leave anyway."

"Why?" she asked, sinking down onto the *chaise-longue,* her energy used up. The energy came only in short bursts as yet; and she'd expended it on anger.

"Because it's a skill I have and so I must use it. Hands-on healing skills come with an obligation. That's all." He took the armchair – the only remaining one as the other one was in her bedroom. "The bloody *chi* has side effects. It can make people think they're in love with their therapist. But you're *wrong!* If you think it was done for any sentimental reasons, girl, think again." He shook his head, ran his hand through his hair. She could see he was agitated.

But this cut close. She stared into empty air, gathering herself. Peridot jumped up on the *chaise-longue* and purred at her, climbing onto her lap, stomach, chest, and eventually shoulder. His purring by her ear was quite loud. She gathered him into her hands and stroked him.

She wished she could reverse to that first time she met Bryan, when he pushed the Arcana into her hands and held her with his amazing blue gaze, and push it right back into his hands and say, "no thanks, sir, I was only joking". Cut the association short right there. It wouldn't hurt so much right now.

Damn Bryan. How dare he? She felt as though *she* had been the one throwing herself at him. Ah. That must be it: He must be tired of having to look after her.

And that was fair. She needed to look at the big picture.

He had done far more than should ever be expected of anybody, friend or rescue worker.

"Listen, Bryan," she told him, her voice low, tired and barely restraining those tears of fatigue. "I'm sorry I yelled at you. You've done so much for me, to get me back on my feet. I can see it's wearing on you. I don't want to hold you back from your life any further. This whole thing with Bonnie and Bex is after all my family karma and has nothing to do with you. So..."

He sipped his coffee in silence, watching her.

"I'll never forget your kindness, and your sacrifice," she said. "I'll be fine now. We're both solitaires, you know. This is why we're irritating each other now. Both of us need our freedom, our space. Locked together like this we're terribly cramped and crowded."

"You're throwing me out," he stated.

"I'm... fine. I'm recovered," said Ivy. "These moments of weakness – I can cope with them. I'll get used to them until they are gone. It's alright. I don't need nursing care anymore."

"You're still scared at night," he mentioned.

Ivy smiled. "What do you mean? I'm a creature of the night. I don't believe in demons. This past time was a nightmare but it's over. If I really can't get over my nictophobia I'll go for therapy. Promise."

"You are actually throwing me out," he stated again.

She gazed at him, with a mix of sadness, desolation and pity for him. "Yes," she said truthfully. "Sorry. I can't watch this work on your nerves any longer. Time you got on with your own life."

Without a further word, he put down his half-drunk coffee, got up, and left.

14

Weird days, reminisced Ivy as she scrubbed out a small pot in which she had heated up a Noodles-For-1. Outside her cosy witch's hut, snow had actually fallen. It was nearing Christmas.

The cottage was all that really reminded her of her witching days now, and the sudden dips in her energy. She had learnt to predict when one such dip was coming, and to replace the missing light by channelling fresh white light into her chakras, a technique she had found online in psychic forums. It was biochemical, but the white light didn't hurt. Something timing out in her metabolism. No imaginary assault from anyone.

Peridot was of course around, her constant companion – so big now, nearly turning into a real cat – nearly. A teenager, gangly and cute. His meow had turned into a demanding meowl, and his tail chatted with her all the time. Sometimes he sang a bit with her; he still liked sitting on her shoulder when she went through her chores. But she hadn't gone flying on anything with him since Halloween. She didn't actually think she could get it right anymore. The Flymo had only flown at night; Flymo II was never taken out at night. She was too scared now.

Ironic, she thought, because logically the danger was over. Jake was dead; Bex was still in jail – they hadn't yet decided finally on giving her community work. And Bonnie, after extensive psychological treatment and rehab, was going to go to the convent school she had chosen. Ivy had put her force behind organizing it for her. Bonnie had converted heart and soul to Catholicism. It gave Ivy shivers to see the feverish devotion in her niece's eyes. But once again she had to agree with her neighbour: It was the only option left for Bonnie to lead a normal life. And Bonnie had decided to embrace life. That was the good news.

Alison popped in often; bubbly and sweet, until one day she was suddenly sad and subdued. Ivy deduced that she'd lost the pregnancy. Well, she and Marc would simply have to try again. Or she and Bryan, damn him. By now Ivy was quietly convinced that Alison's overt flirting with the mystery man was aimed at making Marc jealous and that the girl was actually lethally in love with her husband but didn't know how to get him to respond to her.

Marc also visited Ivy at times. They sat and discussed finances; Ivy showed him some basics of bookkeeping and cursed at the school system that failed to drill this into every child as surely as two-plus-two. His mood seemed to be better than before; whether it had to do with Allie working as Oates's secretary and bringing in some extra money, was hard to tell.

It was in fact Marc who enlightened her about the *chi.*

"Frickin' voodoo," he spat contemptuously. "It's Bryan's main excuse for hanging around my wife such a lot. He claims it's the *chi* that caused her crush on him. I suppose any excuse will do, right?"

Ivy didn't have a response for that. She found it disgusting that Alison flirted so overtly with Bryan.

Ivy was also back at work now; she had returned shortly after sending Bryan home, releasing him from the burden of having to nurse her back to health.

Said neighbour – and that was all he was anymore – had been completely absent. That night, he'd left her cottage; she hadn't seen him since. This was three weeks in the past by now. She waited for him to come through that garden gate, even to visit Alison or Marc; she was ready to intercept him for a chat and a cuppa, but that gate stayed closed. He was apparently ignoring her landlords, too. Maybe that accounted for their marriage seeming better.

A reason, a season and a lifetime, she reminded herself with sadness. Those were the ways people entered one's life. He had been for a reason: To save her life, to rescue her from the onslaught of black magic that had been heading her way. To teach her self-defence without compromising her logical belief system. And then, when she didn't need any more help, to leave her behind and continue on his own path. Why was she feeling bereft?

She finished drying the few items that had been from breakfast and peered out of the window. It was Saturday. She should maybe go to the library, or the second-hand bookshop... or spend the day browsing, online... outside it was miserably cold, and the cottage actually had an old-fashioned fireplace. So maybe going to look for some wood was a nice idea.

The police had stopped chasing her. This was because Bex had dropped her charges after she could see they weren't water-tight anymore. Mr Brown had not tried his luck, as Bryan had predicted.

She missed Bryan's easy friendship. She wondered if she should shake that silly schoolgirl crush and, like a good neighbour, simply walk through that garden gate and knock on his door, say hello. But it was true, what she'd said: they were both solitaires, extremely territorial. He wouldn't appreciate it.

She ended up getting on the Flymo II and visiting her old haunts, the library, bookshop, even killing time malingering around in the malls. Everything was decorated for Christmas. Times like these, she missed her brother. Her parents had passed away when she was so small she could barely remember; she had lived in her brother's house for a good while until she had asked to be allowed to go to boarding school. He'd been shocked by her decision, but she'd felt as though she were in the way for his real family, Bonnie and Bex. Yes, and then she had grown up and become completely independent, pursuing her own career...

She also visited Bex in jail. It seemed as though the parole was not going to be granted; she'd have a sister-in-law in jail for quite some time to come. She'd brought a small gift for her, an iced Christmas cupcake from the markets. Bex appreciated this.

"I've no idea what will happen for Christmas," Ivy mentioned.

"It's a bucket full of commercialism," said Bex scathingly. "Don't mind Christmas, Ivy. It's another opportunity for the shops to make money."

Ivy didn't reply. She'd always loved Christmas, the way her brother had prepared it for his family. Back then, Bex had always got caught up in it and added so many special touches.

She went to see Bonnie too, and gave her what she'd bought for her – an inspirational book about hope. Bonnie would be released from the institution in time for the next school term. She even went to see Janet too, and was happy to meet the elderly lady's older daughter and her grandchildren, who were visiting from Sweden. The younger daughter, the one that was Ivy's age, couldn't come for Christmas, as she had just started picking up speed with her job in New York.

One toddler of perhaps two years, and one baby that was crawling about. Beautiful babies, thought Ivy. They would have had one of those in the cottage by June, if things hadn't gone so deeply evil.

She came away from that visit feeling a bit restored. At

least there were *some* normal people in the world. Should she look up Fareed? She remembered Neeva's unrestrained jealousy and decided against it. She had no business being social with married, jealously possessive couples. Or with lone rangers on Shetland ponies, she thought acidly.

She drifted around her university for a while, sitting down on the stone steps where she had so often sat and studied. Good days, she thought. Well, it was time that she retook her CA. And maybe it was an idea to visit night classes, for two purposes: To make new friends, and to lose her nictophobia.

A nictophobic witch, she thought, what utter nonsense! And just to test her power, she turned a brick that was lying around, into a fluffy toy with a "khazam!". She picked the toy up – a fuzzy white leopard – and stuffed it into her bag. It was good to know that she still had it.

She'd left Peridot at home. The little cat hadn't complained; he was quite used to being locked up by now. She wondered what would happen once he got hormonal and wanted to date a lady cat. But she put it out of her mind. Another day's worries. Each day only had enough concerns for itself. She couldn't shoulder the whole future in one go.

It was really quite easy, she thought. One took the molecules that were there, and rearranged them so they refracted the light... actually she had no idea how she did it. But it could be used to people's advantage.

She returned home in the dusk, lifting the Flymo II off the ground and flying the last piece to her cottage on it just to test if she could. So the little machine did fly, she thought with satisfaction as she parked it behind her home, then rounded the corner to open her cottage door. And she stopped.

Under the trees, the snow leopard crouched, watching her.

"Do you remember me?" she asked cautiously. The leopard looked at her for a while and then slowly came closer. It stuck its head into her hand and rubbed against her. She stroked and patted it.

"Peridot will be jealous," she said with a smile. She hugged and cuddled the amazing animal. The leopard purred and begged for more.

"Wait," said Ivy and went into the cottage to get a blanket to sit down on. Before she could prevent it, Peridot had slipped outside. She turned in horror, expecting the worst -

The two cats were playing, the huge and the tiny, as though they'd always been friends. Ivy didn't quite trust the situation, so she didn't dare leave while the two were together. One bite and Peridot might be history. But that wasn't what it looked like. She could swear these two cats knew each other.

Peridot eventually got tired of the game and slipped back into the cottage. Ivy was left to cuddle and play with the leopard. She talked to the great cat and rubbed the fur behind its ears.

"So! You've been a scarce one! Doesn't your master let you out of the house anymore? I'll come and rescue you if you want me to."

She knew she was babbling, but she'd missed the leopard. Funny how one could get so fond of a wild animal.

They were unpredictable cats, she remembered reading. Nothing to pet and play with. They could be wonderful the one moment and eat you the next, because they liked playing with their food. But tonight she didn't care.

Her brother was dead. Her parents – long gone. Her sister-in-law was in jail and her little niece in an institution. Her friends had drifted away... she liked both Allie and Marc, but there was this awkwardness that prevented her from connecting fully. And *him*... that guy behind that gate... less said the better. So – a perfect dead-end, her life.

She sniffed, allowing herself to wallow in self-pity for a moment. The leopard pushed its head at her, and she hugged it and wailed.

"I'm sorry," she said eventually, drying her tears. "You know, one gets to miss people. Maybe you don't know, leopards are such solitary animals." She felt for its ribs. "Do you get enough food? I can't imagine the hunting is too good around here." It didn't appear too thin though. "So, that Bryan does feed you enough," she concluded. "At least one thing he does well. You'd better not stay away so long again," she added. "You're my only friend, presently. I still don't know how I should handle the thing with Bonnie... whether I should call her over for Christmas, or whether I shouldn't bother. She's gone Catholic, you know... really scary, that. She preaches at me now that I should lay off the magic. As though turning the occasional piece of stick into a flower – *khazam! - i*s magic?" With the 'khazam', she shot some karma at a piece of dry stick and it turned into a single, cut rose. She retrieved that and smelled at its velvet-red petals, sighing. "What can I give you to make your day nicer? Ah: I know." She had some uncooked liver in the fridge. She hoped the cat would eat it, cold like that. So she slipped into the cottage, took the sweetmeat out of the fridge, ripped open the package and offered the liver to the leopard. He gobbled it down thankfully and gave her a purr. And then he got up and vanished into the darkness between the trees.

"So," said Ivy with an ironic little laugh, "typical male! Comes to eat, and then stuffs off again. Yup, that's how it is!" She closed the cottage door with a wistful smile.

Bryan had been on her mind the whole day. Whom was she trying to fool? The whole week, in fact the whole time since he'd vanished through that gate. And there had been absolute silence from his side.

And she knew why.

Damn!

If you love something, set it free, she thought. By that same token she needed to set herself free, too. And she would.

She marched down to Alison's, black cat once again on her shoulder, and rapped loudly on the door.

Alison had slipped into her job as receptionist at Oates, without a ripple. She was good at it. And Biljana was born to zap people's teenage zits and old-age wrinkles. A professional zit-zapper, thought Ivy.

"Yes?" Alison opened the door.

"Allie," said Ivy, "we have to talk."

Alison looked surprised.

"Put on your coat," invited Ivy. "Let's walk and talk. That usually works the best for me."

"Right," said Alison. Within three minutes she was back, in her warm winter mantle.

Ivy walked with her down the long driveway and along the road. It was a dark winter evening; but the street lights took the nictophobia out of it for Ivy, at least in part.

"You've got to divorce Marc," she jumped in with both feet first.

Alison stared at her with her mouth open. "Why?"

"Because – you two – it's not working! I can see it! It's terrible to watch. You're in love with Bryan, and you're breaking both of their hearts."

Alison stared at her as though she'd lost her mind. "But the payment on the house has started working now. I'll lose that if I divorce him. Face it!"

"That's no reason to stay together," said Ivy. "You're young. Anyway Bryan has a house. A nice one. You can spend your money on yourself then."

"Well, I can't see how it's your business," replied Alison, irritated.

Ivy shut her mouth, taken aback. Alison was completely right. It was none of her business.

"Fine," she said eventually. "No problem. I'll stay out of this."

"Good," said Alison. "How's the witching coming?"

Ivy smiled. "Not really at all," she said. "I don't think I've got any significant gift at all." And she kicked at a pebble that lit up as it flew.

"Show-off," laughed Alison. "You know, you've been alone too long. That's *your* problem. You should attend a few more parties."

"Parties," smiled Ivy. "Yeah, I'm so popular, I'm simply going from one party to the next."

"We're having an Esbat on Tuesday," said Alison. "Don't you want to join us?"

Ivy shook her head. "Have fun. But arcane magic is really not my thing."

Ivy returned to her cottage shaking her head. None of her business? *Was* it none of her business, that Alison, though she refused to get divorced, was keeping Bryan on a string? Who had come so close to her, Ivy, during that time he'd looked after her...

The 'chi effect', she thought acidly. Supposedly giving Reiki made people fall in love with you.

No, dammit. She didn't buy that. It didn't gel with what she'd read about the White Light, which was supposedly the substance of the *chi*. She couldn't imagine how every girl – or guy – who ever went for a Reiki session or five came away with a crush on their therapist. It would have been declared illegal by now!

She opened her laptop and connected to the internet, and launched a search.

Hours later, nearly at the crack of dawn, she closed the machine again and fell into bed with an exasperated sigh. Through the night, reading endless articles on her Odyssey, she had got angrier and angrier. She understood now.

There was indeed an effect, well-documented in the *psychotherapies*, in which the patient developed an untoward crush on the practitioner. It was called transference and was based on dependency; the practitioner ethically had to discourage it.

Psychotherapy and counselling psychology was not Reiki, she had thought angrily. It would be comparable to a high-school teacher falling in love with pupils.

She had dug a bit deeper.

The *chi* was pure. It was innocent. This was like blaming the water in a Jacuzzi for developing a crush on someone. As ridiculous. Alison's crush on Bryan was plain old emotional two-timing; he could jolly well stop feeling responsible for it!

Didn't Bryan know? She couldn't believe this. It was basic. The *chi* was divine energy, straight from above. It couldn't be blamed for anything as base as sexual attraction.

Alone the logic in this ought to be clear to him.

The chances were that he did know. In all likelihood he'd used this *effect* to let her know, at an opportune moment, that she meant nothing to him. He had to have seen how she felt even before she got herself shot down at that awful ritual; and while he had to do his best to save her because he felt *responsible* for her, he also had to block whatever feelings she might develop due to his proximity, his obvious caring, his sense of humour... because it would break the situation with Alison.

Alison, she understood now, had him on a short leash with his full consent. It was what he wanted. And *that* made her so angry that she battled to fall asleep and was up again shortly after, making herself coffee at the break of day.

Ivy spent Sunday getting hold of a Christmas tree from a tree nursery, and trawling through the shops for jingles to put on it. Peridot thought this was the best treat, and tried to angle the baubles back off the tree. And by the end of the day, Ivy had come to a decision.

She sat on a camping sheet on the cold ground outside, her arm around the white leopard, telling him of her decision.

"It's no use, you know. This place is not good for me. I'm pretty much alone in the world; what does it matter where I live?" She hugged the great cat tightly. "Only wish I could take *you* with me. You don't have issues."

And she got up, gave her white leopard one last squeeze and went into the cottage to pack.

Monday morning saw her collecting her remaining salary and bonus cheque from a shell-shocked Mr Oates and bidding Biljana farewell. She had already given Alison her notice; she was paid up until the end of the month, and that thing with buying the cottage had never been pursued. She understood the 'ghosts' now. And she'd seen the black markings on Marc's fingers – markings that refused to go away. He had been the one digging in her stuff that night. Why? What had he been hoping to find? One more spell to lift, she thought, but she couldn't get herself to do it. She simply didn't want to deal with magic anymore.

Monday afternoon the moving van was there. She'd found a room on the very northern tip of Scotland to rent; in an isolated village at Little Loch Broom, called Scoraig. There, she was going to help some people put their books in order. Or help out in – whatever shop they had there. Or teach maths to some primary school children. But if she had to move a second time, whatever. She had enough savings to live on for a couple of months, give herself some time to find a job again.

There was one last thing to do, and she put it off until late. She contemplated simply leaving a note, then decided that that was cowardly. By dusk, she finally grabbed the Arcana and went through that garden gate a last time. Her stomach tingled as she did and her knees felt wobbly; she was pretty sure she wasn't welcome here. Especially after her meddling conversation with Allie, which she was positive had reached Bryan's ears by now. But she had to do this.

She knocked on the glass door. Bryan pushed it open seconds later. The sight of him made her swallow a couple of times before she could continue. This was a man, she reminded herself firmly, who was in love with a married woman who was not going to get a divorce, but who was playing him along. She had tried to despise him for his weakness and found that she couldn't. She could only be sad for him, and angry with Alison. Angry with them both.

"Brought your book back," she said with a brave smile, without looking at him, and pushed the Arcana into his hands. "It's worth a lot more to you than to me. I'm really not into the Craft."

He merely stared at her.

"Good luck with Allie," she said, not without some bitterness, and turned, and walked back to the gate, and through it, and to her cottage door. The packing van had already left; all she needed to do was collect Peridot and her Flymo II, and follow.

She had packed a few items for the road into her backpack and into the tiny storage compartment under the Flymo II's seat, amongst others a warm Thermos with coffee. And nostalgia hit. She found her spot at the cottage door, sat down on the ground and poured herself coffee. Peridot came purring around her, wondering what the delay was. She sat there slowly sipping her coffee, and tickling the little black cat.

It had been a mad six weeks. She loved the quiet of her cottage and garden, but couldn't stand the tension. It was time to move along. But, five more minutes in this beautiful wintry garden...

The leopard appeared out of the trees and came strolling up to her. She grabbed its head and hugged it.

"I'll miss you," she said. "But I need a clean break. I can't carry on like this." She buried her face in the thick fur of the animal. "Tell that stupid lout Bryan that I love him. Idiot that I am. I guess I got addicted when he looked after me. Fell bloody headlong. Ah, and it's plain too much. This is ridiculous. Why do we always fall for people we can't have?" She hung onto the huge cat, feeling a bit hopeless. It was no good pining for Bryan. She had to get moving, get her life back on track.

"Don't tell him where I've gone, you hear?" she implored the leopard, scrubbing him behind his ears. "We don't belong together, he and I, see. He needs a lot of women around himself and I – need a lot of space." She got up with an impatient sigh. "Goodbye, Leopard. One day when I own a piece of ground big enough for you, I'll come back and steal you. It's unfair that he has you and I have nobody." And she left the white leopard by the cottage door, mounted her Flymo II with Peridot on her shoulder, and took off.

15

Hammering on the door. Alison opened and peered at Bryan standing in the cold doorway.

"Come in! I'm baking Yule cookies, I'm sure you've smelled it..."

"Hand over that voodoo doll!" he demanded.

Alison shrank back. "What voodoo doll?" she asked with wide eyes.

Bryan pushed past her into the entrance hall, and proceeded into the lounge, where the Circles were held on wintry and rainy nights when the outside was not suitable.

He could see the trappings of a fresh ritual going on right now. Alison was alone; it was Saturday. Marc was in town; one could hope, on Christmas business.

A week since Ivy had left. And still, Bryan could feel the evil vibes that were sent after her, every so often. He knew they would slam into her guts; make her buckle and sit down, make her have to ask for water, wherever she was, and take about half an hour to restore herself. She had thought that by leaving she'd get away from those spells. He had thought so too. She'd properly cut all her connections. But it made no difference; the bad karma still got launched at her – and now he knew from where.

He even knew why. It had puzzled him that Bex should still be managing to attack her young sister-in-law. How? He had managed to search her entire cell, and scanned for any magical implements; she had been rather cooperative, and surprisingly she had seemed sincere when she said that she didn't mean Ivy any further harm. He had indeed found no evidence.

It followed that it wasn't Bex doing this. He had subjected Bonnie to a rigorous stress test that had nearly thrown her into relapse with her nervous breakdown. Bonnie had disintegrated. He was a highly versed and powerful White Mage; even a girl with the natural abilities of the Penningtons couldn't stand up to him. Bonnie had been found innocent on this particular count. And she had practically fled from him, into the chapel on the grounds of the nerve institution. He hadn't followed her there. Let her feel safe at least in that place of worship.

As for the rest, Bryan had by now tracked down each of the little magicians of the dark rite, investigated them, interrogated them and established that none were quite capable of voodoo. Furthermore none had thrown any curses at Ivy – not that their curses would have managed to breach his protective barriers.

So none of the Circle had anything to do with it. He'd tried to catch Marc at it various times; but Marc was brilliant, hiding his psychic awakening behind a cloak of very vocal agnosticism, making overt fun of anything magical or religious.

And not once had Bryan caught him out at magic, even though he knew the man had escaped his spell once.

He'd started to wonder if it was really Marc. The man liked Ivy. Genuinely, it seemed. Maybe Ivy had been right and it was merely metabolic – hogwash. When his instincts said 'black magic', the dark path was involved. Period.

And then Ivy had brought the Arcana back to him with that parting shot, wishing him luck with Alison... wishing *him* luck with Alison! A few things had dawned on him then. But he had so hoped that he was wrong.

Candles were indeed flickering on their shelves, all around the room. Red candles. Alison was too scared to try for the full black magic. He took a look at the implements on the coffee table: Her athame, her crystals, though the crystals looked less than happy. Salt; and the effigy.

It was nothing but a lemon, with some of Ivy's red hair stapled to it and a smiley drawn under the hair with permanent marker. Fine holes marked where long pins had been stuck into it and removed again; but this time it was a nail sticking in its middle. That had to hurt!

He stared at the haphazard conglomeration of magical paraphernalia. Salt? Crystals, which were clearly unhappy with being put to such a negative use? This was a clueless white witch who was side-stepping off the path. She had no real idea about black magic; just enough to do damage to Ivy – and herself.

He shook his head, depressed. This was what he got for

merely being himself. He'd saved Alison from psychic onslaught, years back when they were all at university together. She had caught the brunt of a girl's anger – Angelique – who had vied for Marc's attention – an unconscious witch, he'd like to call that one because she'd been evil without even realizing it. She'd strewed such hectic curses, invoking the saints to help her – the saints! Those hadn't been saints; they had been more demon entities parading as whatever Angelique had wanted them to be. In the name of those saints she had hammered Alison with cramps, nausea, dizziness, headaches, every time Alison came close to Marc.

Bryan had been there and observed this; and he had done what he always did and taken care of the perpetrator, blocked her curses and applied his healing energy to Alison when nothing else worked anymore. In an energy-storm of a show-down he'd bested Angelique at her own game, reflecting her curses and hexes back at her, left her cringing in the sick room. He'd had to go in via distance healing, stealthily, to help the young witch recover her health; not without a warning to Angelique that she had done this damage to herself and needed to stop using magic to avoid a repeat.

Alison had married Marc, who had been clueless about the whole situation; but the *chi* had done what it did sometimes, being pure energy through a fairly raw channel, and had seduced her into wanting Bryan, too. It wasn't something he'd planned, and it didn't suit him at all as it had by now all but destroyed his long friendship with Marc.

Except for causing this seduction, the *chi* and the experiences had awakened the slumbering witch in Alison. She had launched herself on the path of white Wicca, causing Bryan to keeping a constant eye. Alison was the psychic equivalent of a preschooler and needed the supervision; she'd try anything, and the results were, to say the least, unpredictable and chaotic. If there had been no results there would have been no cause to worry. But Alison had quite a decent load of raw psychic gift. It kept Bryan on his toes, and Alison under the impression that he had some romantic interest in her.

Well, there was no denying that she was a gorgeous young woman, with exactly the right balance of coyness and self-awareness. And sometimes it was difficult being a true red-blooded male around a woman such as her, and permanently resist her tempting invitations. If her marriage was in shambles – well, perhaps that marriage wasn't meant to be, in the first place.

If he thought about it, she was also a brilliant actress. Her pose of friendliness and sweetness towards Ivy had been faultless, even though she must have been seething at the way attack after attack seemed to be warded off. It boggled his mind.

Logically, if she really wanted him that much and got him, that should put an end to her practising black magic. It should put an end to all sorts of things, he thought. It would also put paid to the memory of two wild green eyes peering suspiciously at him, asking him what he'd stolen; challenging him every step along the way; resisting his teachings; rejecting his wisdom; rebuffing him for taking care of her wrist; second-guessing his experience-based decisions; doubting his energy-healing; throwing him out... running off...

All this had to be taken care of.

"Alison," he said, removing the nail from the effigy, "we have to talk."

"I don't see what there is to talk about," Alison snapped, for once belligerent with him instead of seductive. "She told me to divorce Marc. Just when things are starting to look up. What the hell? That's after she was permanently throwing herself at you *and* him... really, she's a little whore and deserves everything that comes her way. It's only return of karma, Bryan."

"You're in grave danger," said Bryan seriously, refusing to comment on her jibes at Ivy. "Meet me at the gate, tonight when dusk falls. Use an excuse. Marc doesn't need to know."

Instantly she was compliant. He could see a small smile of triumph flash across her face and disappear again, brought under swift control, and he replied with a small smile of his own. It had to be.

"I'll be there," she said.

Bryan left, taking the lemon with Ivy's lock in it with him.

*

Christmas eve dawned white but clear. Here in Scoraig, winter was in full swing, with Arctic temperatures and metre-deep snowfalls.

Ivy had put her Christmas tree back up, with the cheap plastic jingles on it that she'd bought for Peridot. It was standing in the bay window of the room in the old house where she was sub-renting. Yes – from a garden cottage to a single room, she thought, but she was really just biding her time, this was temporary. She had put feelers out, and there was one neighbour – all of which were hearty, bearded and warm-hearted Scots – who had discussed with his equally kind-hearted wife that he'd build a cottage for Ivy at the bottom of his garden, two rooms, as she was going to be paying monthly rental, and that was not to be sneezed at.

The garden was enormous, not much different from Alison's property. Ivy looked forward to it; but in the interim, here she was in a small outside room with a bathroom but no kitchen.

Bonnie could go hop. No Bonnie for Christmas, she had decided. Nobody for Christmas except Peridot, in fact.

She'd had psychic attacks all week. They *were* psychic attacks after all. She knew this now. They had intensified instead of getting better. Some part of her wanted to call Bryan and apologize for doubting him; but she knew it was just an excuse to talk to him, so she beat down the desire to try and find him in the London phone index. Because his hand-scribbled cellphone number that he had given her originally, had never made it into her phone directory, and of course the paper was goner than gone by now.

Just as well. She endured those attacks and told nobody about them. But maybe she ought to call the police office and let them know to inform Bex that she'd moved – to the end of the world, practically, and that her next move was going to be Alaska? That might stop her greedy sister-in-law from bothering. Or perhaps she ought to call Bex and let her know that she was marrying a wealthy American and was going to cut her and Bonnie in on a hefty allowance – if Bex left off the attacks. And then dodge about the actual payouts. Protection money. Perhaps she ought to learn to do psychic mirroring... no! She'd had more than enough of the Craft!

Of course Bex had a motive! Dennis had left a portion of his estate to Ivy, being her older brother and her guardian of many years, from her fifth or sixth year on. In fact, a lot of what he'd placed into trust for her was her part of their parents' estate. But he'd died before the trust could be signed over to Ivy, so she was still in the strange situation of having to call a trustee to sign over money to her for her studies. By the time she held her first job she'd stopped bothering with this as she found it demeaning; but she had somewhere on her bucket list that one day she'd have to go and sort all of that out.

'Estate' was probably putting it optimistically where her parents had been concerned. They had not been affluent in any way. Still, Bex was obviously not happy with this situation, especially as she had no idea exactly how much of 'her' fortune had been left to Ivy.

Ivy looked idly out of the window and started telekinetically doodling on the windowpane with ice flowers. The ice flowers formed intricate landscapes and images, complete art. But she got bored with that game pretty soon. She ought to be out there.

She got herself dressed in her warmest coat – which wasn't warm enough for these heights, donned a woollen scarf she'd picked up from a second-hand store in one of the larger towns on the way here, lifted the very willing Peridot onto her shoulder and locked her door behind her as she left, and went to climb up into the crags and hills around Scoraig.

Up here, there was a lot of wind, and some grey weather. She climbed up higher and higher, until she was at a fair elevation; then she turned and looked at the panorama.

Little Loch Broom lay quiet and grey in the valley. The wind sang in her ears up here; she could nearly hear the angels with their carols. "Angels I have heard on high..." She didn't consider herself musical in any way, but Christmas carols she had always enjoyed, and she trilled them out at the top of her voice out here, because there was in any case nobody to hear her.

Peridot crawled in under her coat. She couldn't blame him. But she wasn't done yet with this immense landscape.

There was a certain freedom that came with having nobody. You only had to worry about yourself. And your cat.

She clambered around in the hills for the morning; returned to the village at noon, and to her room; opened a tin of baked beans and ate them cold with a teaspoon as she didn't feel like going into the kitchen of the main house and then having to endure company, and cocooned herself up under a blanket with her laptop reading e-books.

Only when she returned that night from a sumptuous Christmas Eve dinner her landlords had invited her to, did she realize that she hadn't had a single attack that day.

The next few weeks passed in a half dream-like state for Ivy. She went trawling for work, not only in Scoraig but in towns nearby. Scoraig had no road leading to it; she had to take her motorbike onto the ferry every time, and it was fifteen minutes to the mainland and the road. This was one of the best things about the place: It was extremely secluded.

When she wasn't scouring for work or roaming the icy countryside with Peridot either perched on her shoulder or tucked under her coat, she was online, looking for work opportunities. She could easily do people's books by email, she thought, if they only sent her everything she needed. There might be privacy issues; she'd need the advice of a good web designer, on how to encrypt what she sent.

By the beginning of the new year, the local primary school had accepted her as assistant maths teacher. She found herself surrounded with children, which somehow helped her psychological healing along. The images of that terrified toddler on the Heath were beginning to lose their vividness. She didn't wake up in terror anymore, at night. Once or twice she had even considered flying out on her Flymo II, to have a look at the Loch from above. But she was scared of taking the machine up, because she didn't know how she'd handle a psychic assault in mid-flight; though since they had stopped a few weeks back, she hadn't suffered even one.

Bonnie skyped her from her convent school and thanked her for organizing it for her. Ivy had to smile. All she'd done was drop the trustees a line that this was what was necessary.

Her landlord and -lady, an elderly couple who had raised their children here in Scoraig but had seen them move away to busier parts of the world, picked up that all was not fine with Ivy, and they tried fishing information out of her. She was as evasive as she was polite. And as time passed, she almost managed to put two intense blue eyes behind her – those secret weapons with which Bryan the woman-hunter snared his prey. When she thought of him now, only bitterness remained.

Winter was slow turning to spring, but eventually by May, the snow finally decided to melt away. It was a lot more fun to watch sunsets from high hilltops when the wind blowing around your ears was not all that nippy. Ivy appreciated the vastness of the place more every day. The children at school loved their young teacher, even though they went to every length to drive her nuts and test her patience. As her energy rebuilt itself over the months, she found the strength to shout at them as necessary.

It was a time outside of time; a world not quite of this world. Ivy knew she was in limbo; but she had no intention of coming out of it. This suited her fine.

*

16

The white leopard moved silently between the people, under a spell of invisibility. It slunk along the platform onto the train, crawled onto an empty bench, and waited.

Several stations later, it switched to another train. Once again it lay patiently waiting on a bench until the train reached destination. Nobody who came past thought of sitting there. It wouldn't have been good for them, in any case.

It was in the high latitudes now. The train stopped at Ullapool. The leopard got off and slunk into the dark.

From here, there was no further public transport. This didn't bother the wild creature at all. He loped silently along fields, hedges and farmsteads, and up into the mountains. He killed a rabbit and had a quick meal; found a loch to slake his thirst, and continued.

He had been there when the Astral Police had dealt with Alison. She still had mostly white light in her soul; but patches had started turning dark, colourless, lifeless, as she had inflicted injury on an already injured woman. Jealousy was a terrible emotion; it had led her to attempted murder. In her eyes it wasn't really attempted murder because she didn't fully believe in the impact of her own spell craft; but the intent that Ivy should die had been there, and later, after Ivy had recovered, the intent that she should suffer.

Purging these dead parts from Alison's soul had nearly taken her sanity. The towering White Mages surrounded her in an oppressively tight circle, and poured their light – pure white light – into her with relentless force. She had screamed in fear and overload. Her head had been hurting like hell – he knew because she had screamed that it did.

When they finally released her from the treatment, she had collapsed to the ground. Bryan had helped her to his guest suite, where she had slept for several hours before returning home, rattled and scared, but purified. She had returned home before Marc had come back from a night of late pubbing with his colleagues; clutching the Arcana to her.

The white leopard ascended a high crag and peered down. Below, the loch curved away gracefully, glistening coldly in the moonlight. He settled on a rock and rested. It was late, not long to dawn now. At first light, he'd continue and skirt the body of water. Humans could only go across by ferry; but to a wild leopard, mountain paths were home.

*

"Walkies," called Ivy. Peridot made a single leap from the floor and settled comfortably on her shoulder, his tail twitching her masses of red curls out of the way. Together they locked the door to her outside room and set off into the mountains. Perfect weather for an early Sunday morning.

This one thing Ivy found a bit cloying in this town. There was a church service every Sunday morning, and every last person in town attended. It didn't help her protesting that she was not a part of any church; good-naturedly, the friendly people of the town had tried to draw her in. But even though she'd tried once or twice to sit there, the sermon made her twitchy, and she couldn't connect to the hymns at all. It wasn't something she could do to herself. She knew that she could never be an automatic churchgoer; it had to come from inside, and it didn't. And that was all there was to it. She didn't believe in hell; not even after encountering Baba Yaga. She believed that there was evil, but for her it resided in what people did, as did the good.

She walked along the narrow path at first, then cross-country up the hillside with Peridot. The larks were up there singing. The sky was actually blue – and what a blue! It was so clean, she felt as though she could see all the way to the north pole. She clambered up to her favourite rock, settled down and unpacked the picnic she'd packed for herself and her young cat.

Peridot was not a kitten any longer. He was nearly fully grown; but playful and funny as always. He chased after butterflies, performed somersaults and leaps trying to catch them, and entertained her wonderfully. She smiled.

The longer hours she spent alone with her kitten, the less she felt the need for human company. Talking to people could be reduced to a friendly greeting. That was enough for her free time; in school hours she was inundated in kids and noise, so it was nice to have silence the rest of the time.

She had located a site by now where she was one of several accountants serving people online; the payments were slow, but they were starting to trickle in. This was nice; it made her more independent of her day job. She chewed thoughtfully on her jam sandwich and watched the birds flutter around in the low grasses.

And she spotted him. Ivy stopped in mid-bite and stared at the white leopard. He stared back and came stalking closer.

This was too much of a coincidence. She stood up and walked up to meet him. Yes, it was definitely her Leopard. She put her arms around his neck and hugged him in delight. She'd forgotten how huge that beast was. The size of a lion.

Oh heck, she'd missed her furry companion!

"How did you find me? I'm so glad you're here! Aw, I love you! Wonderful leopard! Thank you for coming to live with me." She pulled a face as she rubbed him behind his ears. "Sorry, Leopard. I wanted to come and fetch you. Guess I haven't found the right place for you... and I probably lost my nerve, too. Can't face that boss of yours." She stared a hole into the sky, becoming quiet. "I was going to save up, and buy you from him," she said. "If he weren't willing to sell you, I'd have filed a charge against him for that illegal animal smuggling syndicate he runs. I know a bit about the law, my brother was a lawyer." She smiled. "He'd have had to back down then. Leopard, I'd have lost even the memory of him being a friend, but you would have been worth it. He's an idiot anyway." And she thought very fast. "I'll have to move into a house, because I can't expect my landlords to allow you to stay. Doesn't matter, I was going to move anyway. Now I have an incentive. Do you eat a lot of meat? I'll have to step up my income a bit, but it's no issue, my Leopard, no issue at all." She cuddled and hugged the great cat, and Peridot came closer to play too. She thought she imagined a catty wink passing between the two animals.

Ha! One could become so attached to an animal that one thought one understood its language!

"Hope you're going to stay with me now," she told him. "Hope you're not just visiting. Bryan really doesn't need you. He doesn't need either of us. He can have Alison all he likes, damn him. *And* Marc. I hope the three of them are happy in their mutual misery. Because *I...* - have decided to set myself free. I have no business with any of them. Remember, if you love something, set it free..."

The white leopard turned its wintry-blue eyes up and looked at her quizzically. She sighed, and the sadness and bitterness she'd been downplaying took her over. For a while she merely sat there, rubbing the leopard's fur and taking comfort in his great fuzzy presence. Tears ran silently down her cheeks as she gazed out into the vast landscape and the birds of spring flitting about. She let them run; allowed herself this final release of all the rubbish she'd kept bottled up.

Maybe after this, forgetting Bryan would be easier.

"We'll stick together now, you and I," she told the leopard. "You, me and Peridot. I'll never be scared of the night again with you around. And now that I've seen you in the day I know you're more than a phantom. I was beginning to think you only belong to the night. I'm glad you're real."

The leopard purred patiently and allowed her to ruffle its fur all she liked. It had settled down comfortably with its head resting in her lap.

"And if ever by some obscure chance we run into that total idiot of a Bryan," she added, turning vicious, "please bite him for me!"

The leopard blinked. "*That* might be complex!"

She stared. The eyes – it started at the eyes, the metamorphosis. They were the constant in this equation. By the time the leopard had completed morphing into his human shape, she had realized why his eyes were the amazing features they were. Also, she'd jumped up and screamed hysterically, and backed away ten paces. Now she stood there staring, as though she were seeing the wild leopard for the first time, not its human counterpart.

"Bryan?"

"Damn," he said with a grin. "That felt so good, I was going to milk every moment out of it. Maybe con you into months of hugging and caring. But you tricked me into wanting to answer!"

"You're the – white Bryan?" she asked stupidly. "I mean

– you, Leopard, are the cat? You're the same person?"

He nodded, grinning, his hands held out for her. Ivy stared at him, stunned. His grin faded as she failed to move.

"Ivy...?" His mesmerizing eyes were pleading with her.

Damn the man! She slipped into his embrace, defenceless. For a good while they were both inarticulate. His kisses got so hungry eventually that they scared her. They were – a bit wild. She broke free of them and stepped away, towards the ledge where the land dropped away in a vast panoramic display.

"What's wrong?" asked Bryan, bewildered. "What did I do?"

She stared out over the great expanse, Little Loch Broom and the village below.

"Where do I start," she sighed, and shook her head. "This is all an illusion. You're an illusionist. A brilliant one. How did you manage to con me?"

"What do you mean?" he asked, dismayed. She glanced at him. He had moved up right behind her. His hand touched her shoulder. She shrugged it away and stepped aside, her foot catching a loose pebble and slipping a little. Bryan went rigid, his eyes following the pebble down into the gaping drop.

"Bryan, the leopard is your familiar. You can't be both! I saw you two together."

"Impossible," he replied. "When?"

"At Alison's party," she said. "You stormed through that garden gate just as I was about to leave – and the leopard was right behind you. He saw me. You didn't."

"*I* saw you," corrected Bryan. "That man you saw was Marc, not me."

She assimilated this. The two men weren't too different in size and posture; and she hadn't seen his face in the dark. Yes, that was possible.

"What did he want?"

"Beat me up, probably," said Bryan drily. "I didn't have time for his jealous nonsense. I had to intercept you and get to that evil coven first. Slipping past him and locating my keys in leopard shape – that cost me the moments in which I could have saved your life."

She detected quite some bitterness there.

"You did save my life," she pointed out. And she shrugged. "So you really are the leopard? This is no illusion?"

"I'm him," confirmed Bryan.

"So you're a wild predator," she said. "We're from different species. Get it?"

"We're not," said Bryan. "I'm a White Mage, like you, Ivy. Same species!"

"You're a leopard," she smiled.

"I'm a shifter," he said, exasperated. "I'm both. Three parts human mage and one part animal mage. My father was a White Mage. My mother was a shifter. A White Mage, that's a terrible thing, it's a job with never any rest. A White Mage is responsible for *everybody.* Shifting into my leopard shape is a relief – slipping through that garden gate to visit my girlfriend... that lovely red-headed witch who knows exactly how to rub a cat's fur..."

"Your girlfriend, ha!" Months of bitterness came back in a compact black missile, hitting her like a pitch ball. "That would be Alison!"

"Ivy, no!" He grabbed her shoulders and turned her, forcing her to look into his eyes. Passion was burning there, under the iridescent surface. "Alison was a loose cannonball. A White Mage's nightmare. We got her fixed up, just in time." He told her about the voodoo doll, and the mage intervention.

"It was *Alison?*" she asked, stunned. "Not Bex, not Bonnie... not *Marc*... why the hell should *Alison* of all people..."

"Because she wanted something that you had," he pointed out. "Me."

She smiled. "Right," she replied sceptically. "*You* were so bloody standoffish with me all the time! When you weren't drilling the bejasus out of me. And just when I thought we were getting a bit closer -" she stopped.

"You threw me out," he completed with a smile.

"You *chewed* me out!" she retorted.

"Before I could apologize," he added. "Before I could explain. The *chi*..."

"The *chi,* the *chi,*" she mocked angrily.

"I tried to tell you," said Bryan. "The *chi* seduced Alison into falling in love with me, years back. I yelled at you what I'd wanted to yell at her. It wasn't meant for you."

"The *chi* does nothing!" snapped Ivy. "It's white light! It *can't* cause transference! Alison is playing you like a puppet. *And* poor Marc! Bryan, maybe your patients are caught up in thankfulness for your healing, for a little while – note, a *little while*! It takes a true egomaniac to believe they'll fall in love with you over some energy healing! Imagine if every little Reiki healer at a beauty salon..."

He chuckled, wistfully. "Yes, Ivy, I figured that out. Maybe I had *wanted* to believe that Alison's manipulative rubbish was caused by something beyond my control. She was so vulnerable back then, I didn't want to hurt her more by being harsh. But I should have. I was hoping that getting married to the man she loved would sort it for her. And I was mistaken."

"Hell," said Ivy and turned away, studying the panorama below. "I feel very sorry for Marc," she added quietly. "He's really got the butt end of the deal. Why doesn't he throw her out?"

"I organized Marc an architect's job, through the network of mages. One shouldn't abuse the network like that, but – ah, well. Guess I've learnt a few things from you as well." He grinned. "And then I sold him my house. Packed up my stuff – there isn't much, Ivy, those photos, and a few books from my father – it's in storage for when we have decided where we want to be."

She looked up at him in surprise.

"I thought if you had a chance to disappear, the attacks

on you would stop," said Bryan. "But they didn't. Not until I caught the little witch red-handed." He sighed. "You think you know someone! You think you can judge a character! I misjudged her completely. Wouldn't ever have thought she'd be capable of black magic."

"Ha! I considered her a friend," added Ivy.

"She needed your rent," replied Bryan. "She's a good actress. Had us all fooled."

"And I organized her a job," said Ivy bitterly. And she glanced at him. "Thank you, Bryan."

"So...?" he asked and spread out his arms, waiting for her.

"No," said Ivy, stepping away, this time making sure she didn't move any closer to the drop. "I'm not going to be the next in your endless string of girlfriends."

"What?" An incredulous little laugh.

She turned with a hopeless shrug and looked around for Peridot. This was pointless. Time to leave. Damn about the leopard though. She'd miss that beast.

Bryan's hand caught her shoulder, and he forced her to look at him.

"No, you're not," he agreed. "Because there is no endless string of girlfriends. Where did you get that idea?" He gave a cynical laugh. "Of course. Alison. Listen now, Ivy. It's totally illogical. My work wouldn't even allow it, for one."

"Your *work*?"

"As a White Mage -"

"Oh! Of course," she smiled. "For a moment I thought you actually have a job, you know, with earning an income and so on. But of course a leopard wouldn't -"

"I'm in homicide," he said. "Special division, occult."

Ivy stared at him as time stood still, his light-blue eyes that were less azure right now, nearly grey.

"You're a *cop?*" she concluded.

He smiled. "I'm a cop, Ivy."

She laughed aloud. "And here I was thinking you smuggle rare animals for a living!"

He laughed as loudly. "Nice!"

"So..." Didn't she remember asking him just that, the first time he started interrogating her, there in her cottage? "So you actually lied to me?"

He nodded with a wistful smile. "I lied to you."

"*Why?*"

"Because my work is classified."

She nodded, understanding. "Alright. You couldn't tell me because you didn't know me. But of course Marc and Alison do know."

"No, Ivy. *Nobody* knows. We don't get clearance to talk. That's the definition of 'classified.' "

"But you're telling me?"

"I applied for special clearance," he said. "That wasn't easy, especially with those charges Bex was bringing against you! It didn't help that you escaped the police and resisted arrest. I had a lot of explaining to do."

She gaped at him.

"As a shifter, it's an even greater risk," he added. "We never tell *anybody* who we are. Telling people puts our lives in their hands. While we're in animal shape we don't have human rights protecting us. So only our life-long soul mates and our children are ever told the full story."

She peered at him, absorbing this. "And that's the full story?"

"That's the full story," he said.

She gazed speculatively at him. "That's a proposition," she said critically.

"It is."

She walked to the edge of the rock, where the mountainside dropped away underneath, and gazed into the distance. This was a lot to digest.

"I'll never tell anyone," she said, staring out into where white clouds were hanging around on the blue horizon. "Your secrets are safe with me, Bryan."

He came up behind her.

"Don't do this to me," he implored. "My father was human, Ivy. A White Mage. My mother was a shifter. My brother's a shifter like me. I tried to stay sane and carry on with life without you, because I knew you'd object, but the cat – all he could think of was you. I tried, I really tried to forget you, for five pointless months. And then the damned thing literally ran away with me. Brought me to you. He's... wilder than me. He has feral instincts."

She had to smile. "Inconvenient, right? Especially seeing that you and the leopard are one and the same?"

"Damn," grinned Bryan. "You understand shifters a little too well. You know, all that leopard wants right now..."

"Don't say it," she laughed. Her own inner leopard was rather interested in the proposition. It was in fact an ideal moment: The whole village was in church. But... "Bryan – if we do this – if we get together – am I not going to have cubs instead of children?"

He smiled. "No! What gives you that idea? Some of them may end up being shifters like me... want to try it out?"

"That," observed Ivy, "was your third invitation."

"And this time I'm not waiting for you to turn it down," added Bryan and pulled her back into his arms. "I've been a complete idiot long enough."

~ The End ~

www.ingramcontent.com/pod-product-compliance
Lightning Source LLC
Chambersburg PA
CBHW052015020726
47501CB00004B/1070